THE WAY WE ARE

Olivia Norton

To those who walk this world alone.

One

It's an easy kill.

Everyone screams as they attack, charging forward in the mud and rain as the football hits the ground, a classic tale of victory in the making as we secure another touchdown in the biggest sports game of the school year. The crowd goes wild, and with only a few minutes left the visiting school's reputation is truly broken, knowingly unable to save face now being twelve points behind.

As the lights on the scoreboard change and the speakers blare the school chant I slip away from the crowd. The game will no doubt be the talk of the school for the next month. I should be there showing my student pride, but I have a more pressing matter to deal with.

I usually wait for bad weather for such excursions and, as fate would have it, this is the night. With half the town at the game, it's easier for me to get around unseen. Still, I jump behind a tree as a truck passes. It's unusual to see a seventeen-year-old roaming the unlit streets of suburbia in the rain at night, and strangers have a habit of pulling their vehicles over to ask if I'm okay. It is good to know that the state of Georgia still has communities that care, but I usually smile and insist that I simply lost track of time at a friend's house and live just two blocks away. It's a lie, because telling the truth wouldn't go down well. So jumping behind trees it is.

I pass a few more mailboxes until I reach number nine. It's an old villa, probably built in the 1920s before the farming troubles began. It's small but two stories high and has a more modern garage beside it that looks out of place.

I close the front gate behind me then turn back to the house. No lights turn on. I am unnoticed.

"This is a bad idea."

I glance at Cole as he appears at my side. While his sudden presence would startle most people, I don't even flinch. In fact, I expect nothing less from a ghost that's been haunting me, especially one that's been doing so for almost ten years now. I'm used to it, in the same way I'm used to his lean physique, his sandy-blonde hair and warm brown eyes, down to the dimples that appear when he smiles. All the details of him only I know.

Because normal people can't see ghosts.

A few can sense them, and a few of those few may be able to pick up a signal or two from them. But me? I can see them as well as sense them. I can hear them, too. And talk to them. I can even feel their touch, as feather-light as it is. This isn't something I go around advertising to the world, however. In fact, it's something kept solely between me and the dead, and the dead happen to be very good at keeping secrets.

"You don't have to do this," he cautions, looking around for any sign of trouble, being my eyes where I can't see.

"I know," I agree. He's been telling me this all evening. "But I don't have any better ideas."

I pace down the side of the house, escaping the headlights of a passing car. I rummage through the old potted plants along the back door until I find what I'm looking for.

"Ta-da," I mutter, wiping soil off the key. I place it in the door lock and slowly turn it. "Didn't even change the locks. And technically it's not breaking and entering if the owner gives you permission to enter." I smirk at Cole as I creep inside.

"Try telling that to the judge," he replies, following closely behind me.

I hope it will never come to that. He makes a good point, though. No police officer or judge would believe me. Heck, it was years before I believed myself. But that's why I'm here, tiptoeing across some dead lady's kitchen.

It's not like I'm a regular thief; I'm not stealing jewelry or the television set. As I creep down the hallway I wonder what I would say in my defense, but quickly conclude it would be best to just not say anything and hope I reach a good lawyer with my one phone call.

I stop to peer through the ajar door into the living room. A man is snoring in the chair by the ashy fireplace. That would be Roy, a caregiver who has a habit of inheriting quite a few thank-you gifts from his clients once they pass away—gifts that were never intended for him, such as this house.

Call me a vigilante, but I can't let people like Roy get away with what he's doing.

Roy isn't a fan of high school football it seems, which is unfortunate for me right now. But I've come too far to back away and give up, so I creep up the stairs, two at a time to lessen the chance of creaking. My damp shoes squelch instead, the uncomfortable sound too loud in my ears. My soaked leggings and jacket cling to me and I shiver, suddenly freezing in the cold, dark house.

Thankfully I see the first room on the left, just as Ms. Reynolds, the previous occupant, described. I go over to the escritoire and open the drawers, although I'm not surprised to find them empty. Ms. Reynolds mentioned she holds a particular liking for escritoires and cabinets from the nineteenth century, built at a time when inkwells and secret compartments were trendy. Following her instructions, I remove the largest drawer and rummage around until I feel the envelope and pull it out.

"Good. You've got it. Now let's go."

Cole doesn't need to tell me twice. Quietly closing the drawers back up, I shove the envelope into the inside pocket of my jacket and then head back to the stairs.

I freeze at the pair of eyes looking straight at me.

Oh God.

Roy has a dog. A dog with pointy teeth and a spike collar around its thick neck, and claws that would easily rip through my damp skin.

It starts barking as soon as it sees me. I quickly back up to the room and close the door just as it jumps up.

I hear the thump of shoes hitting the stairs.

Roy is awake.

Cole immediately jumps into action, distracting the dog through the wall while I look around. There's nowhere to hide, and only one way out.

I run to the window, heaving it upwards until it loosens and slides up. I peer down before leaning back in again, suddenly feeling sick. There'll be another ghost in this house if I attempt that jump.

Roy's footsteps get closer.

I peer out again and notice the drainpipe on the garage. If I can grab that to break my fall I should be okay. I climb out, closing the window as much as I can while hanging from the ledge, my shoes pressed against the window paneling of the room below. I hear Roy threatening his dog that it will be muzzled if it doesn't stop barking at the clock on the wall, which I assume is where Cole is buying me a few desperate seconds.

I curse under my breath.

Then jump.

The edge of the drainpipe is sharp against my fingers but it takes the brunt of my fall along with it. I try not to yelp too loudly as my body hits the garage wall before I tumble to the concrete ground.

When my double vision fades I see two hands under the upstairs window trying to push it back up. I stumble behind the wall just as Roy peers out the window. Without thinking about the pain in my knees, I sprint through the front gate, turn the corner, and then slide down into the street gutters. The foot-high dirty water immediately soaks through my socks and shoes, but I try my best to ignore it and crouch down in the drainpipe.

"Is he coming?" I ask between short, sharp breaths. "Did he see me?"

"I don't think so," Cole looks back and replies. He stands

there, totally immune to the cold and wet I'm feeling, looking down at me like a parent about to give a life lesson through a long and condescending talk. "You're lucky this time, Charlotte Durane."

"Yeah," I agree, finding my breath. "I am."

"Look at you."

I follow his line of sight down to my knees, now raw and in view through my torn leggings. They're clearly grazed, but any trace of blood is gone with the rain.

"Why do you get yourself into these situations, Charlotte?" he asks, exasperated.

Cole cares, in the big brother sort of way. He's there for me when no one else is, for the laughs and the tears and everything in between. He's like a guardian angel, and I don't know what I would do without him.

The dead aren't all like Cole, though.

Content, fulfilled spirits usually move on quickly. Those that aren't remain behind, usually at protest. Some are just miserable; others are angry. The worst are violent.

Cole keeps the violent ones away as much as possible, but it makes me understand that the purgatory realm of the in-between isn't a great place to be. This is probably why I end up at places I shouldn't be at, doing things I shouldn't be doing, caught between feeling compelled to help those less fortunate—and less physical—and wanting to run away screaming from them. It's a tough situation to be in, and one I don't have an answer for. So, as always, I simply shrug it off.

Cole rakes his fingers through his hair. He does that when he's stressed or feels a lack of control. I feel bad for him when he does it, but it doesn't make it any less sexy.

I hear barking again, which sets me in motion to get away from here. A few blocks later, Ms. Reynolds appears. She clasps her hands over her chest when she sees me holding her will. Her authentic one, that is. The one that gifted her possessions to her children before Roy forged otherwise.

"Thank you, dear. You have no idea how much this means to

me."

"It's okay," I reply.

I take a stamp out of my pocket and place it on the envelope. With a reassuring smile to Ms. Reynolds I slide the envelope into the mailbox. If the mail gets delivered as scheduled, Ms. Reynolds' lawyer will receive that letter within three working days, and a case for her children to inherit what is rightfully theirs will begin, hopefully along with some exposure of the type of person Roy really is.

With one last thanks she leaves, and I know she's at peace now. It's supposed to feel good, helping those less fortunate and less able. And don't get me wrong, it does, even on nights like tonight. But I can't help overthinking how close I was to not having such a happy ending myself, and how I should have stayed at the game instead. And now my favorite leggings are ruined, too.

Cole gives me a reassuring smile. He's proud of me, but I know he has similar qualms, even though he doesn't express them. Cole is someone who lives in his thoughts. He's not one to say more than is needed, rather spending time to process everything in his mind first to ensure the words he does say are more weighted. And when he listens, he waits and takes in every word I have to say.

The world needs more people like Cole in my opinion. Ego doesn't have a place in his heart, which would have made him a good leader or helper to others in need.

Society's loss, I guess.

"You need to prioritize yourself more. Always put your safety first."

There's that voice of reason from him. I should make better attempts to listen to Cole more after tonight.

"Yeah, I'm getting too old for this. In a couple months' time I'll be charged as an adult if I get caught."

He ignores my attempt at humor. "You need to clean those cuts," he says, crouching down and stroking his fingers over my knees.

A simple action, a simple touch.

So why does my heart feel it so strongly?

"It's fine," I reply, trying not to blush.

I've always had a thing for Cole. At first it was a love like that of a sibling, then as our ages neared he became more of a best friend. But he never caused *these* sorts of reactions before, at least not until recently. I did the internet search and marked the symptoms, all pointing to the same diagnosis that I can't get my head around. I can't seriously be crushing on him, can I?

I know the answer to that, but I do my best to hide it from both of us.

He stands, leaving the faint feeling of his touch behind on my sore skin. "I'll walk you back home."

Walking is not something he needs to do of course, but I appreciate the company, if not the reassuring feeling of protection from walking alone at night. By the time I arrive back home, the rain has eased to a silent drizzle with only the sound of a few early season crickets chirping in the sighing breeze. Dad is back early from his fishing trip, no doubt because of the rain. I know because he's left the lights on for me, which is unfortunate, since I told him I'd be home and he's obviously checked.

Cole leaves me to it with the reassurance I won't be seeing any more visitors tonight. That's our teamwork in play: Cole helps to keep ghosts from visiting me so I can function at least somewhat in daily life while I help the lost souls who genuinely need it. The fact that we both keep each other company is a nice bonus.

What I don't know, however, is where he goes to or what he does to pass the days and nights. I can't imagine that there is much to do when you're a ghost, and I have tried asking him over the years to only receive vague or cryptic replies. Perhaps it's some sort of ghost code I'm not privy to know, or perhaps Cole just doesn't want me to know.

I'm not going to get these answers tonight, if ever, so I creep inside, careful not to trigger the canine intruder alarm. I hear the patter of Pippi's paws before she comes into view, but a quick whisper to let her know it's me and a treat from the cupboard keeps her quiet. I lock up and turn off the lights, careful to navigate through the living room past the fireplace when I see her face in the moonlight; the same photograph I face at the beginning and end of every day.

My mother. The one visitor I still hold out for.

I smile, a sad hello. I wonder what she would think of her daughter on nights like tonight. Would she be proud or concerned? Does my reckless side come from her, or is it something of my own? The longer I look at her, the more questions come to mind—questions I've spent far too long pondering over without getting an answer for. I look away, knowing I won't get those answers tonight.

With a quick shower I clean my knees and then flop into bed, the winning results of the night the last thought before I close my eyes.

∞∞∞∞

Even though it doesn't feel like it, I must have slept, because when I open my eyes it's suddenly daytime and my phone alarm is buzzing.

I drag my arm out from my cocoon of warmth and slumber, patting around until I feel the screen of my phone and then flick my finger to stop the sound. I snuggle back under my covers, not caring what the world has waiting for me. It's Saturday after all, and there's still sleep to be had.

"Charlotte," Dad knocks on my door. "Get dressed and come downstairs. I need to talk to you about last night."

Crap.

Suddenly awake, I sit up and rub the remnants of sleep from my eyes before sliding out from my covers. Regardless of Dad's tone, I take my time trudging through the usual morning routine of bathroom, clothes, and then makeup. I usually save looking decent until last; if I give myself too much time looking in the mirror I'll start noticing a pimple or dark circles, how my teeth aren't perfectly straight, or if I should apply more than my go-to tinted moisturizer, mascara, and cherry-flavored lip balm.

Today it's all about the hair, more sprawled out than usual since I didn't fully dry it last night. I don't know where my thick auburn waves come from, considering no one else in my family has it, but it's there, attached to my head, so I have to deal with it.

I sigh, styling my hair into a messy ponytail, just enough to hold the unruly locks in place. I brush my bangs to the side then head downstairs to face the music.

Pippi greets me first with a sniff and lick of my hand. She expects a rub of her beige fur in return, and I comply as I put a slice of bread in the toaster.

Dad enters the kitchen, newspaper in hand. He has his unimpressed parent face on, his frown lines showing above his thick eyebrows. I pour myself a glass of orange juice and take a big gulp, hoping the sickly-sweet taste of concentrate will give me the energy needed for whatever this conversation will entail.

"I heard you come in late last night."

"The game," I reply nonchalantly. "We won."

"The police might want to speak to you."

My stomach churns.

"The police?" I ask as casually as my shaking voice allows. "Why is that?"

"You tell me. I hear they're at the school, talking to students who were there. Something to do with the game last night, no doubt. Probably some pranksters."

"At school?"

"Yes." Dad must have heard my sigh of relief. "You were there, right? Then came straight home?"

I grip my glass. "Yes."

"You didn't do anything stupid, did you?"

I try not to hesitate. "No."

"Is everything alright?" he asks, seeing through me.

I'm a good liar; I do it every day. But Dad is one of those parents that just knows when you're not being fully honest with them.

"Are you seeing things again?" He pauses, before adding, "*Ghostly* things?"

I cringe. It takes him effort to say the word.

Dad is a man of stout Christian tradition; to him there's Heaven or Hell and nothing in between. So when I kept crying to him about seeing ghosts everywhere, I ended up in front of a therapist with a diagnosis of anxiety disorder and given medication to match. Needless to say the medication didn't do any good, and, as I grew older, I learned pretty quickly that parents don't have to know everything about their children. So, with Cole helping to keep the unwelcome visitors away and keep me sane, I lied well enough to have it all thrown under the rug.

Or so I thought.

His gaze narrows when I don't answer.

"We can make an appointment to see the specialist again, if you want."

"It's fine, Dad." I place my glass in the dishwasher to deal with later. "Really. Nothing I can't handle."

"Is it that Cole thing again?"

I had tried telling Dad about Cole when I was younger. Because I improved with Cole around he let it slide, until he realized Cole is a teenager. And a guy. So Cole became another secret: we were living with a ghost. A cute, charming, caring ghost I now undeniably have feelings for.

"No." That technically isn't a lie.

He looks uncomfortable, which is how I feel. "As long as you're not in any kind of trouble."

The toast pops out of the toaster and I snatch it hot.

"I'm not in any kind of trouble." Also not technically a lie as far as I know. "Well, I never thought I'd say this on a Saturday, but I'm late for school, see ya."

I take a bite of toast as I grab my phone and wave bye, which is enough for Dad to let it go. For now, anyway.

Swallowing down the last of my breakfast, I head down the road to school. Foxton isn't a particularly unique place to grow up in. It doesn't have any special features or landscapes that put it on the map, and it doesn't lead to anywhere special either, except other similar towns that dot the state. It's as if settlers got tired of wandering for exciting new lands and decided to set up base here instead. Maybe one day, when the world population soars, all the small towns around here will join and become one big metropolis. But for now it's the type of place where the church serves as the hive of the community, and the older folk still believe in the American Dream.

The younger generation, however, believe more in getting out as soon as we can to make something of ourselves.

"Your hair looks better when it's down." Cole appears by my side, walking in time to my own footsteps. "It's hair that's not meant to be tamed."

I roll my eyes but smile. Cole knows everything about me, including my insecurities. I don't mind; he would never tell anyone, even if he could. He's the type of person who can keep a secret like a Swiss bank keeps gold.

"Good morning to you, too." I smile, feeling the morning sun on my face.

I like the walk to school. It is the same fifteen-minute walk I take every weekday: the same dog barks from the window at number ten, the same birds tweet in the nearby maple tree, the same neighbor who makes it a daily morning ritual to do his gardening has his lawn has his lawnmower out, and the ghost that appears at my side is the same Cole. Except now my heart races when he's near me, and when I look up to see him neither the neighborhood nor anything else seems to matter.

Part of me wants to confess this to Cole, to find out how he feels in return. But aside from the obvious reasons we could never be together romantically, I simply need him too much to risk losing him if he doesn't feel the same way.

I sigh, confused and defeated by my own thoughts.

"You look stressed," Cole says before noticing where I'm heading. "Is it Monday already?"

"No, just checking something out. It shouldn't take long." My mouth movements are now subtle, my eyes looking ahead at other students swarming towards the school like bees to a hive. He knows I'm trying not to garner attention talking to myself. I only hope he doesn't know what I'm really feeling, too.

"Cheer up, only a month left of school to go."

"Five weeks to be precise. Not like I'm counting them down."

It hasn't been easy getting through school. I have learned to adapt though, mostly by being as unremarkable as possible. This means being the quiet, reserved student at the back of the classroom, the one with B-average grades, plain clothes, and minimum hobbies. I'm okay with that; grades and fashion aren't my thing, and I certainly don't have time for hobbies with my secondary lifestyle. But high school is nearly finished, and the prospect of leaving town is becoming more real.

I don't yet know what I want to do or where I want to go. I also don't have the grades or extracurriculars to study anywhere fancy. Not to undermine helping the dead, but I just don't see it being well received on my college applications. But I don't care where I end up, anywhere is better than here, preferably as far away as possible. I also don't care where I go as long as Cole is with me.

"Haunt ya later."

Those are Cole's usual parting words before he vanishes to wherever it is ghosts go. It used to make me giggle every time he said it. It's cheesy now, but I still smile, because it's him. Usually I would prefer his company, but right now I could do with the space to get my emotions in order. Besides, right now I need to focus on doing things like being normal and finding out what happened at the game last night.

"Haunt ya later," I mutter, now alone in a crowd. The buzz of gossip and chatter fills the air, although it's quieter than usual. I guess the police car and news van parked out front causes that effect. Still, I'm half-expecting patriotic school chants and the odd cheer about last night's game to be heard as I make my way to the school entrance.

Foxton High School is the type of school that could be on a postcard: symmetrical front building, red brick, flagpole on the front lawn with the American flag and school sports flag (go, Foxes!) waving lazily in the air. It's almost peaceful to look at. And as with any school, through the doors, the student body of nine hundred students always have some drama to deal with. Most of the students get along reasonably enough with one another. Then there's *The Squad*.

Cole is well aware of The Squad. He calls it his "favorite daytime show" because they are the types of students—rich or athletic or both—who try to live like the popular kids portrayed in movies. Except nobody bothered to tell them movies aren't real.

So it doesn't surprise me at all that talk of Vanessa is the first thing I hear in the hallway.

Vanessa is a girl who carries all the clichés: well-off parents, extroverted, popular, prom queen in the making. So naturally, I distance myself from her. I give her and her friends a respectful nod if we pass in the hallway, or a compliment on the performance I did not watch, creating just enough ego support to not stick out either way. And it works.

Or it did, until the day they saw me arguing with myself. I was actually arguing with the late town mayor about protected forest land losing its status so a residential subdivision could be built, something I still passionately oppose, but obviously she didn't know that. She immediately told everyone in the school, and I've been branded a freak ever since.

I huff as I walk past members of The Squad, expecting some cheerleading team announcement about last night's game or to be given a badge with the words 'VANESSA FOR PROM QUEEN' in block letters.

I am not, however, expecting to see Vanessa's vigil.

"It's insane, isn't it? Vanessa Stalinski, dead."

I turn to find Leslie—the closest thing I have to a friend (who's alive)—standing beside me, only I don't know what to say. Leslie and I aren't close, but we're convenient. We give each other someone to talk to at lunch and to pair with on projects; just enough to get through school comfortably and appear as normal as possible. We even do the odd hang out after school to show our parents how social we are, but it's never for long. She could be a vampire slayer, or turn into a werewolf at every full moon for all I know.

Not that vampires or werewolves exist.

I think.

I stare at the yearbook photo of Vanessa, printed large and laminated, surrounded by flowers and cards.

"What happened?" I ask, still in disbelief.

"You don't know?"

No, because I was too busy spending my night conducting a house heist to catch up on local town gossip. Not that anyone informs me of the local town gossip, because they don't— not even Leslie, it seems. But she was very alive leading the cheerleading team at the game last night, all buoyant and peppy, that I do know.

"I must have missed the memo," I say.

"She never came home after the game. They called the cops and started a search party. It didn't last very long though, because the football coach found her body on the bleachers. Poor guy."

Being a child immigrant from Honduras, Leslie considers herself thick-skinned. Weakness isn't in her lexicon, which is probably why she's not upset like the rest of the students. That, and no doubt because she disliked Vanessa as much as me.

"Why?" I ask, shaking my head. "How did she . . . ?"

"The rumor is alcohol poisoning. The police are waiting for the autopsy results to rule out anything suspicious, but they're taking any witness statements to be sure, and along with *this*," she nods towards the flowers, "we're here on a Saturday." Leslie smiles reassuringly at two girls who pass before muttering, "Pointless if you ask me, since she was found with booze and vomit everywhere you can assume she simply celebrated the win a little *too* much."

I watch Leslie walk over to the nearby table where students are writing messages of love on cut-out hearts when I realize.

"Shit."

Vanessa, the 'it' girl, is dead.

Except Vanessa, the 'it' girl, is also standing ten feet away and looking straight at me.

Two

"Oh my God." She says it first, but we are both thinking it. "You can see me."

I can't say I'm prepared for Vanessa to talk to me, let alone ghost Vanessa. I stand there wondering if I should respond or run away, until she says, as clear as day, "Of course the freak can."

I cower at the words, then roll my eyes and take off in the other direction.

"Wait," she calls out above the low murmurs from the students.

I don't look back. Instead I pace into the toilets, only they're full of upset girls reapplying their makeup.

"You can hear me too, right?" She shouts in my ear. "Right?!"

I flinch.

"Hey!" She calls as I snake between the crowds of students in the hallway.

I rush into a classroom and close the door behind me, keeping my back against it. Not that it stops Vanessa from coming through the wall like there's nothing there, but it is a comforting reflex, nonetheless.

A few faces look my way, but then disregard me. They're used to my weird quirks. Most of the students are still in the hallway anyway, crying or calling their parents.

I walk to a desk, taking my phone from my pocket and putting it against my ear.

"Can you not!" I hiss, intimidated by my own sudden assertiveness. Why couldn't I be like this all the time?

"Who are you talking to?" Vanessa asks.

"I'm talking to *you*," I reply.

"Why can't anyone else see me?"

I look at Vanessa for a punchline that doesn't come.

"Because," I murmur under my breath, "you're a ghost."

Vanessa glares down at me. "Bullshit. If I'm a ghost then why is it you can see me but no one else can, huh?"

"I . . . I don't know." Which is the honest-to-God truth.

"This is just some weird dream. Of course you're also weird in my dream."

I raise an eyebrow at her. Denial is a common trait among the newly deceased, but this is some determination. I mean, she just walked through a wall. Students are crying at her locker. We're at school on a *Saturday*.

While Vanessa starts berating me I message Dad to let him know what happened. A few more students soon trickle inside, including Dylan, Vanessa's boyfriend, who looks like he's been through hell and back.

Everyone suddenly goes quiet, including Vanessa.

He makes his way to the side of the classroom, pulling out a piece of paper and pen from the drawer before leaving with Vanessa in tow. As much as I don't want to feel it, the heavy atmosphere lurks and is hard to ignore. People actually liked Vanessa Stalinski, and are genuinely upset she's gone.

But she's not gone, I think in silence. *She's still here.*

Except, of course, only I know that.

Principal Headley enters the classroom, looking as glum as everyone else, and we are ushered into the school auditorium to await questioning. As well as officers calling in students one at a time to question, volunteer therapists are setting up group talk sessions on social drinking and peer pressure, and I overhear a few adults discussing the need for a self-defense workshop.

Standing on stage is a congregation of Vanessa's closest friends that make up The Squad, all eight of them (nine including Vanessa, but I guess she doesn't count anymore), taking turns saying how great she was, and how she will remind them to make the most out of their lives. Ryan and Liam share funny stories, followed by Sven who even wrote a poem. Gwen, Vanessa's number two in The Squad, puts on quite a performance before Stephanie and Mandy ushered her off stage.

Vanessa—her ghost, that is—appears in front of the stage, but instead of being moved by her friends' efforts, in the classic Vanessa manner she stands there, arms crossed, complaining.

Not that I'm surprised. She was always one for theatrics, even with those who put up with her, and that clearly hasn't changed.

"Most of you know I was with Vanessa since junior year. I loved Vanessa . . ." It's Dylan's turn to speak, not that I could pay attention because Vanessa is suddenly at my side.

"Pfft, Dylan didn't love me," she mutters, I guess to me. "You don't need to lie anymore!" she calls out to him before turning to me. "Tell them I'm here."

I frown uncomfortably, keeping my gaze on Dylan. For all the times Vanessa's presence made me shy away or take a detour to class, this time I can't run or hide.

Dylan struggles for composure until the rest of The Squad usher him aside and Jordan, the star quarterback that won last night's game and who would otherwise be the spotlight of celebration, now stands center stage to read aloud his hastily put-together speech.

"Tell them I'm here!" she demands again, but I keep a straight face, ignoring her.

Not now, Vanessa.

"Bitch, listen to me!"

She raises her fist in the air. Fighting the urge to wince away I brace for impact. While it wouldn't leave me with a black eye, I would certainly feel an unpleasant force of energy strike me.

"Don't." Cole appears, his hand catching hers.

My heart flips inside my chest.

Vanessa seems taken aback by this sudden interruption. She yelps as if, well, she's seen a ghost.

I look at her as if to say, "What, did you think you were the only ghost around?" but her eyes are still on Cole.

With *that* look, the innocent startled double-eyed blink one.

"Who, who are you?" her voice turns high and soft and I can feel my face curl up in disgust.

"I'm Cole," he replies in his usual benign tone. "Tell me what's wrong, Vanessa."

"What's wrong?" she starts, choking up emotion. "Nobody will talk to me. I keep disappearing and reappearing at places. Everyone's saying things about me that aren't true. And if what they're saying is true then I'm going to miss out on prom!"

I give her a look, but I'm really not surprised. Prom was probably the pinnacle of her existence.

"I'm sorry for what you're going through. But what you're doing here won't help," he replies, remaining perfectly calm. "Come, let's go talk outside."

Cole and I meet eyes and I twitch a grateful smile. He nods back, our teamwork in play. My relief is cut short, however, when I then notice Vanessa's fist is now loose fingers entwined with his as he leads her away.

My nostrils flare. She better not be doing what I think she is doing! I roll my eyes and slump in my seat. Great. While I have to sit and watch fake nice things being said about poor gone-too-soon Vanessa, she's already moving on to Cole. It's when I am tapped on the shoulder and see a police officer wanting me to stand up and follow him that I wish it really is some weird dream. I knew I should have stayed in bed this morning.

∞∞∞∞∞

Thankfully the questions were few and easy enough to answer, especially once I said I left early because of the rain. But even after hanging around to watch the rest of The Squad talk about Vanessa for any new information, I am still confused.

Vanessa is dead, but the how and why are still under investigation.

Everyone is suspicious and scared. Parents are being vigilant, including Dad, who has made it clear I am not to be outside after dark. And, as it is with teenagers from small towns, gossip rages like wildfire. The rumors in the school hallway already range from a new deadly party drug to a football score revenge prank gone wrong, and even cold-blooded murder, which is probably why that self-defense workshop is now happening. And the real story, straight from the horse's mouth herself: nothing.

Yeah, nothing.

Now, I can't speak from experience, but I would assume your death is something you'd remember pretty well if you suddenly found yourself, well, *dead*.

Apparently not.

"Death isn't always an enlightening experience, Charlotte," Cole remarks. "Some rather not remember. Some don't let themselves remember."

Cole has a fine line when it comes to talk of death, especially his own. He was eighteen when it happened, which means he's still eighteen now. But aside from his birthday (April 18) and his age (twenty-seven if he were still alive, but who's counting?), his cause of death is something I don't know.

Of course it is something I want to know, however. I mean, we've been friends for nearly a decade, and that should count for something, at least in my opinion. I've brought it up here and there, but it's something that obviously still bothers him because he always avoids talking about it. And if he doesn't want to talk about it then what can else I do? So I don't push it; a price I pay for keeping what relationship we have.

Nonetheless, I can't help but notice the look in his eyes as he says that. Even after knowing Cole for all these years, there's still a mysteriousness that surrounds him. It sometimes peeks through his light and shows in his eyes, a weight on the thoughts he keeps inside himself. And right now they are dark, as if fighting back unwanted images; memories he'd rather not remember.

"It will come back to her," he reassures me. "Being dead gives you a lot of time to think."

I guess, considering when you're dead you don't have to

work, or sleep, or study for exams, or wait for the bus, or eat, or anything really. I wonder if that's all Cole does when he's alone: think.

We're lying on opposite sides of the trampoline in the backyard, facing the sky. It's one of our usual thinking places, chosen for the privacy and backdrop. My house is at least fifty years old, sitting on the border of suburbia and countryside. It's a renovated farmhouse, now blending old beams and brick with modern interiors in a unique way that differs from the cookie-cutter newbuilds that grow like weeds from an urban sprawl. The first houses erected tend to get the spots with the best views, which is why I get a nice view of the dwindling hillside to the township from the back garden.

When I was younger I would jump high on the trampoline, trying to see the span of the whole county area. I enjoyed it, right up until one time I lost my balance and fell off, spraining my ankle. I don't need the trampoline anymore, but to Dad's annoyance, I insist it stays, for Cole. It's one of his favorite spots, along with the water tank and front porch decking. He likes to watch the clouds and stars from it while losing himself to his thoughts, and since he is such a quiet and conscientious tenant I figure keeping an old trampoline for him is the least I can do.

"You and this bloody trampoline," Dad says as he approaches me.

"It's still not going anywhere, Dad." I sit up to face him, Cole already gone. He's respectful of that, giving me privacy for personal conversations even though he doesn't have to.

Dad places a plate in front of me. "Rhubarb."

Dad manages a small truck stop diner just outside of town, which is ironic given his vastly limited culinary skills. He leaves the actual food part to other staff though, and keeps himself busy behind the scenes with everything else from accounting and deliveries to maintenance.

Making pies, however, is something we do very well. It started as a therapeutic coping mechanism after the car crash that broke my family of soon-to-become four down to just the two of us. Considering Mom was the main cook, pies were the only thing Dad and I knew how to make. So, after she died it was oven foods, microwave meals, and various pies that became the new staple diet of the Durane household, at least until we bought some basic recipe books and got the garden productive again.

I never complained, though. Making a mess in the kitchen with Dad was a fun distraction, and vegetables were yucky anyway.

"Everything's better with pie," I say before taking a bite. "Even days like today."

I know what's coming, which is why I said it.

"How are you feeling?"

Bingo. The question I hate most after "Are you okay?".

It always starts like this from strangers or relatives or therapists, and they always expect some strewn-out answer. Except sometimes there just aren't any answers to give, like right now, because I simply don't know how I feel. Vanessa and I weren't close (at all), but she was (is?) still a classmate, and now she's a life no more.

So I simply answer, "I'm okay."

This is probably the answer Dad expects because it's the answer he always gets. He puts up a short-lived smile, then an awkward silence ensues as he rubs his chin, something he does when he's entering uncomfortable territory.

"Did you . . . know? Last night, that she had passed away?"

I don't know if he means from gossip or other-worldly phenomena, but I answer truthfully. "No."

"Oh." He sounds relieved, if anything, as if maybe his daughter isn't as crazy as he fears. Because of all the spirits I claimed had visited me, surely the people I actually knew who died had come to me? Aside from my mother's parents who passed away when I was just a baby, there are now two people that fit into that category: Vanessa and my mother. Vanessa didn't come to me when she died, which is fine, I'm not complaining. Except that when my mother died she didn't come back to me, either.

That was the question asked in therapy, the question I still can't answer. Which is why I was signed off as having anxiety with abandonment issues.

"I have to do some things at the diner but Patricia is on her way over. Do you mind sorting out dinner?"

Patricia works at the town library, which is not a place Dad would go to, except that one time I was sick with the flu and begged him to pick up some items I had on hold. I don't like to brag, but I knew their shared interests in vintage motorcycles and permaculture lifestyle would create a lasting connection, which may be why I made Dad pick up the apiculture book and motorcycle magazine I just *had* to have.

But like Dad, Patricia also experienced loss in her life when her late husband passed away from cancer. The connection through grief is a special one, a bind that others simply can't understand nor should ever have to. And although they are only friends, I'm just glad Dad has someone in his life to confide in— that is, when his tough exterior allows for it.

I'm not surprised he called Patricia, though. I know he doesn't want to leave me alone, especially at a time like this. I don't blame him; Foxton isn't the type of town to have such things happen, whether accidental or not.

"Sure. I'll have a pick in the garden for things to go with the fish you caught."

Dad nods. "I'm considering starting the hives up again."

I glance to the two empty hives at the back of the yard, past the greenhouse and fruit trees. The garden was Mom's project, but Dad's admirably kept it up with the odd help from Patricia and myself—a living shrine to her passion for conservation.

"Sounds like a good idea." Cole, who fondly takes to watching bees in all his spare time will be pleased. "I'll make sure the hives are clean and ready."

"Thanks, bub," Dad replies before heading off to work.

I sit there finishing the pie, wondering if Cole will come back. When it becomes clear he won't, I take Pippi for a walk and then get on with chores. By the time dinner with Dad and Patricia is finished (lemon and pepper-flavored grilled fish with fresh vegetables and the last of the rhubarb pie, Patricia's favorite) I excuse myself to get ready for bed, reassuring them both that I'm fine and just craving the sleep lost from the night before.

Pippi follows me as I head upstairs to my room. Cole is waiting for me at the top of the staircase. He never enters my bedroom without my permission, fully respecting my personal space.

"Patricia is here."

"Yeah, Dad's on protective parent mode, making sure Vanessa's death isn't triggering some trauma in me from when Mom died."

I'm no scientist, but since the universe is made up of energy, that's what I assume ghosts are: the energy of their consciousness, based on the soul imprint of their physical bodies. This energy changes based on their emotions, so when they carry positive emotions they become lighter and more luminous. But if negative emotions are brought up, their glow darkens.

This means even Cole, as reserved as he is, can be easy to read when there's strong emotional variance involved. Which means when he's happy he can look jovial, but when he's sad he can look devastated. And it's not even big things that trigger such reactions within him; it's the small things like watching a butterfly emerge from a chrysalis that makes his aura glow, or words like the ones I just said that dims it.

"I'm fine," I reassure him as I close the door behind us. "It's not like Vanessa and I were close. If anyone needs help it's her boyfriend Dylan. I didn't think I'd ever feel sorry for a member of The Squad, but the poor guy looked so broken."

It takes Cole a long moment for his aura to return to its usual soft glow. "It's certainly not an episode of The Squad I was expecting."

"Me neither. How is Vanessa now, anyway? Minus the amnesia."

"She's upset she can no longer have everyday experiences like painting her nails or dressing up."

The dead don't exactly look like their moment of death (and thank goodness; seeing ghosts is one thing but seeing ghosts bloodied or charred or with other gruesome ends to their lives lost would be a whole higher level of freak-out), but instead they have a habit of taking on their last stable form before their body succumbed to whatever sickness or accident that killed them.

That's why Vanessa is still wearing her cheerleading uniform, and Cole, for whatever reason, is always wearing a white t-shirt and dark navy-blue jeans. His hair looks lightly styled with hair gel, and if I look closely I can see he shaved not too long before it happened. But that's it. Nothing substantial, nothing distinguishable. Wherever he was, whatever he was doing before his death, he probably wasn't expecting it.

"Do you miss it? Everyday experiences, I mean."

I know I shouldn't, but sometimes I can't help but slide such a question into our conversations. I only hope he doesn't retreat away like he has a habit of doing in such moments.

"Not really," Cole eventually replies, his energy holding steady. I notice he's watching a spider weave a web of silk on the corner of my bedside table. "In some ways I think I experience more."

"Well, she better get over her afterlife hangover and sort herself out. I don't think I can take too many more of her outbursts."

I slump down on my bed, mindlessly throwing Pippi her tennis ball to catch across my room. After two bounces she catches it in her mouth then circles herself down between us. She accepts Cole as family, whatever it is of him she senses, although she still barks once at his entrance or exit.

"I'll speak to her, but she's very distressed right now, and she's going to need help getting through her dying process."

I huff at the directing tone of his words, shaking my head.

I mean, I get it. I help ghosts; it's what I do. Some just want to relay messages to loved ones that are simple and sweet, while others cause a lot of conflict with those on the receiving end. But I don't pry; that's not my business, not my burden to carry.

Vanessa, however? She's my business. Which sucks, because I doubt she even thought about me unless the opportunity for a taunt came up, whereas I thought about her every day, always on the defensive for what she would say or do to me.

And now *I* am supposed to help *her*?

If Vanessa's untimely demise really is as distressing as Cole suggests, I will have to put past grievances aside and help her where I can. And I know this is what Cole wants with the look he's giving me.

"Yeah, I get it. I'll try to help her. It won't be easy, though."

Cole smiles and sits next to me. Cole is a gentle soul; I can tell it in his eyes. He has always been kind, even when he's angry or when his energy is dark.

I look into them as he says, "That's the amazing thing about you, Charlotte. Even if it's difficult, even if it's tiring or you simply don't want to, you help because you care."

I smile back and glance away, fighting the need to stick my head in the freezer downstairs to cool my burning cheeks. Whatever it is I am feeling right now I have to stop it before it gets too noticeable and I risk ruining everything we are.

Cole's eyes narrow and his head turns. Suddenly Pippi barks repeatedly as three ghosts appear in the center of my bedroom.

"Uhm, have you heard of knocking?" I say angrily at the three young women. Each one is wearing a different colored cocktail dress that matches their hair and shoe color. Had I not known otherwise I would have passed them off as members of The Squad. "What if I was naked?"

"Well *he's* here," one of them says, nodding at Cole.

There's a big difference between Cole seeing me naked and them seeing me naked, but I quickly bury that thought.

"Sorry," Cole says, now standing defensively. "I let my guard down."

Okay, I really wish he would add more context. Does he mean he let his guard down with me or with keeping the dead at bay, possibly because of me?

"You're not the problem," I reply sweetly before scowling at the three uninvited guests. "Office hours are closed."

"Vanessa said that you can see us," the one with short black hair to match her short black dress, short black bag, and short black heels says. Her arms are crossed and she already looks bored of waiting.

Of course she knows Vanessa. I bet they're already besties.

"Seeing you and *seeing* you are two different things," I say between clenched teeth.

"That's like, so trippy you can see us," the redhead in the middle says.

"She said that you'd help us," the other one sporting neutral tones adds. She's petite, in the real vulnerable young woman sort of way. Her voice is squeaky and she has a long face that makes her look unintentionally glum.

"What happened?" I question them.

"We took some bad drugs," the redhead says.

"Really bad," the one dressed in black adds. Maybe it is how half her head is shaved down, or the various tattoos and piercings on her body, but I can believe she is the type to consume such substances. The other two, however, not so much. They probably followed their social leader to their own reckless demise.

"We want to let our boyfriends know it's not their fault," the glum-looking one says.

"Why would it be their fault?" I ask.

"Well, they supplied them to us," the redhead sheepishly replies.

"But they didn't mean for us to die."

"We feel really bad."

I roll my eyes.

"We want to let them know that we're okay."

"Just a phone call. Or three. That's all we ask."

"Vanessa said that you're so helpful. She's telling everyone what you can do and how well you help."

"Is she now?" I raise an eyebrow in Cole's direction.

"Do you want me to get rid of them?" Cole whispers to me.

I shake my head. They'll only come back in higher numbers tomorrow from the sound of things.

"I'll go talk to Vanessa. You'll be okay for a while?" He smiles sympathetically at me, which is enough to make me nod and smile back.

Pippi barks once as he leaves.

I sigh. It's going to be a long night after all.

Three

It took a couple of days, but the initial shock of Vanessa's death eased. Conversations were getting back to normal again. Students were still cautious while the investigations around Vanessa's death were still ongoing, but the school routine was taking over, making our days more manageable.

My feelings for Cole were getting more manageable, too. They hadn't gone, but, like everyone else in the hallways, I carry on as my thoughts and feelings about those no longer alive linger in the background.

Quite literally, in fact.

Unbeknownst to them, Vanessa does all she can to make herself known. If there's one thing I've learned from all my years of ghost watching, it's that the dead are just as emotional as the living, and when they throw a tantrum, it *really* shows.

And there are moments—as rare as they are—when ghosts can conjure up so much emotional energy that they become more physical. That's my theory, anyway. It explains how really angry ghosts can do things like move a glass off a shelf or punch a picture on a wall hard enough it actually falls off.

Most people usually shrug it off as an odd draft or a rusty nail. Pets tend to bark or hiss, sensing something in their territory that shouldn't be there. Some people get a sudden chill down their spine or the feeling they're not alone. They're usually right.

So when I see Vanessa storming through the hallway towards me, leaving a gust in her trail, I know it isn't going to be pretty.

"You!" She points her finger at me, raging energy blaring off from her. "You have *got* to tell them I'm still here."

I stand there in shock. Students pick up their papers falling to the floor, probably assuming it's just a wind tunnel from the open windows and operating ceiling fans due to the early high coming in from the Gulf. Some kid bumps into me and mutters for me to move it, which is a daringly rude way to speak to a senior, but nonetheless gets my legs moving.

"Don't just turn away from me!" she bellows behind me. "Hey!"

I shakily search my bag for my phone. Just as I grab it I dodge walking into a student, dropping my textbooks in the process.

"I said——" She now stands in front of me. "—you have got to tell them I'm still here!"

I can't believe what I'm hearing. Vanessa, expecting me to do the very thing she mocked me for, without even asking, with her same bitchy tone as always? Has death not changed her attitude even the slightest?

"No," I hiss back.

"Fine, I won't help you then."

I look up to see someone stand and walk away from me, muttering a nasty name my way.

"I wasn't talking to you," I sheepishly say in vain.

Oblivious, Vanessa carries on being the center of attention she's always seen herself as. "Are you listening to me?"

I pick up my belongings, balancing them in my arms as I pull my phone to my ear.

"Yes, I heard you!" I seethe.

Cole is suddenly next to us.

"*Vanessa.*" There's exasperation in his voice, his arms crossed. "What did I say about harassing Charlotte at school?"

"But they're questioning Dylan!"

"Who are?" I ask.

"The police! They're even asking him if he wants to call a lawyer. A lawyer!"

"Is he in handcuffs?" Cole asks.

"No," Vanessa replies.

"That's good. I'm sure it's just routine questioning," Cole reassures her.

"But he didn't do anything to me, he wouldn't."

"What makes you so sure?" I ask.

"Because I am, okay?" she snaps back at me.

I look up to Cole, my expression jaded. This is what I have to deal with? I'll raise the white flag now, she's on her own.

Cole takes the reins. "If you're sure he didn't do anything wrong, he'll be let go."

"You think so?" Vanessa's newfound soft voice makes me want to gag.

Cole smiles warmly at her. My stomach jolts. It's a good thing my emotional energy doesn't show like theirs because they'd be seeing some very wild, dark colors right now.

"Go keep a watchful eye. It'll be alright. You'll see. You'll laugh later on about how worried you were."

"Okay." She sniffs. "See you later then." And after a small touch of his arm she disappears.

I huff. I have no words.

"You're angry," Cole eventually says, following me back down the hallway. The bell rings and as quickly as the hallways became packed are now becoming deserted. I put my phone in my pocket.

"You think?"

"Why?"

"What?"

"Why are you angry?"

I scowl. I don't have time for this.

"We've dealt with worse than Vanessa."

"Vanessa's different, because—" I swallow, blinking away the tears that want to escape my eyes before Cole notices. "—she made my life hell for years, and by some cruel trick of the gods she is even worse dead than alive."

"Trick of the gods, eh?" Cole asks, raising an eyebrow.

"You know what I mean."

I cannot say God or the Bible or any religion for that matter is something I overly believe in. I've seen too much death and suffering with spirits gone too soon, too young, or spirits that feel lost and left behind to believe that there's such a thing as a loving god out there.

Not to mention all the Vanessas that exist in the world. No deity in their right mind would allow such a thing to happen.

"Fate can be cruel," Cole simply replies.

Cole is a mystery, but it's fair of me to assume that his beliefs are similar to my own. He's clearly not in a rush to move on to whatever afterlife there is, not that I'm complaining. And based on his aversion to talking about his death, I often wonder if he even cares to find out what awaits him.

Maybe one day he'll open up about his philosophies. But honestly, right now Vanessa is taking up enough of my time. And patience.

"Vanessa died. Yes, boo-hoo so sad. But can't she just remember and move on already? She's overstaying her expiry." Cole gives me a look as his light dims. I curse under my breath. "Sorry, Cole, I didn't mean it like that."

"She's still trying to remember. She feels like things don't quite add up."

"Can she add them up quicker at least?"

"She just needs more time. And support."

Cole gives me a pointed look; the same one he's been giving me the past couple of days. I know where this is going.

I quickly enter my locker combination and place my pile of books inside, my arms feeling like jello to the sudden release of heavy weight.

"Look, I *will* help Vanessa, okay? After all, the sooner I help her the sooner she'll leave, right?" I close my locker door, harder than needed, then rest my head on it in defeat. "Just not today."

"You're tired."

Cole's voice is soft and silky in the quiet of the hallway. I wonder if he was ever into singing. With a face like his he could be living a very different life right now if he were still alive.

I swallow, the thought disheartening.

I feel the slight press of his hand on my shoulder as he mutters, "I forget what being tired is like."

I turn to him and smile, his calm energy soothing my pent-up frustration. There have been many times when the ghosts became too much. And when they did, when I didn't want to leave my room to face the world, Cole never wavered or criticized. He was always there, to be funny, supportive, or understanding. Even now he makes me feel safe, secure, even *ordinary*. I snicker at the word.

"What's so funny?"

"Here I am, standing in the school hallway talking to a ghost about how to handle the unruly dead. Why can't I be focused on regular seventeen-year-old girl things like friends and makeup and clothes?" I sigh heavily. "Oh, to be ordinary."

"Ordinary? Why would you ever want to be ordinary?" He leans in closer, his arm resting on the locker next to mine, his warm amber eyes in front of me. And in his soothing voice he says, "You're *extraordinary*, Charlotte. Don't forget it."

I smile, trying hard not to blush without much success.

The bell rings again, making me flinch. Cole stands straight, back to his usual self, the past few seconds gone. "And you don't need makeup and your clothes are fine."

"Thanks."

"That's what best friends are for."

Best friends. The words leave a strained feeling within me, like my heart was doing cartwheels but suddenly tripped and tumbled to a halt.

Cole doesn't seem to notice, though. "What class do you have now?"

I think for a moment. "Shit," I mutter, now serious. "The trig test. I forgot all about it since I've been so busy lately with all the extra visitors I've had—thanks to Vanessa, that is."

Cole looks at me sympathetically. "I can help you."

"You know trigonometry?"

"Heck no, like I remember that. I mean, I *am* a ghost. I could just happen upon the answers the smart kids at the front of the class write down and say them out loud."

"Cole!" I say pacing down the hallway, "I can't cheat. That's wrong."

"It's just a dumb test," Cole replies, unconcerned. "It won't haunt you. Trust me on that."

"Still," I say, reaching for the classroom door. "It's immoral."

I apologize to Ms. Kennerson for my tardiness. She looks annoyed, but hands me the test papers anyway. I take the last empty seat and grab a pen from my bag.

"Last chance." Cole's at my side. "Nod or shake."

I open the first page and already all the letters of one word seem to blur onto the next word and so on. I sigh but shake my head.

"Suit yourself," he replies as he walks to the wall. "Haunt ya later."

He vanishes, and I slouch into my elbow on the desk, keeping my pen on the paper with one hand and rubbing my temple with the other. I close my eyes and try to remember all the angle equation methods from class. I really do need a little shuteye time, as Cole recommended.

Cole. I hear him say my name. The throatiness of his voice is thick and sexy, his tone serious with an intonation of wanting. I hear him again, louder this time. I open my eyes and perk my head up. Was I dreaming? I look around. No sign of Cole; everyone is still writing and not a minute has passed on the clock.

Just as I slump back down I hear it—a shrill scream from the hallway.

I jolt upright, eyes full and alert, fatigue now long gone.

I cast around wildly to see if anyone else heard it, but only a few heads turn—and they're looking at me.

I hesitate, not sure how to excuse myself. Even Ms. Kennerson has paused from scrolling on her phone to look at me.

But then Cole screams my name, and I'm out of the classroom door.

At first I don't know what I'm seeing. A janitor stands by a cleaning cart, his back to me in dark green overalls, and there's a strange haze in the hallway in front of him.

Then I see Cole—or what's left of him, already half-consumed as he struggles in vain to stop getting sucked into it.

"Cole!"

I sprint past the janitor and latch onto Cole's chest, gripping him tight to me. He clings to me, his energy so strong that it feels almost like I'm holding someone alive.

I want to take in this feeling more—to feel *him* more, but the haze is making him slip through me. It creeps up from the ground onto his body, like overgrown vines of marble-white hues of light. Looking at it makes me feel lightheaded and queasy, like the travel sickness I used to get as a child on summer vacation road trips. My arms start to feel flaccid, and Cole slips more.

"No!" he panics, gripping me tighter.

I flinch and throw my leg over his, trying to block the haze that's now starting to cover the both of us.

"What is that?" I strain to ask.

"The afterlife," Cole replies through clenched teeth.

A clammy sweat ripples down my body and I feel the adrenalin pump from my chest. The afterlife? Like, Heaven? Or . . . Hell?

I don't have time to ask. I use my legs to push up from the floor, yanking Cole from the haze with me as I fall on my back with my shoulder blade taking the impact. I groan in pain then look up to see the haze gone and the janitor standing frozen in shock, eyebrows furrowed over wide eyes, muttering something incoherent.

I then turn to Cole, who is still gripped onto my arms like a helpless child. But he's still here. With me.

"It's him," Cole stutters, lifting his hand to point. "The janitor. He tried to exorcise me."

"Exorcise?" As in . . . *exorcism?*

I turn to the janitor, my face hot with fury. I shove him against the side of the lockers with a metallic crash, and punch him in the face.

In front of half my class and Ms. Kennerson, I realize, but by this point I don't care. It's too late to do anything about it, so I go all in and punch him again just as Ms. Kennerson shouts my name.

"You . . ." the janitor whispers, his words intense.

"Charlotte Durane!" Ms. Kennerson bellows, yanking me away from him. "What has gotten into you?"

I ignore her, my attention now on Cole. He looks up at me with wild eyes; that mix of confusion and shock that an animal has after a lucky escape, trying to put together what happened, how close he was to . . . I swallow. Cole was preyed upon. By whoever that janitor is.

Ms. Kennerson clicks her fingers in front of my face. "Charlotte!"

Two guys from my class help the janitor to his feet. He looks at Cole, then to me in bewilderment and I wonder if he's trying to piece together what I just did, or if I really hit him that hard. His eye is already swelling, just above his cheek by the crow's feet of his eye.

I glower at him in warning. I'm pretty sure he got the hint.

Two teachers attend to him before I'm motioned away by Ms. Kennerson. Not that I care.

Nobody harms Cole, not with me around.

∞∞∞∞∞

I spend the rest of the trig test and lunchtime sitting outside Principal Headley's office to think about what I did. It's a tactic for children, but it works. It didn't take me long after the walk of shame down the hallway, as teachers gave me scornful looks and tutting, to fully realize I'm in trouble.

Big trouble.

The door opens and another class peer walks out, not daring to look at me. He's the last of the students to give their witness testimony to what they saw, and thanks to the low building budget of the school district I could hear almost every word they said through the thin walls.

"He didn't see anything else, either." Cole is on translation duty between the walls. I could tell him I can already hear but it keeps him feeling useful while I finalize my story.

"That's good," I reply. Being seen picking a fight with a janitor is feasible. Being seen struggling on the floor and talking to myself, not so much.

Since (thankfully) none of my classmates cared to follow me out of the classroom, they only heard the janitor hit the lockers and went to look at what was going on just in time to see the punchline—literally.

I wonder what the janitor told them. He could say the truth but they'd have him in for concussion. Cole the ghost-fly-on-the-wall would have been useful then, but I glared at him to stay away and he didn't need the warning twice.

Thankfully, this means I just need a story that compensates for why I rushed out of the classroom to pick a fight with the janitor. I ponder my excuses: there's always the truth, that I was saving my ghostly best friend and major crush from being exorcised by the janitor who obviously omitted a few things from his résumé. But such a claim wouldn't get me anywhere other than the psychiatric ward. I could scream attempted assault, but I would never stoop that low. Would they believe I have an irrational fear of cleaning products? I sigh. Maybe the 'going mad' excuse would be easiest.

The door opens. "Your turn."

"This is ridiculous," Cole huffs, not that anyone but me can hear his protest. They have invited the school counselor for emotional support and Ms. Kennerson as a witness. They also called Dad in, and I can't even look him in the eyes. Instead, I sit across the long mahogany table facing the condescending gaze of Principal Headley and Jesus on the cross behind her looking down at me while they all wait for me to explain myself.

"Just say you had to go to the bathroom, real bad, because, well, girl things," Cole suggests.

"I had to go to the bathroom. Real bad." I pause before adding,

"Girl things."

My father coughs awkwardly while Principal Headley wiggles slightly in her chair.

"Yes," Cole continued. "Say your tampon exploded inside of you or something."

I blink twice. "I . . . needed a tampon. Badly."

"And how did your *feminine emergency* end up with Mr. Beasey having a black eye?" Principal Headley asks, as if periods need a euphemism. Women like her belong in the 1950s.

"I . . ." I glance at Cole who comes up empty. I then glance at Dad, a disappointed look across his face, waiting for some validity from his daughter. Why can't the ghost standing right next to him be valid enough? Why can't I just be believed for once? Why can't Vanessa just cross over already?

"I was startled. And, in my panicked state I slipped. The janitor—Mr. Beasey—tried to help me by catching my fall." I should stop there, but I don't. "And with all the rumors about Vanessa—" The name makes Principal Headley's eye twitch. "—I thought I was being attacked. I've never seen him before. So, as taught in that self-defense workshop, I punched him. Twice."

I lower my head, hoping they believe my words. I don't realize I'm crying until I see two teardrops fall onto my pants. Using a dead student as a get out of jail card, how callous. But why am I crying? I'm not the one who died, or who almost fully died. Maybe I am getting so good at lying to the world I can even fool myself.

"He did say it was just a misunderstanding." The words come from Ms. Kennerson. "Some students are still troubled by what happened. They hear all sorts of things."

Troubled would be a word to describe seeing Cole getting exorcised, yes.

"Charlotte, is this true? Do you have anxiety about what happened to Vanessa?" the counselor asks.

"She has a history of anxiety. She lost her mother at a young age," Dad fills in for me when I don't speak. "Death is . . .

sensitive for her."

"She's not a bad student, but she has seemed out of it recently," Ms. Kennerson pipes in. "Late to class, dozing off on her desk."

So she wasn't just looking at her phone. Teachers really do see everything.

"Her grades have slipped a bit, too."

"I can recommend some light dose sleeping pills," the counselor says. "Perhaps some one-on-one sessions should be scheduled?"

They carry on talking as if I'm not there, saying how I need help more than punishment. Maybe they are right, maybe I overreacted. Maybe I *am* going mad and imagining things. I look up to see Cole pulling a face in front of Principal Headley. I bite my lip and quickly look down again. Nope, I couldn't make him up if I tried.

I hear my name and flinch.

"This school does not tolerate physical violence of any kind," Principal Headley starts. "Usually this would end with you leaving the school and not returning. However, this does seem to be a one-time occurrence, and Mr. Beasey has insisted it was a simple misunderstanding. You're too close to finishing school to ruin things now, and quite frankly, with everything going on right now this school doesn't need any more attention than it already has.

"Nonetheless, punching a member of staff is a serious act of misconduct you won't be getting off lightly with, regardless of your reasons. I would have you on cleaning detention, but I don't think having you near him would be the best idea."

"I'll help Mr. Beasey with the cleaning duties," I say before I've had the chance to think it over.

"You will?" Dad asks, surprised.

"You will?" Cole echoes, just as surprised.

"I will," I reply. Of course spending my free time at school cleaning is the last thing I want to do. But this Mr. Beasey clearly knows things, and for the sake of Cole and any other ghost out there, I need to find out who exactly he is and what he knows.

It beats the logistics of stakeouts and Friday night break-ins, at least.

"But you hate cleaning," Dad mutters to me.

"I know." I sigh. I'll hate myself for this later. "Which is why it's a suitable punishment."

"No. It's dangerous," Cole objects.

"It's the best option," I say to Cole more than everyone else in the room.

"She really does hate cleaning," Dad reassures Principal Headley.

"Fine. You will be assisting Mr. Beasey after school with cleaning duties for the next week. Is that clear?"

"Yes."

"You will also have a counseling session tomorrow during lunch break. Take the rest of the day off to get some sleep and reflect."

"Okay."

"Consider yourself lucky. You should also be thankful that Mr. Beasey isn't going to press charges. It's his first week working here, too. This is not the impression we want to make."

"I'll be sure we express our gratitude." Dad stands and shakes Principal Headley's hand.

Cole looks at me concerningly.

I smile back.

He's still here, that's the main thing.

But I never had to worry about something happening to Cole before. As I get up and leave, I feel like nothing is certain anymore.

We don't speak a single word to each other as Dad drives home. I inherited Dad's stubbornness which makes for long awkward silences in situations like this. He knows it, too. That doesn't make the inevitable any easier, though.

"Charlotte," Dad caves in first, his voice a shock to the quiet. He places his truck keys on the counter and kicks off his shoes. "What happened today . . . I know that isn't you." He waits for a reaction, but I have none to give. "Now I didn't know that Stalinski girl, but I do know you didn't like her. You might have fooled the school, but your ol' man here still has his nuts n' bolts screwed on." He taps his temple.

"I wouldn't think otherwise of my old man." I manage a small smile.

Dad rubs his chin. "I want you to tell me . . . is there anything I should be concerned about?"

I open my mouth to speak but quickly close it again, not knowing what to say. I could mention how I nearly got dragged into the afterlife while protecting my secret ghost best friend and crush—who happens to live with us—from the school janitor, but I don't want to see what disbelieving look he would have from hearing that. Or, worse, if he did believe me, I wouldn't want to let him down with my dangerous recklessness.

"No, Dad," I say instead, making my way to my room. "Everything's fine."

"Charlotte," Dad calls back sternly. "I don't believe in ghosts," he struggles to say the word. "But I do believe in you."

I smile, and it's genuine. "Thanks, Dad," I say. Then I head to my room before the emotions hit me.

∞∞∞∞

"Wait, so exorcisms are real?" I ask as I brush out the last knots of my blow-dried hair. It's only been ten minutes since I had possibly the longest shower of my life, but already my hair is forming waves at the ends. I like taking long showers; it's the only time I feel truly alone in a safe space where I can go over my thoughts and let my emotions drain out with the water. I had a lot on my mind it seems, because Dad ended up knocking on my bathroom door to check that I hadn't drowned.

Cole looks at me like I'm stupid. "Well, clearly."

"I've never heard of that before. Aren't they for demons or something?"

"Charlotte." Cole sounds exasperated. "Demons aren't real."

I shrug in defeat. "Geez, sorry Cole, I must have slept through pneumatology class."

Cole smirks. "I'll ask around, find out what he's doing."

"Great. You do that while I get some sleep," I reply as I get into bed and pull the sheets over me.

"Your hand." Cole crouches down in front of me, stroking his fingers over my knuckles. I didn't even notice they are bruised. That will hurt tomorrow.

"It's fine," I say. "It hurt him more than me."

"I'm sure it did. And what a performance it was," he replies with a smirk before getting serious. "You're in trouble because of me, though."

"No, I'm in trouble because someone tried to exorcise you. I don't care who that janitor thinks he is, he doesn't have the right to dictate when ghosts cross over."

"Our voice of justice. Our savior." He smiles at me with his warm brown eyes and my heart starts doing that cartwheel thing again.

"What was it like?" I ask to distract myself. "Being exorcised, I mean."

Cole pauses to ponder this. "Weird, I guess. Like being sucked into something. It was . . . I don't know how to describe it. I was worried, not knowing what would happen . . ."

"Scared?"

"Yeah, scared. I felt scared." Cole's forehead creases.

"Ghosts usually do the scaring," I say.

Cole turns to me. "Boo."

I snort. "You'll have to do better than that."

Cole snickers. "It seems I'm losing my touch. Maybe I'll have to haunt you in your dreams, instead."

I turn to the clock. It's late. "I'll look out for you."

"Haunt ya later." He walks to the wall but he stops and turns to face me. "You saved me, Charlotte." He looks at me with an appreciative stare and it makes me melt inside.

"Anytime," I reply. We look at each other another long

moment, our eyes deep in trance, then he leaves.

I smile down at my heroic bruises but it's short-lived. Had I been a few seconds later Cole would have probably been gone forever. And I would have never known where he was, or had the chance to say goodbye, or tell him how much he means to me. And whoever that janitor is, he can see Cole. Under normal circumstances that would have me excited to feel less alone, but now I just feel concerned.

I sigh and stretch my arms out like I'm on my own cross awaiting judgment. I feel the weight of my tiredness pull me into my bed and I close my eyes to images of the abyss into the afterlife replaying in my mind. To think that's where we end up when we die. If that is what it even was. But that janitor could see it, too. There are others like me.

"Others like me," I whisper the words and they follow me into sleep, along with the anxiety it brings.

I won't sleep well tonight.

As expected, I didn't sleep well, but that excuse doesn't go through Dad enough to get me out of going to school to have a lunchtime counseling session to prove my sanity, followed by afterschool detention with the janitor who exorcises dead people. School is officially a ghost no-go zone while this janitor is around, which means I feel oddly lonely without Cole popping by here and there. At least that means I also get a day away from Vanessa who still hasn't gotten over her untimely passing. Or maybe she has, but she has new unfinished business now: Cole.

I cringe at the thought of Vanessa and Cole alone, her sweet innocent act playing on cue. So although I'm sure somewhere in some small crevice of my mind an analysis of Shakespeare's *Othello* does hold interest, I can't pay attention to anything the teacher says at the front of the classroom while not knowing what they are up to.

Then again, maybe I don't want to know.

I sigh. Guy dramas are the worst.

The bell rings and I stiffen at what comes next. I lag behind, taking my time to pack away my books. Mr. Beasey slips in through the back door, his eyes—one of which has a bruise underneath—straight on me. Nobody else seems to notice his early intrusion, but I doubt they would care even if they did.

The teacher reminds anyone still listening to read to the end of Act Two at home as Mr. Beasey, hunching over, fiddles with his cart of cleaning supplies and props up the wet floor sign.

Then as soon as the door closes behind the last student to leave, his demeanor changes, now standing straight, arms crossed, his face stern with frown lines bordered by an early beard and hair somewhere between dark gray and black.

He has a surprisingly bulky frame for a janitor; that should have been the first warning sign. I mean, I highly doubt vacuuming classrooms develops biceps like *that*. Perhaps he is ex-military. Perhaps exorcisms—or whatever it actually is he does—requires quite a bit of muscle power.

In any case, I can't back down, so like the stubborn fool I am I mimic him, making sure he sees my clenched fists instead of my biceps (because, well, there's nothing to show there). We stare each other down, daring who will be the first to concede.

"He's not here." I give in first.

"I can see that," he replies.

"You won't get him."

"You seem very attached to it."

"I am attached to *him*, yes. So back off, unless you want another purple eye to match."

This would stir up most people, but not Mr. Beasey. He smiles, in the way the side of his mouth creeps upwards and his eyebrows lower to show he's not swayed.

"You have quite the spunk for a Communicator."

"Communicator?"

"People like us."

"People like us?" I repeat, now feeling nervously excited.

While I've had moments of curiosity that led me to the odd internet search or library book over the years, most self-proclaimed psychics or mediums disappointingly turned out to be fake or nowhere near as able to see or hear or feel ghosts the way I do. To save myself from disappointment, I gave up, which means I don't know how many people in the world are like me (if any), or if so, what people like me are called.

Until now.

"How many of you . . . of *us* are there?"

"Sixty. Maybe seventy."

"In the United States?"

"In the world."

"Oh."

"That's how many I know of. So you can understand how surprised I was when I saw you coddling up to a spirit in the hallway of Foxton High School."

"His name is Cole," I inform him.

"Yes, well whatever its name is, it needs to move on."

"That's not for you to decide," I protest. "Especially not against their will."

"Not all ghosts want to be your friend, Charlotte. In fact most don't. It's for your own safety. Mostly."

"Yeah, well, like an actual communicator, I prefer the more compassionate approach of *communicating* with them."

Okay, that's not entirely true. In fact, I prefer to avoid them at all costs. But since I can't always do that, a simple listening ear or reassuring sentence can go a long way for both them and me.

"And how has that been going for you?"

"Pretty well, actually." I think back to Vanessa. And Ms. Reynolds. And the many other encounters over the years that could have easily ended far worse than they did. "Mostly."

I doubt he believes me because he snickers.

"What's in it for you, anyway?" he asks. "If you're not doing it to serve God then surely you have better things to do in your free time than play mother bird to broody spirits?"

"I do it because it needs to be done." I pause before adding, "And sometimes, as a favor in return, I ask them to pass on a message."

Mr. Beasey raises an eyebrow. "A message?"

"To my mom. Just an update on how I'm doing." I look to the ground, embarrassed. "So she knows."

Mr. Beasey catches on quickly. "To know she didn't stay behind is a blessing. She led a good life."

"Yeah. Just one visit would have been nice, though."

Mr. Beasey sighs, taking pity on me. "There's a reason why people don't see the dead. It gets too complicated. We have to judge God's finality in that."

"Except *we* can see the dead."

"Indeed. And it is a gift that was bestowed upon us. But it comes with responsibilities, including not getting attached to them."

I roll my eyes at his words. "Cole's different. We're a team. He protects me from the more problematic ghosts while I try to have as normal life as possible. And it was going just fine. Until you came along."

"Don't worry, I have no intention of receiving another black eye."

"Good," I reply.

"So you don't befriend them all, like you did with Curt?"

"Cole."

"Right, Cole."

"No. But I like to believe there's a Cole in every spirit. You can't just shoo them away like vermin. They were people, too."

"How admirable of you. Naïve, but admirable."

I cross my arms defensively. "So why do you do what you do then, hmm?"

Mr. Beasey walks over to the window at this. Students are still lounging around in the parking lot, enjoying the warm weather and socializing with one another, oblivious to the conversation going on in their classroom. Probably for the best, though.

"When I was thirty years old I got into a construction accident," he starts, placing the palm of his hand out to my face. It had the wrinkles of a fair number of decades and the odd large blue vein line, but none of that measured up to the star-shaped scar about a dime in size next to his thumb. "The apprentice didn't turn off the electricity properly. One touch and flash then suddenly I'm watching people run across to where I landed and administer CPR. While I was watching myself die I noticed so many spirits around, roaming aimlessly, sad, guilty, angry. They were suffering. Suffering from their lives now gone." He closes his fist. "I obviously made it, but from then on I could still see them."

"Sorry to hear that."

"Sorry?" He shakes his head. "I had always felt purposeless before the accident. But afterwards I had a gift, a second chance, a divine purpose given to me. So I turned to the church. I got my degree in theology, became a priest, then went to Europe and researched."

"I thought Christians aren't into ghosts. At least not the ones I know of."

"Oh, some are deeply invested in it, even if not outspokenly."

"And?" I ask. "What did you find?"

"Through the priesthood I found the Communicators," he replies.

"The people like us," I confirm.

"Yes. People who can communicate with the dead and make them cross over."

I recoil. "This isn't *Ghostbusters*. Besides, you're a janitor at Foxton High School. Forgive me for taking what you say with a grain of salt."

"Janitors can get anywhere," he casually replies. "Hospitals, morgues, care homes, schools. Heck, I could probably infiltrate the White House if I wanted to."

I take to the thought of this guy exorcising old Abe in the Oval Office.

"Smart," I admit. "So let me get this straight: you're some rogue priest who, like me, can see and communicate with ghosts, are part of some type of *Ghostbusters* underground priesthood from Europe, and now roam around the USA exorcising every spirit you can find?"

"Well, I wouldn't use those words, but you have the elements correct."

"Huh." I don't know what I was expecting from Mr. Beasey, but it certainly wasn't that.

"Spirits talk, you know. I heard of a Communicator in this area, and followed the trail of whispers to Foxton.

"So you've been tracking me?"

"Just following the breadcrumb trail," he replies. "They said you were young, but I didn't know you'd be a *child*."

"Hey, I'll be eighteen soon."

"Still so young. May I ask, how did you come to be able to communicate so clearly with those that have passed?"

I shrug. "I've been able to see ghosts for as long as I can remember."

"Fascinating." Mr. Beasey looks at me in the way a scientist would look at bacteria splitting into two, or a lab rat growing an extra ear.

"So, what are we doing first?" I ask, examining the cleaning cart for a distraction. "Mop, trash, vacuum?"

Mr. Beasey slides something across the table to me, a black book. It's leather-bound, with an inscription in gold block letters: LIBER MANIUM.

"The Book of the Dead," he says as I pick it up. "Sixtieth edition. Everything we know about spirits, from recovered scrolls from the Library of Alexandria to the Vatican to our own testimonials."

"Woah," I look over the pages of old inscriptions and diagrams. "I haven't seen this in the local library."

"It's not the type of book you'll find with a Google search. Only members get one."

"Members?"

"Communicators who join the cause." He flashes a small grin. "By invite, only."

"Ah."

"Don't worry, membership is free."

"Nothing's ever free. There's always a catch."

"The catch is the discovery of your own potential." Mr. Beasey leans forward, his hands gripping each side of the desk between us as he looks at me intently. "You're lost, Charlotte, confused as to who you are. You're unaware of your own potential. But I can teach you."

"I . . ." I lose my trail of thought.

All this time I thought I was some outlier, and now suddenly I'm not alone, and presented with the chance to find more people like me, people who understand me, even if it is through someone like Mr. Beasey.

Plus, if it's in detention time then it beats hours of cleaning I would otherwise have to do.

"Fine," I agree cautiously. "But on one condition: no harm comes to Cole."

"Oh, I won't exorcise Cole. Not for now, anyway. You have my word," he replies a little too furtively.

"How can I trust you?" I ask suspiciously, crossing my arms.

"I say it how it is, Charlotte. I'm a man of my word," he replies. "Besides, I'm now interested in seeing how it goes with Clint."

"It's Cole. And you'd better be a man of your word," I warn. "Vanessa, though? She's all yours for the taking."

"Vanessa?"

"The cheerleader with the attitude problem. Surely you've heard her if not seen her?"

"Yes, I am aware of what happened. I was actually on the lookout for her when your buddy showed up instead."

I cringe.

"Tragic what happened to her, nonetheless. Kids are so young, so stupid."

"Hey, we're not all stupid," I object. "Besides, she thinks there's more to her death than a few too many vodka shots."

"A mystery, eh? I love a good mystery. In that case I won't exorcise her, either."

I frown. Since when was this an all or nothing deal?

"Fine, but the deal is for Cole and Cole only. Remember that when her tantrums get on your nerves."

"Noted. And please, no more Mr. Beasey. Just Beasey is fine since we'll be establishing a more personal relationship from now on."

I cringe, instantly regretting my agreement. "Okay then, *Beasey*. Where do we start?"

I pick up the book and start flipping through the pages.

"We'll get to that soon enough. For now though," he takes

the book out of my hands and replaces it with a cloth, "it's desk cleaning time."

∞∞∞∞

It's over an hour later by the time I finish detention, and I would be cursing out loud if Cole wasn't standing by the school entrance doors waiting for me. He straightens up from his usual slouch and half-smiles, his hands casually in his pockets. It would make me swoon if it weren't for the clear anxiety on his face, so as soon as we're outside I relay to Cole everything this Beasey guy said as I make my way to the school parking lot.

"So there are more of you?"

"Apparently so, if only a few." I can't help but smile at this. It's reassuring to know that I'm not so alone, even if that includes Beasey. "It seems he knows what he's doing, too, what with that book 'n all."

"Those poor spirits," Cole mutters.

"I thought there were fewer ghosts around than usual. You don't think—"

"I know," Cole interjects. "From what I've found out, he's been doing a purge. He now works weekends at your church, too."

"Ha," I blurt out. "So he's making a career out of it."

"It would seem so."

"Maybe we should get Vanessa to go to church on the weekend?"

"Charlotte!"

"What? Everybody wins!"

"Vanessa doesn't."

"Like that matters."

Cole looks at me disapprovingly.

"Well, you're off limits, at least," I say.

"What makes you so sure?"

"I made a bargain."

∞ 51 ∞

"A bargain?"

"Yes. I get to learn more about what I am, and you get to keep your life—or afterlife, I should say."

Cole's eyes narrow. "You shouldn't have done that for me."

"It's not just for you. I do less cleaning this way, too. It will make the next week of detention more survivable."

"I'm not happy about it, but if you're sure."

"I'm not happy either, but what choice do we have? He obviously knows more about what I can do than I do, things I need to find out. And," I swallow. "It's just nice to not feel so alone anymore."

Cole looks at me sympathetically. He knows of my angst on the subject, and why I'd rather keep to myself. I know from helping spirits communicate with their loved ones that the truth of me is tough to face, and I never know how people will react. Some will do whatever they can to believe, but most people choose not to, even relentlessly. And to be fair to them there are a lot of scammers out there, so I'm not overly offended by the resistance and backlash I face. Heck, *I* probably wouldn't even believe someone like me if I didn't experience it first-hand. But Beasey gets it. I can learn, and maybe I can even teach *him* a thing or two.

"That doesn't mean you should trust him," Cole replies before adding, "I certainly don't."

"He says he's a man of his word," I reassure. "Besides, I think we're the most exciting thing he's seen in a while."

Cole smiles briefly at this. "I'm surprised he can still see with the way you hit him."

I try not to smirk too much.

"I need to read that book. Find out more about who I am and what I can do. And if I can persuade Beasey to go easy on the dead that would be good, too."

"Looks like you're onto something. You have my support."

"Speaking of, how is Vanessa anyway? Or do I not want to know?"

"She's still upset, naturally. I'll spend more time with her to support her."

I cringe. She'll like that, I'm sure.

Cole looks around. "Where are you going?"

"Picking up a few groceries. You go ahead," I say as I reach Dad's truck, the last in the parking lot except for the small motorhome parked in the far corner I can only guess belongs to Beasey.

Cole nods. "Haunt ya later."

And with that he's gone, probably to Vanessa, but there's nothing I can do about that.

Dad took his motorcycle to work so I wouldn't be walking around by myself in the evening, which is good because I feel rain coming in the air. Even though I hurry along, it's dusk by the time I get home, the solar lights lined along the stone driveway lighting up upon my return as if to announce my arrival to the Durane household.

I have dinner with Dad, a quick mix of food I picked up at the store, and then wash up before excitedly walking out to the trampoline where Cole lies, staring up at the cloudy night sky, lost in his usual thoughts.

He looks my way, noticing the silver balloon I'm holding, then with a chuckle he rolls his eyes. "Is it *that* day again?"

"Yup. Every three hundred and sixty-five days," I reply, holding the balloon out to him. "Happy eighteenth again."

Cole looks back up to the night sky. "Every day feels the same when you're dead. No work schedule or deadlines or appointments to remember. Just the motions of the sun and moon, again and again."

"Sounds peaceful."

"I was hoping you'd forget this year."

"Why would I forget?" I ask as I get on the trampoline. I don't give him the chance to reply though, because before he can protest I pull the balloon by the string in front of him and say, "Make a wish."

"Are we really doing this?"

"It's tradition," I persist.

Every year since I first started getting allowance I would buy a balloon for Cole on his birthday—the nicest biodegradable helium one I can find, of course. Then he makes a wish and I release the balloon for the heavens to receive. This was back when I still believed in the possibility of magic and prayer and angels, but since it has become our special thing I continue to do it. That, and because it's not like he can eat a cake or spend a gift card.

Cole sighs, but it's bashful. He places his hand on the balloon. I like to think it dips under his weight but it's more likely a trick of the lighting coming from the house.

"Close your eyes," I tease.

Cole gives me a look, but with a smile forming in the corner of his lips he complies. I give him a moment before asking, "Do you have a wish?"

"Yes. It won't come true, though."

I pout. "Not with that attitude."

He opens his eyes, his light dimming to a tint of gray. "It hasn't come true all these past years."

"Well, it has to be believable. And you only get one wish every three hundred and sixty-five days so make it count."

The corner of his mouth twitches but his light doesn't come back. "You're right."

He sits up straight this time, placing his hand back on the balloon. He closes his eyes, looking still and calm. I wonder what he's thinking, and selfishly if those thoughts include me, then he opens his eyes.

I smile questioningly and he nods, his gray tint from before fading to his usual light. I look at the balloon joggling to be free. I then let go and watch it rise up into the sky until it's seen no more, a message on its way to the stars.

We keep our gazes on the clouded night sky, the quiet of the night with light misty rain trickling on my face oddly soothing.

"What did you wish for all the other times?" I eventually ask. "If you don't mind me asking, that is. I mean, maybe I can help?"

"I don't think you can help with that one, Charlotte. Not even with your abilities."

"Try me."

Cole doesn't move, his eyes still on the dark above. "I wished to go back. To the day I died. To be given a second chance."

Oh.

I swallow. And here I was thinking he wished for the chance to witness a UFO zoom by or to see a long-lost pet or something. Of course a ghost lingering in the land of the living would wish for a second chance at life again. I suddenly feel so stupid.

"Who knows?" I try to sound positive as I sit up, too ashamed to face him. "Maybe someday time travel will be possible."

"Time is an illusion," he agrees. "I mean, right now—when the clouds allow, that is—we are looking at remnants of entire worlds and stars that no longer exist." He pauses before adding, "But some things are just fated to be, I guess."

I look at Cole. I don't know why, but the words slip out, nonetheless. "What was it like to die?"

Cole turns to me before looking back at the night sky. If his energy darkens I can't see it as the sky has now fully clouded over. Oblivious to the drizzle, he contemplates this for a moment, forehead slightly creased in concentration. He then opens his mouth, an answer to give. "Rather shit."

I can't help it; his bluntness makes me smile.

Cole notices this. "My death is funny to you?"

"I'm sorry," I say, biting my lip. "I just expected something a bit more . . . philosophical."

Cole is also holding back a smile now. "Philosophical?"

"Yeah. Or poetic or something."

"Poetic? Like," Cole suddenly sits up, arms outstretched to the sky, yelling, "I defy you, stars!"

I hold back laughter. "Is that why you like the night sky so much? Do you like, cry to the moon or something?"

"I'm not a wolf, Charlotte."

"Sorry."

His forehead slowly frowns, his mouth starts to twitch. "I . . . I'm . . ."

I lean in closer, suddenly worried.

"A werewolf!"

Cole suddenly jumps to his knees and howls so loudly I cover my ears as I snort back laughter, tugging at him to make him stop. His howling also soon breaks into laughter as he rolls over and pins me down on the trampoline, now visible by the glow from the porch, a warm reflection on his light as our laughter settles.

Then it happens. His eyes go distant, his gaze drifts, his grip on me weakens. Sorrow peeks through the light of his eyes, his aura darkens into the surrounding night, a weight pulling on the thoughts he keeps within.

"Cole?"

It was only a few seconds. Then he blinks twice, back in the present, his usual light and self again.

"That's enough howling for one night." He leans back. "It's late. And it's raining."

"Yeah," I reply, wiping my exposed arms of raindrops. "I guess."

He's suddenly standing by the backdoor, composed yet closed off. Why is he suddenly acting so . . . *ghostly* all of a sudden? I guess death is still a sensitive issue for him, after all.

I step onto the porch when he turns back to me, his eyes heavy with things untold once again as he says, "Thank you, Charlotte. For remembering."

I open my mouth to reply but he's already gone.

I dreamed of Cole that night, but not in the way I wanted to.

He was being taken by the haze. He was calling my name, reaching out his arms, saying he's sorry. And as much as I tried, I couldn't get to him. Except once the haze consumed him it turned black, choking him until he vanished.

I woke up in a sweat, an hour earlier than I'd needed to, but I didn't fall asleep again. That may be why I've been a bit moody since first period. Or it may simply be because Vanessa hasn't left me alone since then. Both very probable reasons.

I enter an empty classroom before turning to face her. Although Beasey said he would leave Cole alone, I still told Cole to stay away a while longer just to be sure.

Vanessa, however, I figured could take the risk.

"Okay, Vanessa, what is it now?"

"My body is in a refrigerator. A refrigerator! Soda belongs in a refrigerator, not my body! And it's pale and gray and this old fat lady in a lab coat cut me up and did all sorts of gross experiments on it!"

I focus on the Vanessa in front of me instead of letting the imagery of her words form in my mind. Even though she's clearly been crying her makeup and hair is still perfect. It may just be an imprint of consciousness, but still. It must be nice not having to worry about such things.

"It's just to find a cause of death," I try to reassure her, but she only wails louder at the words.

"I don't want a cause of death. I want my life back!"

I sigh. "Look, Vanessa, you need to accept you're not that body anymore and move on. I know someone here who can do that for you—"

"Cole said you would help me do whatever it is I need to do."

"I said I'll try to help you remember. Just not now. I have class."

"Oh, I get it. Say anything to please Cole."

"What?"

"Didn't know the dead were your type, Durane. But I can't say I'm all that surprised."

"What's that supposed to mean?" I snap.

"You. And Cole."

The bell rings and I already hear students approaching. I don't have time for this. Nor patience.

"Cole and I are best friends."

Vanessa rolls her eyes. "Sure. Whatever."

I snap back, "Look, Vanessa. I have class. You want my help? There's a light—go into it."

"Charlotte?"

I have already opened my mouth, prepared to argue my case hoping she will take the hint. Except her mouth is closed. The voice is low, and for a moment I assume it's Cole, except I know Cole's voice, and it isn't Cole who said my name. I follow Vanessa's line of sight, her eyebrows high and her mouth slightly skewed.

My eyes bulge, realizing I'm not alone.

"Oh, uh, hey, Ryan." Ryan Hill, assistant captain of the football team, member of The Squad, classmate, and all-round liked guy is standing in the doorway. "I was just—"

"Telling Vanessa to move on into the light."

Crap.

I open my mouth, begging my brain to come up with something good. Except nothing comes out.

Thanks, brain.

His eyes dart around the classroom. "Is she here?"

He seems neither scared nor excited, and totally oblivious to Vanessa cajoling over him. I wonder what to say, but students start brushing past us into the classroom, including a teacher who coughs conspicuously for Ryan to move out of the way. He takes one more look at me before he grabs a pencil case and heads off.

I close my eyes and take a deep breath, my anger and embarrassment high. Vanessa is still a very sensitive topic within these school walls, and for a student to be casually talking to her . . . well, that's a wildfire of gossip in the making.

I fling my bag over my shoulder and pace after Ryan, trying to keep up between the crowds of students.

"Uh, hello? What about helping me?" Vanessa calls behind me.

I ignore her in the way you try to ignore a pimple. You want it gone, but attacking it only makes it flare up worse, so sometimes you just have to leave it be until it goes. That is Vanessa. A big, ugly pimple in my life.

"Fine. I'll just go to Cole then, since he's the only one that cares!"

Great. More drama for later.

I enter the classroom and see Ryan already seated next to members of The Squad. I start walking up to him to demand a word in private, but the teacher walks in and calls for us to settle into our seats and get our textbooks out. Trying not to tremble, I walk past them to the last empty desk and take out my economics textbook.

Not that the world markets are on my mind. At all. Between free trade agreements and issues of outsourcing I can only think about how to deal with Ryan. I decide I will catch him at the end of class and say I was relaying something on the phone to someone, gossip from a friend. Not that it makes much sense, but with my combined fatigue and Vanessa headache it's all I've got.

That opportunity doesn't come though, because a small thud jolts me back to see Ryan's textbook is on top of mine in front of me.

"Hey, let's pair up."

I prefer to assume it's because of my other-worldly side gig that I don't engage in socializing with guys (that are alive, anyway). But I know, down in a part of me that doesn't want to think too much about it, it's because I'm not the type of girl who gets the attention of the opposite sex—not in the attraction sort of way, at least. I'm not particularly stand-out material in looks or sports or the arts. I'm not rich or charismatic. And that's fine, whatever. Besides, Cole keeps me distracted enough. And while it would be nice if he were more, well, *physical*, considering he hasn't made the slightest move or hint of reciprocating my feelings, I believe maybe such things are just not meant to be for me right now in my life.

So when Ryan Hill walks over to me out of all the students in this class and wants to pair up, I naturally do a double-take.

"Huh?"

"Page seventy. Let's pair up."

It's not a request as much as an order. I glance at Leslie, my default go-to class partner, who's eyeing me with an intense shrug.

"Uh, sure," I say, making room for his stuff on my desk.

I glance back at Leslie apologetically. She nods in understanding, then turns to the desk behind her.

"That was some knockout you pulled with the janitor."

Crap. That's the last thing I want to talk about.

"You saw that?"

"Yeah." Ryan looks amused. "I'm not surprised you did it; he seems like a creep. The others don't like him, and say they even sometimes hear him muttering gibberish to himself in his cleaning closet." He flicks his textbook open to the chapter we're on. "*You* weren't muttering to yourself though, were you?"

Okay, that's *the last thing I want to talk about.*

"I don't know what you mean."

"In the other classroom. I went to grab my pencil case. I heard you. You were talking. To Vanessa."

"What? I was on my phone," I lie.

"Talking to Vanessa?"

"Talking *about* Vanessa."

"Okay, okay, if you say so." He starts chewing on his pen as he says, "I just think it's kinda cool."

Kinda cool.

Cool?

I must have asked that out loud, because he smiles back.

At me.

He smiles back at me.

I could have sworn the other members of The Squad in this class were giving us looks, but he either doesn't notice or doesn't care. We do the textbook work together and talk about trivial things like the weather and sports. He doesn't bring Vanessa up again, though. We get through our work and I assume that's it until he follows me out of the classroom when the bell rings.

He starts talking again, but it doesn't last long because an eerie silence forms with each student as Dylan passes down the hallway.

Everyone except Leslie, that is.

"Ow, watch it, thug!"

Leslie is an outcast like me, but unlike me she doesn't care. She will turn up at school wearing jewelry that doesn't match or dark red lipstick (which never gets brought up with the teachers, unlike that one time I tried a peach kiss on mine), or fishnet tights with boots that would surely kick ass in a zombie apocalypse. She has a punk chic look, especially when she braids her hair, and she rocks it with full confidence every day.

I wish I had a personality like Leslie. It would make being me easier, but I don't. I'm also not into the fashion she flaunts. In fact, with my discount rack jeans and collection of plain cardigans and t-shirts that scream ordinary teenager, I look like the least susceptible person who would have an otherworldly connection to the dead. It helps me blend into the crowd, I guess, at least when I stand next to people like her. Which certainly helps in moments like this, because suddenly everyone looks at Leslie for a change.

Dylan stops and turns back, his eyes like narrow daggers.

Except he looks pained. Angry and pained.

I try not to let my pity show, but I think it does, because when he locks eyes on me he lowers his head and storms off, not taking his gaze off the ground as he leaves. Squad member Liam turns the corner and after a near-miss, shrugs at Dylan when he pushes past with no words.

"Okay, it wasn't just me who felt that, right?" I ask.

Ryan, still lingering at my side, responds, "What, Dylan? Yeah, it's weird, yo. The police were questioning him. Just standard procedure, apparently. But he was, like, her boyfriend 'n all. And he was AWOL half the time, leaving her to come up with excuses as to why. Not to mention the last message Vanessa ever sent said that she was meeting him."

"I don't care how guilty or innocent of murder he is," Leslie interrupts as she massages her arm. "He's a thug with a bad attitude, just like the rest of The Squad."

"Squad?"

"So he's hiding something?" I reply to Ryan, hinting to Leslie that Ryan is still here, as weird as that is.

"That's the assumption," Ryan replies. "Do you know anything?"

"Why would I know anything?"

Ryan gives me a look, one of expectation of something I'm not willing to give. He quickly gives in with a small smirk. "See you around, Lottie."

Lottie?

"Lottie?" Leslie mouths my way.

I shrug and we part for our next classes. Okay, so Lottie is a name I never liked, but he doesn't know that. He called me a nickname, though. I bite down on my excited smile. My day suddenly feels so much better, I doubt even detention will get me down.

∞∞∞∞∞

Gum.

A timeless décor of the modern classroom. One I absolutely hate cleaning.

"The thing is, Charlotte," Beasey continues his speech. He's rehearsed it well, using fancy words, as if reciting from scripture. Maybe he is. "God has bestowed upon us a gift, a gift to help guide His lost children in the purgatory of life and death by returning them to the heavenly realms of His home."

"If what I have is a gift then tell God I want to return it."

Beasey has finished mopping and is now watching me scrape gum off from under the desks. My mouth shrivels at the pile of white and green clumps in the bucket next to me. "Besides, returning them? What if they don't want to be returned?"

"I think your account on that is a bit biased based on your personal, uh, affiliation with a certain spirit, hmm?"

"Answering a question with another question doesn't answer the question, Beasey."

"Nor does deflecting," Beasey shoots back.

Damn. He had me there.

"Tell me about Cal, if you don't mind."

"Cole? Well, he first appeared when I was seven. My mom who was pregnant at the time had died in a car crash, so you can understand I wasn't in a good place. I was scared of ghosts, but he was the only thing that made me smile. He kept the ghosts away and taught me to get used to them. He made things better. He made *me* better.

"That's a long time to be playing life coach. And how did he die, exactly?"

The bluntness of his words make me wince inside. "Privacy is a term with different interpretations nowadays it seems."

"There's that deflection again."

I sigh in annoyance. "I . . . don't know," I admit.

"Oh?"

"He never seems to want to talk about it. And I don't push it."

"If you are as close to him as you say you are, why hasn't he opened himself up to you?"

"Because unlike you, Beasey, I respect his privacy," I retort defensively, except he's right. Most ghosts tend to mull over and yap on to me about how they ended up that way.

But not Cole.

"We all have secrets. When he's ready, I'll listen," I say, reassuring myself more than Beasey. "Besides, as you now know, he's quite content being here."

"Indeed it seems so," Beasey responds. "But have you ever asked yourself why?"

Dang. He got me again.

Cole never came across as one of those lost helpless souls stuck in the void of purgatory. As a kid I always saw him more as *Peter Pan*, wanting to play in Neverland as a kid forever; a childish big brother that never grows up. I had always assumed that if Cole really wanted to cross over then he would have done something about it. But since he hasn't—at least to my knowledge—then who am I to intrude?

I shudder in disapproval. It was a selfish assumption, I realize. I can't help but want it to be true, however.

"Cole just doesn't want to move on yet," I reply. "Who am I to judge?"

"So what exactly is he to you? A friend?"

"Friend. Best friend. Big brother. A guardian angel without wings." I can't help but grin as I think back to memories of Cole making me laugh out of bad situations. "The big brother demeanor has lessened as I've gotten older, though."

"Do you love him?"

"What?" I bang my head on the table. Thankfully there's no gum left on it.

"Do you love him?" Beasey casually asks again, as if he's asking something trivial like if I love pineapple on pizza (yes, by the way).

"Cole's like family to me." I avoid eye contact. I feel like I'm in therapy again. Beasey is good at this.

"Would you let him go? If he wanted to cross over, would you stop him? Or would you let him go?"

I glance down, blinking away the sudden water in my eyes. The thought's been there, at the back of my mind, something I've kept suppressed for years. He is here today, a life trapped in time, but one day he won't be. One day he may grow bored of me, or the world, and decide to leave. And I know when that time comes I'll have to support his decision, even though I know it will be the hardest thing I'll ever have to do.

"Of course I'd let him go," I reply quietly. "If that's what he wants. I'd support him."

"So why hasn't he?" Beasey asks out loud. Whether it's for me to hear or not I don't know, but I roll my eyes.

"For the last time, I don't know and I don't care." A total lie, because I suddenly and frustratingly do want to know.

And I do care. A lot.

"You're holding him back."

Ouch.

"You're the key."

"Leave us alone!" I snap back. "Just let us be."

"Charlotte," Beasey says, not affected by my sudden mood, "ghosts are the embodiment—minus the pun—of the negative karma from their lives keeping them from God's love which resides in Heaven. They don't remain behind because they're happy. Not for long, anyway."

Well, that hit me like a brick.

"The fact that you know so little about him concerns me. And it should concern you, too."

"As I said, it's his choice and his only. Conversation over." I place the bucket of gum I'm holding on the desk. "Done."

"Good. Classroom number twelve down, just three more to go."

I groan.

∞∞∞∞∞

It's nearly dark by the time I get home. Seriously, aren't there laws about this? I should complain to the school board, except I highly doubt learning all about the dead counts as school time. I did learn about some of the earliest records of ghost encounters, and how secret studies are beginning on the genes of Communicators as to why we can see ghosts, which is admittedly pretty cool.

But what lingers uncomfortably in my mind over dinner is how Cole has been in my life for nearly ten years and it hits me just how little I know about him. And it is when Pippi barks once and I look up to see him across the living room that I feel like I'm looking at a stranger. And now, for the first time since I have known him, I feel spooked by his presence.

"How was detention with the grim reaper?" he asks.

"Terrible," I casually reply, looking back at the computer screen in front of me. "Scraping gum from desks."

"Gross."

"You bet."

"Did he at least teach you anything good?"

"Hmm, only that what I have is a gift from God, yadda-yadda."

"Don't toot your horn too loudly."

"Yeah, I wouldn't want to keep the neighbors up."

"You look stressed." The humor dies, and Cole's eyes are on me.

"Just been a long day," I reply nonchalantly. "Assignments, homework, class peers. Vanessa didn't help, either."

"I'll try to keep her occupied during school hours. Maybe the distraction will be good for her." He bends down and greets Pippi with a stroke behind her ear. Her ear flicks at his hand, her sensitive nerve endings sensing his presence. "As for the rest of your neurotic school peers, as long as I'm here you don't need them."

I smile, hoping it hides the concern in my eyes as I wonder how long that will be. We have never spoken about his eventual, uh, *departure* since it is something I've never wanted to bring up. I have always feared the answer he would give, but now I feel the overwhelming urge to know, weighing up that not knowing may in fact be worse than knowing.

"How long?" I ask.

"Hmm?" He angles his head to me.

"How long will you be . . . *here* for?" I say, pointing to the ground.

Cole looks straight at me, eyes deadpan. For a moment I don't breathe as I brace for the worst. Maybe he notices this, but he leans forward slightly and without blinking he replies, "As long as I need to be."

As always, an answer as vague and mysterious as he is.

"You want to watch the stars for a bit?" he then asks casually, the topic over with. "It's a full moon tonight."

"Actually, I'm really tired. I'm just finishing up on some homework then I think I'll go straight to bed. Tell Vanessa I'll help her after I'm done with Beasey tomorrow if she'll stop bugging me."

Cole nods coolly. "I'll leave you to it. Haunt ya later."

Pippi barks once, but I still turn to make sure I'm alone. I pull the browser tab back up and click the search bar on Google, my fingers hovering above the keyboard, not knowing what to type.

Sure, I know things about Cole. Things like how much he enjoyed the outdoors, especially hiking, and he even gave me lots of tips when I was on school camp. He likes country music, not to mention he once said he could play the guitar pretty well, all through self-learning. He admitted he did the occasional graffiti, although he saw it as art more than vandalism since he was improving the dilapidated walls he sprayed on. He liked running, had a best friend called Heath, and like most guys his age he thought school was boring most of the time. He once mentioned he was born in Tennessee but spent most of his life in Georgia. Part of the PTSD with dying is that he can no longer fathom eating another creature that once lived, but he still misses food, especially pineapple, which is why I tell Dad I don't like pineapple so that it's not in the house. He's a sucker for romance movies, although he'll never admit it, even after I caught him crying during *Safe Haven*.

More snippets of Cole's revelations to me over the years come to mind, all affirming that I do know a lot of things about him. Heaps of things, in fact.

Except for who he is.

I start with typing the obvious 'Cole' then 'Cole Georgia'. It would be helpful if I had a family name to include. I've asked him more than once about this over the years but he always replied that he doesn't have one anymore because the dead don't need last names and left it at that. I didn't question him at the time; I figured it was a ghost taboo by the way he acted. I mean, he had a point. He never answered the question, though.

After eight pages of no useful search results I frustratingly try 'Cole Obituary Georgia', then 'Cole memorial', 'Cole eighteen', even 'cute eighteen-year-old named Cole'.

Nothing, nothing, nothing.

I thump the keyboard in frustration. Who is Cole, and why do I know so little about him? I sigh and turn the computer off. I wash up then hunker into bed, my curiosity now burning to find out who this ghost really is.

I hate everything about running. The heaviness on my lower back, the sweat, the difficulty breathing, the inability to think through the discomfort. How do people enjoy it? Nonetheless, thanks to the weather I'm doing just that, hoping for some of those endorphins people rave about. I pass two streets when Cole appears, both surprised and amused at my efforts.

"Nice weather for ducks."

I shoot Cole a glare. He doesn't feel the rain of course, but a little sympathy wouldn't hurt. At least today's rain is a warmer rain from the Gulf, a sign that summer is approaching.

"I don't know how you ever enjoyed this," I pant as I turn the corner.

I should have taken Dad up on his offer of a ride on his way to work, but I got too distracted getting my hair looking nice. Not like it's any good now.

"It grows on you. Give it a couple miles and you'll find it exhilarating."

I slow to a speed-walk. The rain is light enough now and I have my raincoat on. Besides, I don't want to arrive at school sweaty as well as wet. The rain means few people are on the street so I don't have to be so subtle when talking to Cole. Which is good, because my mind is full of things I want to ask him.

"Did you ever enjoy the rain?" I decide to start with something simple.

"No," he replies rather solidly.

Cole doesn't tend to go for long answers, but there's something different in the way he says it.

"Why not?"

He takes a second to reply. "I guess you could say it puts a damper on things."

Another answer as enigmatic as his personality. To think up to only yesterday I would think it was broody, sexy. Now it just makes me unsettled.

"Well, I like the rain. I think it's calming. I just don't like being caught in it."

I notice the neighbor is getting ready to mow his lawn again. Even in the rain he still has his lawnmower out.

"Since the rain is keeping you calm, I'll remind you now that you're seeing Vanessa after school today, remember?"

I sigh. "Yes, I know. Maybe I'll actually be able to concentrate in class today if Vanessa behaves."

"Don't worry, I'll be with Vanessa today."

That only makes me worry more.

Suddenly it starts pouring so I run for cover in a nearby bus shelter.

"Still like the rain?" Cole asks, looking out to the sky. "It'll pass. Give it a few minutes."

"Yes, I do. Because now I have a few minutes to talk to my best friend."

Cole looks my way and smiles. Now is not the time for blushing, though.

"Something on your mind?"

"Yes. I can't remember if you've ever mentioned it, but there's something I need to know."

Cole goes serious. "Oh?"

"What's your favorite color?"

Cole relaxes, a short smile as he contemplates before answering, "Red."

"Red? Really?"

"Yeah. Why?"

"I just pictured you as more of a blue or green admirer."

"Red is bright. It dares to stand out. I respect that."

"Fair enough," I say, making a mental note of it. "Mountains or the beach?"

"Mountains. Unless it's July 4th, then definitely the beach."

"Republican or Democrat?"

"Both are different sides of the same coin."

"Public or private health care?"

He raises an eyebrow at me. "Seriously?"

"Sorry." My cheeks go hot in embarrassment, but as long as he's answering I don't let it stop me. "What about your favorite sport?"

"Running. You know that."

I do know that, but I just want to confirm that he's being open and truthful.

"What was your favorite subject? Wait, let me guess, history? No, math. Definitely math."

"Aside from running track? Probably biology."

My mouth gapes slightly. "Biology?"

"Yes. Why do you sound so surprised?"

"I . . ." I guess I really don't know Cole as much as I thought. "I just didn't take you for a science geek, that's all."

"My grades were never geeky. I just liked how the world has so many equations, so many secrets, all compiled up to the formula that is the natural world today. Like there's some grand, intelligent design behind every leaf that falls to the ground or every drop of honey a bee makes or everything that can be told in one drop of blood."

Another enigmatic answer, but one I smile at. "I wish I had that enthusiasm when it comes to biology."

"You'll have a lot more of it if you pursue sciences in college."

I cringe.

"It'll be worth it, though. To become someone you will be proud of."

"What did you want to be, before you . . ." I close my mouth.

"You can say it, Charlotte. Not saying it doesn't make it any less real."

"Before you . . . died."

"Dunno." Cole looks out to the rain hitting the roadside. "I didn't have any plans. Just to leave town. And I couldn't even do that . . ."

Cole zones out into an intense stare, one which makes his forehead slowly furrow and mouth scowl as his aura seeps into gray. I always thought ghosts are just good daydreamers. I mean, what else do they do in their spare time? But according to Beasey's fancy book, while people can think back to a time while remaining in the present, ghosts, as states of consciousness that they are, return to the memory itself. It's supposed to be part of their purgatory process of sorting through their trauma to make peace with themselves and their lives in order to cross over. But in order to protect themselves, sometimes the consciousness prevents or restricts them from doing so, like a safety valve.

This reminds me of what Cole was saying about Vanessa struggling to remember what happened to her when she died. I also think that is what Cole is experiencing right now. Wherever he currently is, he's trying to unlock that safety valve.

Or tighten it.

He then shakes his head, the gray energy now gone, his demeanor a one-eighty.

"I think if I had a second chance at life I would want to be a teacher."

"Really?"

"Yeah. Help little kids grow into something great." He turns to me with a cheeky grin. "I guess you were my lab project."

"Glad to be of service," I reply. "I could see that though. You, being a teacher."

Cole smiles, but it falls short. "Maybe next time 'round."

I suddenly feel terrible. And angry. Cole is kind and helpful and a natural with kids—in my experience, anyway. So much potential to better the world in a person, lost.

"Hey," Cole teases. Sometimes I wonder if I have an aura he can see and is not letting me in on knowing. "Chin up. It's stopped raining."

Cole is right; it is now only lightly drizzling and the best opening I am going to get to make it to school on time. So while I want to continue this rare moment of open communication between us, I sling my school bag back over my shoulder.

"You might have turned out to be a cool enough teacher to let me off for being tardy, but Ms. Kennerson sure won't."

"You don't know that. I could have made you pick up trash after school or something."

"Not much different to what I'm doing now." I turn to face Cole. "Thanks for the talk."

"Better get running."

"Haunt me later?"

"Always."

With a shared smile he shimmers away.

I pace to school and make it just as it starts to pour again.

"Lottie." I turn to see Ryan eye me up and down. "Heard of an umbrella?"

"I got caught out," I reply as I take my raincoat off. Ryan is right; the lower half of me is uncomfortably damp.

"I can see that."

"Charlotte." Leslie bursts between us and grabs my arm. "You have *got* to see this."

Without a chance to respond, Leslie pushes me through the small group of students by the lockers, including members of The Squad.

I hear Ryan behind me read my mind when he says, "Well, this is weird."

Weird is an understatement, but I've seen worse.

Liam, Gwen and Mandy start talking to Ryan, but I ignore them, more focused on the blood slowly flowing out of Dylan's locker.

"Has anyone opened it?" I ask.

"Eww, no," Gwen answers. "What if there's, like, something dead in there?"

If there is anything dead inside the locker it's fresh because there's no smell, not to mention the lack of anything that only I would be able to see. So I slowly reach for the handle, and after hesitating in my own doubt, open it to see a tipped vile.

Everyone leans in to get a look of what's inside, including Gwen who was so grossed out only seconds before.

The sound of Dylan startles us all.

"What the—ugh!" He pushes through us and takes out his textbooks. He only had two in there, but the bottom of the pages are red. Gwen squirms and cowers to Mandy as drops of red dangle from his books to the ground.

"What the hell is this?" Dylan demands to know. The few lurking juniors scuttle away when he slams his locker door shut, ignoring it opening again with the force of the swing before turning to me and shaking his books in my face. "This your idea of a joke, you freak?"

"Me?" I stutter.

"It's more your scene right now, Dylan. Collecting your own trophies, are you?" Leslie asks.

At moments like this it's good to have someone like Leslie by my side.

Dylan darts his eyes between me and Leslie, his nostrils flaring as he clenches his fist and inhales deeply. I want to feel bad for him, I really do. But between calling me a freak and wondering if he's going to hit us it's pretty hard to do so.

"Dude," Ryan interjects, placing a firm hand on his shoulder. "She didn't do anything. She just stepped inside from the rain. Look at her, she's soaked."

Sven, Stephanie and Jordan walk by at that moment and I assume it's the first time all members of The Squad have come together since Vanessa's school memorial service because I can sense tension in the air.

"Is that?" Sven asks.

"Blood?" Jordan follows.

"Oh-em-gee, gross!" Stephanie squeaks.

Leslie, however, smirks. "I think it's cool." She places a finger along the bottom of one of the textbooks in Dylan's hand.

"Eww, oh my god!" Stephanie squeals in disgust at Leslie

before hiding her face in Sven's chest.

"Calm your tits, O'Brian. It's corn syrup," Leslie replies, licking her finger.

Stephanie turns her head from Sven as he gives her a reassuring pat. "How were you so sure?"

Leslie turns to Stephanie. "Real blood would have a brownish tint by now." She then smirks. "Or maybe I just don't care either way."

Stephanie gags in disgust before storming off with Gwen and Mandy in tow.

Jordan takes out the vile. "That's the flag blood."

"Flag blood?" I ask.

"It's school tradition to pour fake blood on the opposing team's flag after a game. Except it never got to that last time," Sven explains, wiping remnants of Stephanie's makeup off his shirt. I think this is the first time Sven has ever spoken to me despite being in most of my classes. I almost feel like I should introduce myself, but of course I don't.

"We couldn't find the flag blood," Ryan says before swallowing. "Then we couldn't find Vanessa."

"What do you mean?" I ask.

"Vanessa had it." Everyone turns to Sven. "She went to get the flag blood. That was the last time any of us saw her."

An awkward silence follows. I don't know how much they've spoken about what happened that night. I assume they've talked it over quite a lot, but the tension is high, especially with Dylan when all eyes turn to him. Suddenly he's not the tough act he tries to be, a vulnerability sinking over him that strains his eyes.

That doesn't last for long, though.

He suddenly turns and eyes up Sven, his arms flexed, fists clenched. "Just say it. Go on!" he coerces.

"Why do you have the flag blood in your locker, Dylan?"

It is Ryan who asks, breaking the death stare between Dylan and Sven.

"It's nothing to do with me," Dylan says defensively to anyone who's willing to believe him. "I leave my locker unlocked half the time. Someone put it in there.”

I glance up to the ceiling, my thoughts confirmed. While the entrances and exits appear heavily fortified with security to ensure students are kept safe inside, the school still believes in the good of mankind enough to not have CCTV in the hallways. Not that I blame them, it’s how it should be, which is why I also don’t bother with the code combination on my locker half the time, either. I mean, I don’t keep much in there anyway, and if someone wants to read up on trigonometry or borrow my spare eraser that badly then they can. I guess that’s how Dylan felt, too. But no CCTV or witnesses means whoever did this will probably get away with it.

“Maybe Vanessa put it in there,” Jordan suggests, although it is more of a snarl. And I can’t help but notice his eyes are directed at me.

I don’t think anybody noticed the bell ring because the hallway is now empty except for us and Beasey.

“Someone told me there’s a bit of a mess that needs sorting out.” He strolls by with his cleaning cart, his hunched stance and lighter tone in his voice far from the Beasey I know. It just goes to show you don’t know who people really are. “I’ll sort this mess out, you kids run along to class now.”

Dylan doesn’t wait up. He storms off to the toilets to wash his books. Leslie gives me a quick reassuring grip of my arm before heading off. The rest of The Squad also disperses, including Ryan with a wink at me that I manage to only swoon a little at.

“Don’t want to be giving the janitor another black eye now, do we?” Jordan smirks before walking past with Sven.

As soon as it’s just me and Beasey left standing there, Beasey—the truer version of him, that is—returns.

“Do I want to know why the energy here was so tense that even the dead don’t want to be around?” He picks up the mop, his hunch now non-existent. “Not to mention *this*.”

“It’s just some prank gone wrong. I think Vanessa might be right, though. There’s something not quite adding up. And while humans aren’t as easy to read as ghosts, there’s clearly something going on. I just don't care for the people who may have the answers."

"You know there's a simple solution to this," Beasey says, wiping the locker with a cloth. I hold my disapproving stare until he acknowledges it as my reply. "Well, how long do you want this Vanessa to be haunting you? Because the dead are in no rush."

I cringe at the thought, but he's right. I might not have a normal life, but I actually miss the normal that I had before all this. Which is what I need to work towards getting back again. The sooner the better.

"Life is messy, Charlotte," Beasey continues. "And so are people. You just need to slap on some gloves and scrub away at it, one stain at a time."

"I hate it when you're right."

"You're getting there."

My pout breaks into a small smile as I sling my bag over my shoulder and then pace to class.

∞∞∞∞

Thankfully I only got a verbal warning for being late since I still looked like I got caught in the rain, and classes were a breeze without the pandering of Vanessa in my ear. I actually managed to forget about the locker situation for a few hours. That is until the end of lunchtime, when I see Dylan behind the gymnasium. He's by himself, leaning against the wall in the light drizzle, lost to whatever music he's listening to through his earphones. I don't want to, but I tell Leslie I left my book in class so I'll catch her later, then walk over to Dylan.

I have to wave to get his attention; the music he's listening to is so loud I can hear it through his earphones three feet away. Nothing like some heavy rock music blaring into your eardrums to forget the world around you. I know.

"Hey, Dylan."

He pulls an earbud out of his ear before scowling at me. "What do *you* want?"

I decide there's no patience here for waffling, so I get straight to the point. "Did you find out who made the mess with the flag blood in your locker?"

His eyes narrow. "No."

I wait for more, but nothing comes. "But you didn't have the flag blood, did you?"

"Did Ryan put you up to this?"

Now *my* eyes narrow. "No."

He stands up at the ring of the bell and starts walking away. "No, I didn't have the flag blood. Why would I care for that shit? Football's not my thing. What does any of this have to do with you, anyway? What are you, a detective?"

No, I'm not. But I'm starting to wish I was, because maybe then all this would make more sense.

Pacing behind him I ask, "Uh, do you know why someone would do that though?"

Dylan stops in his tracks and I quickly swivel to my side to avoid knocking into him.

"You don't get it, do you? They think I had something to do with her death."

I shrug helplessly. "Did you?"

"No!" he seethes. "And how many times do I have to say that? The police, my family, my friends—or those I thought were my friends."

"But you were the last person to see her, right?"

"No, I wasn't! I never saw her that night."

"But her last message said she was—"

"That was never the plan!"

"Plan?"

Dylan curses under his breath then pinches his nose between the creases of his eyebrows. "Look, I was out. I have an alibi. I'm not a suspect. So back the fuck off!"

He storms off before I can ask anything else, but if what he said is true then there's nothing else to get from him.

I sigh. I miss Cole. Cole would do something funny or say

something reassuring right now. Instead he's with Vanessa.

Lucky her.

I dash off to English class. The teacher is even later than me thanks to a scuffle between two juniors in the hallway and I sneak into my seat just as he enters. To be fair, the absence of any ghosts gives me some well-needed catch up on schoolwork. Ryan also stays behind after class to chat with me which is nice if not weird. He mostly talks about football and his part-time job at the sports store, but he then talks about his grandfather who passed away last month. Apparently they were close and it was sudden so he never got to say a proper goodbye.

"So would you mind coming to the lake and meeting my grandpa? He'll be there if anywhere; it's where we scattered his ashes."

"He's dead, Ryan."

"Sure, yeah, right. But *if* you happened to pick up on something, you could let me know."

Ryan then turns to me. His eyes are hazel like mine. Hazel with a pale blue ring on the outer iris. I can tell because he's close, looking at me quite intently, a quick sly grin peeking through his lips. "I won't tell anyone."

I sigh. "Ryan, I would, but I've got detention now and my dad doesn't want me out after dark right now with the ongoing Vanessa thing."

"Oh, you don't need to worry about that anymore. The autopsy results just came out."

"Oh?" My eyes shoot up. This is news to me.

"Yeah." He waves his phone. "Just heard the news."

"And?"

"Drowned in her own vomit, unconscious from alcohol poisoning. No drugs, no signs of a struggle. She just overdid herself. Case closed."

"Oh."

I don't know what else to say. I mean, yeah, I'm glad there's not a psycho murderer after teenage girls out there, or that I'm taking classes with one. But I can't help but feel a *little* deflated at all the surrounding drama Vanessa has caused regarding this.

Ryan scrolls through a message on his phone. "They'll release her body tomorrow. The funeral is this Saturday. Foxton Park Cemetery. Four o'clock."

"Oh."

"Why, did she say anything otherwise?"

"No," I quickly reply. "Nothing at all. Case closed."

"How about it, then? You've got detention, I've got practice. I can pick you up afterwards?"

I smile nervously. Am I about to spend time with Ryan Hill outside of school? Okay, it's so he can find peace with his grandfather, but that still counts for something, right?

"I'll have you back home by sundown, Cinderella," he adds at my hesitation.

Cinderella had to be back home by midnight, but I don't correct him. Instead I smile sheepishly.

"Sure."

"Cool. See you after practice, then."

With a quick wink he leaves to go to his afternoon ritual as I go to mine.

So it's final. After all the drama, she drank herself to death. That's it.

I huff. Whatever. Case closed. Now she can move on, from her life, from Cole, and from pestering me.

"You look happy."

"Cole!"

"Had a good day?"

I can't help but beam at him.

"I missed you." I cough, lowering my voice. "I mean, it was a busy day."

"Oh?"

"Yeah. Good news, though: Vanessa died of alcohol poisoning. Well, not that that's good news, but the autopsy came out saying it was simply a few too many shots. Well, technically she drowned in her own vomit, I mean, eww, that sucks. But no foul play." I clap my hands. "Case closed! Vanessa can move on now."

Cole looks contemplative, not showing the satisfaction I thought he would.

"She still needs to get over her grief to move on."

I roll my eyes. There's always a catch.

"Well how does she do that?"

"Remembering will help. As well as compassion and care."

"Comp—" I pinch the ridge of my nose and press my lips together to stop myself from saying something I'll regret. Cole is right, though. It's not as over as I briefly had the pleasure of thinking. Vanessa hasn't moved on yet. Someone is out for Dylan. And if I want to get back my normal I need to help Vanessa as much and as quickly as possible.

"You're walking faster than usual."

"Yeah," I reply as I head inside. "Busy day, remember? I'm hanging out with Ryan after I see to Vanessa after detention with Beasey which I'm already late for."

"Ryan? From The Squad?"

"Yeah. He seems alright."

Cole raises an eyebrow. "If you're sure."

I'm not sure, but I don't say that.

"I said I'll help him with his grandfather, bring some closure to him."

"Wait," Cole touches my arm which stops me in my tracks. "Charlotte, why would he ask you that?"

"Don't worry, I didn't tell him anything. He's just suspicious. And you can thank Vanessa for that, the drama queen."

Cole lets go of me. It was a light touch, but my arm now feels oddly incomplete, the remnants of his energy lingering on my skin.

"You seem a lot more keen to help Ryan than Vanessa."

"Ryan asked nicely."

"Hmm."

"You're too kind to Vanessa," I say. "I still think we should throw her to Beasey."

"Grief is a process, Charlotte. It takes time."

"Yeah, but while the dead have plenty of time, the living are on a timeline with schedules to uphold." I open the door to the classroom Beasey is in. "Starting with detention."

Cole is gone in a flash, but I don't hold it against him. He's not exactly on talking terms with Beasey, and I find it comforting that he is still being extra cautious regardless of how Beasey claims to be a man of his word.

Beasey walks over and hands me a broom. Straight into it. Good. A quick start, a quick finish.

"The spirit, I assume?"

"*Cole*. And yes."

"He's not keen on joining us?"

"He's not, as I'm sure you can understand."

"Hmph." Beasey sprays the teacher's desk with disinfectant. "So did you talk to Carl—"

"Cole—"

"And figure out his life story?"

"I'll have you know I had a lovely chat with him this morning. But no, not yet."

"Oh?"

I put the broom down and start pacing back and forth with the mop. "I'll ask him when the time is right. But right now getting Vanessa to the other side is my priority. Her autopsy results just came out and it was simple alcohol poisoning. Nothing suspicious. She just needs to accept that. Which is why straight after this I'm going to help Vanessa remember what happened, go over her death, and see if it lifts any anchors that are holding her here."

"Isn't that what Cliff is helping with? I see those two spirits together outside a lot of the time," Beasey says as he sorts through recyclables in the trash.

My lips curl in disgust and it's not a reaction to Cole's incorrect name. I'm sure that if going over her death was all they were doing she would have crossed over by now.

"She's . . . complicated. The sooner she goes, the better," I grumble as I slosh the mop in the bucket, watching the water turn murky and dark. "On that note, if you were to, you know, do what you do, but to her, I wouldn't protest. Just a reminder."

"Charlotte." Beasey exasperates, but the small smirk as he looks my way is telling. "Are you trying to pick and choose who gets to stay behind and who should go?"

"No!" I snap back defensively before muttering, "Only her."

"Charlotte," Beasey leans forward over the desk and I know he's about to go into lecture mode. "Since you want to do this your way, do try to remember that ghosts are souls that have trauma from the life they had. They carry that trauma with them and cannot move on until they find peace with themselves. Usually this means self-reflecting at their funeral or watching their loved ones pick up the pieces and carry on without them. But for others it's not so pleasant."

My mind relays back to this morning, the way Cole was distant in his memories, and all the times he's done that before. This suddenly makes me feel sad for him. What has he been suffering through, and why is he so closed off?

I pick up a cloth and spray then start wiping desks. "In that case, I'm sure being ambushed and thrown into judgement against their will doesn't help."

"What I do isn't an ambush, Charlotte. It's tough love."

Beasey suddenly smiles and waves to a teacher who walks in. She nods and smiles back, doing an awkward tiptoe walk over the wet floor to her desk where she grabs her keys from the drawer. Once she's out of sight, Beasey drops his smile and carries on talking as if we were casually debating the best cleaner for the desk graffiti.

"Besides, I don't just throw them into the void of the afterworld. That's not what I'm about. I am a priest, after all. An exorcism cleanses them of their darkness. By then they're at peace enough to cross over themselves. Usually, at least. Your friend Cliff—"

"*Cole—*"

"Was determined not to find that enlightenment."

I stop and turn to him. "Do you think that's why Cole is still here? Because of trauma?" I swallow. "Because he's holding onto something from his life? Or his death?"

And not because of me?

I mentally curse at myself for the ridiculousness of such a thought.

Beasey looks at me, void of emotion in his voice as usual when he confirms what I don't want to hear. "Yes."

I bite down hard on the inside of my lip.

"Cole finds purpose in helping other spirits," I defend as I wipe at the permanent marker on the desk a little too sternly. "In helping me."

"I would like to follow up on that theory. I wouldn't mind talking to him myself, actually. For research purposes."

"Research purposes?"

"Research purposes," Beasey echoes innocently, holding up his book.

"I can't say he'd be keen, but I can pass it on," I suggest.

"Splendid. In that case, I think you're finished here for today."

"Already?"

"Don't you have a ghost awaiting your help to remember her trauma? Your duty calls. Duty beyond using toilet cleaner to wipe graffiti off desks."

I look at the spray bottle in my hand. *Whoops.*

Ignoring embarrassment, I drop what I'm doing and grab my bag and raincoat.

"Thanks!"

"See you tomorrow, though. And don't be late again."

"I won't!" I call back, already out the door.

Seven

The hallways appear to be empty, but I know otherwise.

"You don't have to hide," I call out loud.

"So you say, but I still don't trust him," Cole replies, now visibly by my side. "That was quick."

"Yeah. Apparently communicating or whatever is a get-out-of-jail card," I reply as I step outside.

There's still an overcast sky, but the rain has passed, so I sling my raincoat over my shoulder and make my way across the school grounds.

"That was nice of him."

I look at Cole. Now is the time to ask, if ever. "Beasey spoke about you actually. He seems interested in getting to know you a bit more."

"No."

His reply isn't strong, but it's final.

Before I can come up with something to reply with he says, "Vanessa is by the bleachers."

Suddenly I miss detention.

"I still don't get what the big deal is for her. I mean, she had a good life and it's not like she was beheaded or skinned alive. Of all the deaths to have, going out on a drunken high doesn't sound all that bad."

Cole gives me a look. I would say it's a look of disgust or condemnation, but his features quickly soften back into his usual deep-thinking self.

"Dying is more traumatic for some than for others, Charlotte."

There's that word again.

I probably shouldn't, but I dare to ask, "Was your death traumatic?"

Cole's face suddenly drops, a slight twitch of discomfort, a gap in his composure. He does his best to hide it, but it's already seen: the darkness that momentarily shadows him.

"I'm not the one you need to worry about."

The football team jogs by and the conversation evaporates along with him. Ryan notices me and waves quickly. I smile and wave back. I wait until they're gone before giving Vanessa any attention.

"About time," Vanessa tuts as I approach.

I bite my tongue. I don't have time for petty verbal showdowns. "Well I'm here now. So, where'd it happen? Where'd you die?"

Her eyes widen before quickly narrowing. She points not far above us. "Back row."

I look over to the back benches, then to the football team. They're set up at the other end of the field. Two juniors are nearby, but they're now moving to get a better view of the team to ogle over. The back rows are also shaded. Good. We should be out of view.

"Let's do this, then. Tell me what you remember, step by step."

Vanessa huffs. "I've done this with Cole already."

I shrug. "I can leave then."

Vanessa sighs and rolls her eyes, as if *I* was inconveniencing *her*.

"Fine." She starts by pointing to the field. "I remember the game. Thirty–eighteen. That won't be forgotten anytime soon."

"What were you doing at that time?"

"I'm the cheerleading captain, what do you think? Or, at least I was. Gwen must be so happy now, finally getting what she wants."

"Did Gwen have anything to do with your death?"

"Her? No. At least, not that I can remember."

"Okay, so back to the game. You were cheerleading. And

then?"

"We celebrated the win. It was crazy! Our first state finals win in eight years! Everyone was too ecstatic to care about the rain. We were going to party at Steph's place because her parents said we could use their house to celebrate if we won, which was great because they have a pool *and* a hot tub. I had the cutest white Peony bikini in the backseat of Gwen's car to change into as well. You have no idea how hard it was to get my size before they sold out—"

"I don't care," I speak over her. "What does this have to do with your death?"

"Well, it's just such a waste, considering I never got to wear it. I would have liked to have left a lasting impression, at least."

"Wait, Dylan wasn't there, though."

Vanessa snickers. "Yeah, that's not exactly his thing."

"Why wasn't he at the game supporting his friends?"

Vanessa snaps, "He was busy, okay? What's your deal with him? Come to think of it, I don't recall seeing *you* there."

Touché. But I doubt Dylan was out serving justice for those whose voices are no longer heard.

It's clear Dylan has secrets. And yeah, okay, I too have secrets, as does everyone. But mine don't involve murder (well, only on one or two occasions, but not *because* of me). Not that Dylan murdered Vanessa, because the autopsy results came out stating otherwise and he supposedly wasn't even there. So if anything, he was just a shit boyfriend, and considering it's Vanessa, I honestly don't blame him on that front.

"Okay, so Dylan's not important. Tell me what happened next, Vanessa."

"Well, we snuck into the boys' locker room. Ugh, the stink. Seriously. Gag. They were loud and proud and all that when they came through the doors. We started drinking—"

"In the locker room?"

"Yeah. We even used the trophy as a drinking goblet."

I roll my eyes. "Of course."

"And that's where things start going fuzzy. And the next thing

I remember I'm standing over my body in the rain." She takes a few seconds to process it. "It was weird; I remember feeling divided, like I had a choice to go back or go . . . *home* I guess is the feeling of the word." She folds her arms into herself as she contemplates her thoughts. "Whatever that means."

"Go back? You mean into your body?"

"Well, I tried that." Her voice dies as she says, "It just didn't work."

"Do you know what happened to the others that night?"

"How should I know? I only remember them drinking. Except for Jordan and Gwen. They were the sober Ds."

"Jordan, the captain, was sober?"

"Well, yeah, there were scouts around. He couldn't exactly go shaking hands smelling of rum and coke."

"And Gwen?"

"Busy trying to impress Jordan, probably. She's been clawing her way into him for months now. Only it wasn't her he wanted."

Vanessa smiles smugly, then rolls her eyes at my confusion. "Me, Durane. He wanted *me*."

I roll my eyes. The Squad sounds more like a serial drama with every sentence she says.

"What about the flag blood?"

"What about it?"

"You had it when you died."

"No I didn't."

"Yes you did."

"No. I. Didn't." Vanessa persists. "It wasn't there when . . . when I . . ."

"Died."

"Thanks for the clarification," she scowls.

"Not saying it doesn't make it any less real," I quote Cole from earlier. "But you went to find the flag blood. Sven said you leaving to get it was the last time they saw you."

"I guess that makes sense. I made it, after all. But I wouldn't have kept it."

"So who did? Oh, let me guess, you don't remember?"

"I don't. But I do know, from before things . . . *changed* for me, that the fake blood was Jordan's responsibility, being team captain 'n all. I wasn't going anywhere near that stuff."

"Are you sure, though? You could be confused—"

"Charlotte, get a clue already. Why would any female in a cheerleading uniform—especially a white-colored one—mix with fake blood, do you not even realize how bad that would look?"

Okay, she had a valid point there.

"That stuff stains. And I told you already I was going to wear my white Peony bikini. *Peony*," she emphasizes as if I'm supposed to know what that means. "I don't care how drunk I was, there was no way I was going to risk anything except chlorinated pool water get on my Peony."

"Okay," I raise my hands. "Protect the Peony at all costs. And the flag blood was Jordan's responsibility. So why was the flag blood in Dylan's locker this morning?"

"What? I don't know."

"Really?"

"Yeah, really." Picking up on how unconvinced I am she adds, "How could I know? I was with Cole all day, thanks to you."

I curse under my breath. She's right.

"Jordan said perhaps you put it there?"

"Oh, did he now?" She crosses her arms and tuts. "Jordan's an ass."

"You just said he wanted you."

"Doesn't mean I wanted him."

"So the head cheerleader *doesn't* want the star quarterback?"

"This isn't a television show, Durane."

"Could've fooled me," I mutter. "Is there anything else? Anything at all?"

"Maybe if I could remember, but I can't."

"I don't know what to suggest, Vanessa. Have you tried meditating?"

She looks at me unamused. "You think this is funny, don't you?"

"What? No."

"There was something else," Vanessa insists. "I know it."

I sigh. Now *she* was the one keeping *me* waiting. "Are we done now? Because I've got places to be."

"Oh, like with Ryan? What is that, anyway?"

"None of your business."

"Whatever. Like it will work out. He doesn't do friends."

"What's that supposed to mean?"

"He's not your type, Durane. Besides, are you going to ignore the obvious crush you have on Cole?"

"I, I don't know what you're on about."

"Seriously, your denial is embarrassing. I've seen the way you look at him like a lovesick puppy all the time. You're totally into Cole, and you know it."

I scowl at her, trying hard not to make my cheeks flush red. "Cole and I are best friends. I don't have a crush on him."

"Fine," she says, pouting her lips into a smirk I want to smack. "So you won't mind if *I* do."

It's a shame there are now others around because that's the only thing holding me back from punching her here and now. It wouldn't do much, but I would probably feel better for it, at least. Instead, fed up with being on the receiving end of Vanessa's mouth, I decide to take Beasey's advice and attempt—what did he refer to it as? Ah, yes—*tough love*.

"I think you want there to be something else when you died," I say, rage filling up within me, "because you're in denial about how you were stupid enough to drink yourself to death."

I notice Cole across the bleachers, giving me a hunched stare. He's too far to hear, but he's certainly picking up on the tension of things. I should stop, but I don't want to.

"What, did you think some knight in shining armor was going to swoop in and save poor little Princess Vanessa? CPR by some handsome paramedic?"

Okay, I *really* should stop. But I don't. "Well, newsflash, Vanessa: they didn't. Your autopsy results came out: you died, alone, with a mouth full of vomit and a bottle of vodka in your hand. And it's only because of you. It's *your* fault."

Vanessa is fuming, her eyes wanting to kill. And just when her fists clench and I know it's going to hurt, her stare slopes off to the side, her eyes doing that distant gaze thing as her energy quickly darkens, and then she vanishes.

I blink in confusion. Too much tough, not enough love? Cole appears in front of me and gives me another look. It's clearly disapproval this time.

"She was being a drama queen!" I retort defensively.

"Really? Because *you're* the one acting like the drama queen." And leaving me with that blow he disappears after her.

I huff and kick the step in front of me, as if that exertion of energy will make me feel better. Instead, it stubs my toe, but at least that distracts me from the vented frustration seething through me.

Ryan notices my mood as he approaches. "You know that's exactly where they found her, right?"

"I am aware."

"You're probably the first student since that night to stand there. Everyone thinks it's haunted now."

"It's not. Not right now, at least."

"Oh?" He looks around suspiciously. "Is she . . .?"

"No," I snap as I grab my bag and raincoat. "Let's go."

∞∞∞∞∞∞

I'll admit Ryan is a good distraction. Not that there's much conversation beyond how his training went, but such casual conversation is all that's needed. Just two teenagers hanging out. Teenagers with air in their lungs and beating hearts. And, okay, he may have some ulterior motive with his grandfather, but I prefer to think it isn't the only motive he has.

I believe this from the way his hand rests next to mine during the drive to the lake. I try not to look up at him, one hand on the steering wheel, sunglasses on, chilling to the country music playing on his car radio, because I don't know how I feel about him in *that* way.

He pulls into the parking area right beside the boat ramp. The wind is noticeably absent as I step out of his car. It is still. Quiet. With not even a single ghost in sight.

"He spent the best years of his life fishing on this lake," Ryan says, skimming a pebble across the surface of the water. The late afternoon light makes it hard to see the gray of the pebble beyond the ripples it leaves behind. "He loved to fish. If there's anywhere he'll be, it'll be here. So?" Ryan asks hopefully. "Do you sense him?"

"I'm sorry, Ryan," I say sympathetically.

"Are you sure? We can rent a boat and go out to his favorite spot if that'll help."

I shake my head. It wouldn't help. And I doubt alone time on the lake with Ryan Hill—as romantic as that sounds—would help him.

"Can't you summon him or something?"

I raise an eyebrow. "That's not how it works." As far as I know, anyway. Beasey has raised a lot of questions in my mind lately.

"Oh."

"Sometimes they don't hang around, you know? If they lived a satisfied life and made their peace." I smile reassuringly, but I don't think that is the answer he was hoping for.

His forehead furrows as he kicks a stone down the boat ramp with his foot, but he calms as he looks out across the water. "Yeah, I guess so."

"For what it's worth, I think he would have been flattered that you came here."

He shrugs. "Sorry for dragging you out here."

"Don't be. It's a cool place."

"Vanessa liked to hang out here, you know."

"Really?" It's probably bad timing, but I feel obliged to ask anyway. "Did you see anything suspicious the night Vanessa died? I mean, did anyone act weird, or . . .?"

Ryan shakes his head. "The whole thing's fucked up. Like,

there we were, arm in arm, one of the best nights ever, then hours later we're being told by police that Vanessa had died."

"I'm sorry, Ryan."

"Like, how does that even happen? Being so alive to being so . . . *gone*."

"Did she say anything or do anything weird that night that you can remember?"

"No. She was happy. Drenched from the rain, we all were. But she was happy. Then, as we were getting ready to go to Stephanie's place for the big afterparty, she said she was going to get the flag blood and that she'd hitch a ride with Jordan and meet us back at Stephanie's place." He throws another pebble, only this time it doesn't skim along the surface but falls straight in. "I didn't realize she was *that* drunk. Nobody did."

"It's not your fault," I reassure him.

"Exactly."

He didn't need the reassurance, obviously.

"Nobody thought anything of it. We left with Gwen. It wasn't until Jordan finally arrived over an hour later that we realized Vanessa wasn't with him, but he showed us his phone, she messaged him saying she was going to meet Dylan."

Vanessa didn't mention this, but she probably doesn't remember. However, Dylan said there was no such plan for them to meet that night. And since Dylan was cleared by the police, Vanessa either made new plans to meet Dylan, or lied to do something else.

"Except she never got that far," I finish.

"Right. Because when we finally realized she still had the flag blood we messaged her to no reply. Then we messaged Dylan, who had no idea where she was." Ryan swallows. "That's when we started to get concerned."

And, according to word of mouth in the school hallways, that was when they contacted her parents, who contacted the school, who contacted the police, who then contacted Vanessa's parents to say that they had found her, dead. Then they told The Squad.

I rub his back. He's slouched forward, clearly not in the best of states.

"Sure, she was high maintenance," he says. "She was terrible, actually. But she shouldn't have *died*. Not like that. What was she thinking?"

"You don't think, not when you're drunk. Not when you're young."

Two cars pull up nearby, hooded figures exiting and giving us uncomfortable stares. Ryan catches on, too.

"That's a drug deal waiting to happen if I ever saw one." He stands up. "The sun is setting, Cinderella. Time to go home."

The drive back is filled with stories about Ryan and his grandfather which seems to boost his mood again. I guess having a listening ear helps with these things, and I'm glad Ryan chooses me to confide in. I just wish Cole would feel the same way.

He pulls into my driveway, stopping by the front porch.

"Are we late? Did you make it back before sundown, Cinderella?"

"Don't worry, my dad won't pull his shotgun out on you," I say as I unclick my seatbelt.

"That's good to know," he replies. Then in one swift motion he so casually puts his hand behind my head and pulls me in to place his lips on mine.

What the—

Oh.

I mean cool. My first kiss.

It's about time I experienced things like kissing and dating, I guess. Does this mean we're dating now? Maybe he'll ask me to prom.

Ryan's lips gently push into mine more, opening them up for—*oh*, hello tongue. We're now full-on French kissing. This must constitute confirmation we're a thing now, right? I mean, Ryan isn't bad. Not that I know him very well, but he seems okay. Kissing him feels alright at least.

"Uh," I catch my breath as Ryan's hand starts to explore. "If my dad sees this he may just go get his shotgun after all."

I wonder if I pulled away too brashly, or if I'm leaving a bad impression. Ryan, however, takes the moment in his stride with a calm nod. "See you around."

I exit his car but stop at the sight of Cole leaning back on the outside chair, legs resting on the porch handrail, watching us.

"What's wrong?" Ryan must have caught my trail of sight because he turns to look.

I glance at Ryan then back to Cole, wondering if he will start shouting, or make a lightbulb explode in a fit of rage or something. Okay, I hope at least for some reaction that makes me a little bit worth fighting for. A twitch of sadness at least? Or a small indication in his aura?

But instead he merely looks back, hands now pillowed behind his head, a half-smug expression plastered across his face as he says loudly enough to be heard, "Well, this is an exciting episode of The Squad."

"Nothing," I mumble, my eyes still on Cole. "Nothing's wrong."

"You are weird," Ryan says, turning back to me, emphasizing the *are* as if confirming some preconceived notion about me. Great.

I turn to him and smile sheepishly, not knowing what else to do.

He winks, then drives off, leaving me standing here, alone, with Cole.

"Had fun?"

"I guess." I step inside and lock the door behind me. With a hello to Dad who's preoccupied watching a sports game on television, I head upstairs to my room.

"I have to say I'm surprised," Cole says, following me. "It's not like you to fall for a member of The Squad."

"Ryan's different."

"In what way?"

"Well, for starters, he's open with communication."

"Yes, I saw that. Very open, articulate with his tongue, too."

"*Ha-ha.*"

I shoot him a scowling stare as I open my bedroom door and gesture for him to enter. Naturally he's now in front of me, watching as I grab my pajamas hanging over my chair and head to my bathroom. I don't bother closing the door as I get changed, though. Cole won't look. He never does. "Anything else?" I ask.

"Do you like him?"

"Huh?"

"Ryan Hill. Do you like him?"

I peer my head out the doorframe, repositioning my singlet over my torso as I do so. It's not his teasing voice anymore, nor is his face.

"I mean, it's early days. I can't say I know a lot about him. He only just kissed me."

"You kissed him back."

"Yes, thank you for that clarification." I turn on the tap and wash my face. Over the water I say, "I figured that was the appropriate response to such a situation."

"Clearly."

I pat my face dry with my towel before saying, "Any last clever comments to throw in? I've had a long day so get them out quickly."

"Nope, nothing. I'm going to see Vanessa anyway. She's still worked up about before. That wasn't like you."

"Beasey said to push for results," I say through the toothbrush and toothpaste in my mouth. "Tough love, he called it."

"Since when did you start following what that guy says?"

"He makes some valid points." I rinse my mouth. "And he's been right so far, I'll give him that."

Cole frowns at this. "I still think he's hiding things."

I walk back into my room, giving him a firm look as I say, "Who isn't?"

This causes him to falter slightly, his frown quickly loosens. I give my hair a quick brush, waiting for his response.

"Did you find out anything else about Vanessa?"

I sigh. "Nothing in particular."

"She needs answers."

"You know, you two live in the same astral plane, why don't *you* do some more investigative research?" I snap back. "Anything else you want to lecture me on? If not, I'm going to sleep."

Cole watches wordlessly as I get into bed and pull my bed sheets over myself.

"You're right. The dead can wait." He starts to walk away. "I'll keep an eye on Vanessa. Sleep well, Charlotte."

Just like that, he's gone.

And so am I.

I wake up before my alarm, something that doesn't happen very often. I don't need Dad's parental alarm either, as my mind seems to be well-rested and oddly perky.

Maybe it's because Ryan Hill kissed me last night. Maybe that's why I got out of bed early and spent an extra ten minutes in front of my vanity mirror making sure I look good. I even get my hair tamed enough to settle in a bun and put on extra cherry-flavored lip balm, finishing with a touch of blush and mascara. More than usual, but hopefully not too much.

Once I'm satisfied I head downstairs. I hear Dad working in the garage so I grab an apple and then let Pippi out to do her business. I follow her down the backyard to where Cole is inspecting the two hives we now have. The clouds are still gray, the ominous warning signs in the air of another rainy day.

"How are the bees?" I ask before taking a bite of my apple.

"Settling in well," Cole replies, watching them crawl into the little entrance along the bottom of the hives, probably to shelter from approaching rainfall. "They've taken a particular fancy to the neighbor's primrose."

"Was there any place you ever took a particular fancy to?"

Cole seems caught off by the question. I can tell he doesn't want to talk about it, but surprisingly he does anyway.

"I guess there were a few places. There were some good hiking spots . . ." Cole disappears into himself, daring to go back in his mind. "The waterhole, by the old watermill in the valley . . ." His thoughtful stare then breaks into something else. It's quick; his lips quiver, a contest between emotions. He blinks once, twice, then he's back to normal. "A good swimming spot."

"Ah, I miss swimming," I say with a stretch. "You'll have to show me that place sometime."

He doesn't answer. Maybe I pushed it too far.

Raindrops make themselves known.

"You're wearing makeup."

I usually do, but since it's only minimal I don't hold it against him. Guys are useless like that.

"Is it a problem?"

"Not at all. It's perfectly normal for someone your age. Or, as I remember you saying, *ordinary*."

"Surely you did ordinary guy things back in the day of existence?" I defend. "So you were eighteen when you became spiritually immortal. But while I assume you never got to experience the power of Maybelline, you didn't miss out on all things, surely? I mean, I assume you had a beer or few?"

A slight smile grows. "A few."

"Right. And you got your driver's license?"

His smile falls. "True."

Pippi now joins us and Cole bends down to stroke her. Should I push it while he's distracted? I have to know.

"Did you ever have sex?"

Cole's stare keeps on Pippi, his eyes move straight to mine, his expression blank and untelling. "Yes."

Oh.

Well, of course. Cole is good-looking, charming, funny. Why wouldn't girls want him? Why did I even think otherwise? He was alive once, his own person. Of course he could have had a girlfriend or a lover. Or many girlfriends or many lovers.

"There you go," I say, trying to keep my voice from cracking. Why was my voice cracking? "See? Not all experiences lost."

I'm relieved to hear a car coming up the driveway. I joke all too sheepishly, "Maybe you could talk it over with Beasey?"

Cole's expression doesn't change.

I turn to the house as I hear a car door close. Pippi barks once so I know there's no point in turning back around. Instead, I follow her to the front door.

"Ryan," I say surprised. I try to hold Pippi back from doing circles around Ryan as he approaches. She sniffs the hand he offers, then licks it twice before settling down.

"Hey," he says, stroking Pippi behind her ear. She clearly approves as she sits by his feet.

"Who do we have here?" My dad walks out from the garage, rubbing oil off his hands with a rag. He looks straight to Ryan, a quick, stiff nod followed by an outstretched arm. Ryan doesn't hesitate to shake his hand with a nod back.

"Ryan. Hill."

"Hill, eh? Hugo's kid?"

"One of them, yeah."

"How's your old man doing? Still crop dusting on the planes?"

"Yes, sir. Apparently here'll be a good haul of produce this year."

I press my lips, studying this male-on-male interaction. Males marking status, establishing social links, weaknesses. Threats to their own.

"Let's hope so." Dad finally stops shaking Ryan's hand. Threat level lowered. "So, you know my daughter?"

"Dad," I mutter through my near-closed lips.

"Yes, we have some classes together. I was actually passing by to see if she wants a lift. She got a bit wet yesterday."

Dad quickly glances between the two of us before smiling indiscriminately. "I'll get back to the garage, then. Orange juice is in the fridge."

He leaves, which I think is a bit odd considering his values make for what is usually a parental blockade from the dangers of the opposite sex. I guess at this stage he's just relieved that I'm socializing with actual people.

When the quiet starts to become awkward I ask, "Would you like some orange juice?"

He shakes his head. "You have a pretty cool place here. It

looks different in the daytime.”

He leans back on the railing of the front porch, one leg crossed over the other. He then pays attention to my windchimes hanging down, pushing the copper wire to hear the light clanging of metal meeting glass.

“Did you make these?” he asks.

I look up to my windchimes, the different colors of glass still showing in the gray sky as they twirl in the light wind. I used to make them out of Dad’s old beer bottles; the different colors of different brands from different parts of the world excited me whenever Dad finished one. Thankfully he stuck to his limit, especially when going through some very rough years where I’m sure if it weren’t for looking after me he would have drunk a lot more.

“Yes.” I smile. “Recycle and reuse.”

Ryan makes a little noise, a grunt of acknowledgement. “You going to Vanessa’s funeral this Saturday?”

His question catches me off guard. “Uh, no. I’m pretty certain she would not want me there, anyway.”

Ryan smirks my way. “Pretty certain, aye? Can’t blame ya.” He looks back to the windchimes. “So there’s going to be a party afterwards. Liam’s place. Just a few people, a few drinks. I want you to go with me.”

Woah, wait. What? Ryan offers to drive me to school, then asks me out? If it even counts as asking me out, that is. I don’t know where on the definition of date being invited to an after-funeral party lies, but he *is* technically asking me out. I mean, not that there’s a problem with Ryan asking me out. Because there isn’t. I think.

“Go with you?” I echo.

“Yeah. Unless your dad’s still all anal about you staying out late.”

All *what*? I cringe internally at the connotations of what he just said. My father may be a traditionalist, but he means well and is certainly not *anal*. I bite my lip casually and reply, “Nah, he’s not like that.”

"They *are* kinda cool." He taps the windchimes again, this time harder, the clanking sounding unnatural and chaotic. "So you'll come?"

"Um, I mean, yeah. I guess." Because why wouldn't I? My mind was blank, void of any reasoning or excuses.

"Cool." He stands. "I'll pick you up at seven."

I feel butterflies. "Sure."

Rain starts falling. With a quick nod he hops back into his car calling back, "You coming?"

I grab my bag then join him, a glimpse of Cole standing on the porch just visible enough through the raindrops flowing down the car window.

Cole, who clearly had a whole other life I know nothing about.

Not that I should be bothered. Who gets caught up on what some dead guy got up to years ago? I mean, I was still learning how to read when he was . . . doing other things.

"You're quiet."

Ryan's words blink me out of my thoughts. "It's the rain," I lie. "It's melodic. Thanks for the ride, by the way."

"Thanks for last night."

Ah, yes. Last night. I almost forgot. I flash a smile at him.

He glances at me. "You enjoyed it too, right?"

I don't know if the 'it' he is referring to is the lake, the time spent with him or the kiss we shared, but my money's on the kiss.

"Yes."

"What's on your mind?"

"Is sex really that common for eighteen-year-old guys?"

"What?" He glances between the road and me. "You're serious? *That's* what is on your mind?"

Shit, did I really just ask that out loud?

"Yes. No." I sigh. "I dunno. Forget it."

I bite my lip, annoyed with myself. Ryan's going to get the wrong end of the stick with this, thinking I'm giving off a strong signal. Except it wasn't him I was thinking about.

"I mean, I guess so. Sports and sex and Smirnoff aside, what else is there for guys in these parts to do?"

"So you've done it?"

"Yeah. Cousin's wedding. Hot bridesmaid," he smirks. "Good food *and* good fun."

"Charming."

"Then a few others since."

Of course. I'm not even surprised.

"So . . . what are you implying here? I mean, we've got twenty minutes before class—"

"No!" I recoil. "I mean, so for guys it's just to let off some steam more than romantic dedication?"

Ryan shrugs. "I guess. I mean, Liam's stepbrother fell for Clara—hard—and with a shotgun wedding ended up becoming a husband and father at nineteen. Sucks he became a divorced dad at twenty-three, though."

I have no idea who Clara is, but I can't help but wonder if Cole had a Clara in his life. Maybe he still does, even. Maybe that's where he spends all his time. With *her*. Or worse, *them*.

I shake my head at the thought. We pull into the school parking lot and Ryan slides into a space and then turns off the engine in one quick motion. Even in the rain, faces turn our way, especially a cluster of juniors who suddenly don't care about the weather they were running from.

Just as I scowl at them to stop staring, Ryan leans over, his lips firmly finding mine.

I imagine their sad faces of envy as I kiss him back, wondering what exactly it is I'm doing.

Being ordinary.

"I think you've just prevented me from being able to focus on anything in class today," he says between kisses.

Liam stops in front of the car to imitate a sexual gesture which causes others to laugh. Ryan flips him the bird but it's all in good spirits. We make a dash for the school building, then with another quick kiss, we part ways to go to our classes.

∞∞∞∞∞

Things start becoming different from then on. Ryan waits for me at my locker between classes. His hand always finds itself in the back pocket of my jeans in the three or four minutes we stand there complaining about teachers or homework or assignments. Sometimes it's just the two of us, and other times one or two members of The Squad join us.

Although Gwen, Jordan, and Stephanie still shun me, Liam doesn't seem to care either way, Mandy is polite enough to talk to me, and Sven has started chatting to me like we've known each other for years. Maybe it's a guy thing to just get into it, whether it be friendships or relationships. Then again, that would only solidify how Cole probably feels about me, which makes me wonder if the mystery of Cole sounds better than the fear of the reality of him.

"What do you reckon?" Ryan whispers quietly in my ear.

"Huh?" I hadn't been listening to a word Liam was saying.

"Vanessa's funeral. Reckon she'll be there?"

"Oh." My eyes widen. "Oh, of course she'll be there," I laugh nervously. "Embalmed and boxed up."

To my surprise Ryan laughs at this. But Gwen, overhearing, gags. "What the hell, Durane! You better not be invited."

She walks away. Jordan must have overheard too, because he stares at me, his eyebrows low and face stiff, before following Gwen.

"Mr. Hill, take your hand out of Miss Durane's back pocket!" Ms. Kennerson scolds him as she walks past. Ryan utters a word that, luckily for him, gets drowned out by the sound of the bell above us. I tell him I'll meet him on the field after a quick bathroom break so he heads off first.

"Hey, Jordan."

Both Jordan and Gwen turn around, surprised to see me pacing up to him. "What?"

"I was just wondering, how did the scout meetings go?"

"Good. Why?"

"It was just such a stellar performance at the game. How many scouts turned up?"

"Three."

"Wow, three. So how'd it go?"

This seems to ease Jordan. "Yeah, it was great. It's not even a matter of applying for two of the scholarships now; it's choosing between them."

"They're negotiating contracts," Gwen adds proudly.

"You must have been talking with them for a while. How long did it take to finish talks with them all?"

"I dunno. An hour, maybe? Coach did most of the talking. Why?"

Enough time to drink yourself to death.

"Well, it's just . . . if Vanessa was last seen getting the flag blood, then why would she go to see Dylan without first giving it to someone?"

The only someone who was still around.

"I dunno. I was with the scouts after the game," Jordan tenses. "Ask Dylan, he seems to know."

I already did.

"What are you implying, Durane? Got a problem?" Gwen sneers.

"No. No, I . . ." I straighten myself, force a smile.

Ordinary Charlotte, remember?

"You're right. Someone just played a foolish prank. Anyway, I just think with all that happened regarding Vanessa, nobody really got a chance to celebrate your success. You did, like, such a great job, you're a school legend! I just wanted to congratulate you."

Jordan loosens up at this. "Cheers." He takes a moment before adding, "You're coming to the party Saturday night, right?"

"Yeah. Ryan invited me."

Jordan nods. "Cool."

On that terse reply he leaves.

"Lucky you," Gwen sneers before trailing behind him.

The hallway empties but luckily I have a free period so there's no teacher scolding me for my tardiness. Instead, I meet with Leslie and we head out to the bleachers. The library is our usual study spot, but I convince her to spend our free period outside now that the rain has passed.

Unlike the rest of the student body, Leslie doesn't care that a student died nearby and the area could be haunted (which wouldn't be a wrong assumption). I wonder if it's something she came across all too often in Honduras, but I don't ask. In any case, it makes for a nice place to study because it's warm, we are free to talk as loudly as we like, and since Vanessa is here with Cole I just want to make sure she is actually working on herself and not, well, Cole. The fact that Ryan is nearby immersed in football practice has nothing to do with it. Mostly.

"So," Leslie slurps the last of her juice carton through the small white straw. "You and Ryan, huh?"

I had almost forgotten that Leslie is sitting next to me, my eyes so intently spying on Vanessa as she shimmies up close to Cole across the far end of the bleachers. She knows I'm here; she even waved at me as I sat down while she laughed at something Cole said.

I aggressively tear a bite of my granola bar and give myself a few chews before answering. "Maybe."

"Maybe?"

"Ryan is cool," I admit.

Leslie raises an eyebrow at me and says, "I mean, try not to complain any louder. He's not exactly a consolation prize."

"He's not," I agree. Most girls would squeal in delight to have Ryan Hill occupy their school day as much as he is occupying mine.

"But?"

"But . . ." I look back to the field and see Ryan taking the brunt of a tackle quite admirably. As the coach blows the whistle he takes his helmet off, notices me and winks my way. I smile and wave back. Under normal circumstances my heart would probably be doing backflips in my chest right now. Instead, I'm more focused on spying on Cole and Vanessa while using my phone to search up watermill sites in this corner of the country.

I sigh. "It's complicated."

"Complicated?"

I nod. As cliché as it sounds, it's true. Ryan heard me speaking to his dead friend, yet it didn't seem to concern him. Maybe that is enough to assume there is something there between us. Maybe the stars are aligning and I just need to open up a little. Maybe I just need to put my phone down.

"I'm just a little apprehensive. He is a member of The Squad, after all."

"True."

The coach blows on the whistle and the team starts patting each other on the shoulder at their touchdown. Gwen claps her hands loudly on the sideline next to her entourage who, like me, appear more interested in their phones.

Leslie sighs. "Doesn't it suck that the hot guys here are football jerks?"

I look back from my phone to Jordan. I mean, I try to feel girly looking at his six-pack and noticeably large biceps as he takes his shirt off, or at the way he swings his wide shoulders as he strides across to the benches, and at how he flicks his shaggy-black hair aside as he takes a drink from his water bottle.

I then watch Ryan, with his sun-bleached light brown curls and gold-tanned skin as he leaps up on Jordan with a tousle of his hair and a pat on the back. But my eyes can't help drifting to Cole across the bleachers, leaning back, laughing at something Vanessa says. Then, as if on cue, he turns, his lean body, sandy hair, warm amber eyes, and alluring smile now focusing on me.

Not all the hot guys here are football jerks.

I cough awkwardly, as if I can cough out such thoughts. Distracting myself, I look back at my phone to a place called Winston Watermill:

A watermill built in 1878 with strong optimism for the growing township of Richmond until it struck financial trouble with its owner, Winston Hayes. Despite starting conversions to change it into a roller mill to reflect the changing times, it ended up being decommissioned in 1908

I scroll through the text, flicking back up to the picture of kids jumping into the water and surrounding hillside.

I sit up. This has to be it.

I check the location on my phone. It's just under thirty miles away.

I stand. "I gotta go."

"Where are you going?"

I stop in my tracks, noticing that Cole and Vanessa are also looking my way. I also notice the football team packing up. Checking my watch I realize that school is nearly over for the day and I have detention with Beasey.

Dammit.

"Uh, detention. I've got cleaning duty for punching the janitor, remember?"

"You still owe me a truthful explanation for that, by the way," Leslie replies.

"One day," I call back. It's an empty promise, one Leslie doesn't deserve. But it's for the best.

I make it to detention before the bell rings. I thought that would mean hanging around until the classrooms are empty, but we don't seem to be doing clean-up duty today, and I dare not bring it up. Instead, I find myself reorganizing the cleaning cupboard and noting expired products. Judging from the age of some of these bottles I'd say it's in much bigger need of cleaning out than the classrooms across the hallway. Maybe even a hazmat suit or two is required.

"Exorcism," Beasey begins, "is not a punishment. It is a form of blessing, a release of judgment, so that they can move on into the Lord's realm."

"So you keep saying. But I still don't buy it. Ghosts should cross over on their own terms." I hold up a bottle. "Three expired disinfectants."

Beasey scribbles that down on a clipboard. "And what if they can't on their own terms, hmm?"

"Then I help them to." I dump a bottle in the black trash bag. "One very expired sanitizer."

"You can't save the world, Charlotte," Beasey says as he scribbles on the stock order form. "Imagine if every ghost came knocking for your service. The queue of the dead would only get longer and longer, you would never get anything done. You'd go mad."

"I know." I pause, then dump two more bottles in the trash before saying, "But I can make a difference, one soul at a time, right?"

"That's not very efficient, Charlotte."

I roll my eyes. "Two drain cleaners. Expiry unknown." I pick up a backpack from the floor by the wall, the contents of candles and various liquids in bottles visible. "What's all this stuff?"

Beasey looks up from his clipboard. "Communicator supplies."

I cringe. "You mean your torture tools?"

"They are not torture tools. And I've been exorcising ghosts since before you were born, kid. I know more about all this than you."

"I don't care if you've been exorcising ghosts since the days of Noah's Ark. This is the twenty-first century, I like to believe people have rights, whether alive or dead."

Beasey sighs. "Not every spirit is sad, Charlotte. Some are just bad. They won't leave you alone. They will beg, persuade. Some will even terrorize you. So you need to be ready, ready to protect yourself."

"Ready to exorcise them, you mean."

"Yes. Especially when Clark isn't around. What will you do then?"

I shudder at his words. He's wrong about Cole's name, but he's right with what he's saying. As much of a slap in the face that sentence is, he's putting forth the thoughts I refused to think about until now.

My silence seems to be an answer because he opens his book on a page and slides it across the table to me.

"What is this gibberish?" I ask as I pick up the book.

"Ancient tongue."

My eyes widen. "Woah."

"It was gibberish to most. Not to people like us, though."

"What do you mean?"

"People like us have been popping up throughout history, to varying degrees. Some were feared, killed even. Some were revered and worshiped like deities. Nowadays, many are probably off their rockers on medication."

I cringe at his words, hitting too close to home.

"Unfortunately, there are a lot of scammers out there that waste everybody's time and put us in a worse light. Needless to say, it's hard to know how many of us there are as we are generally well-hidden folk." Beasey winks. "But we have our ways."

I follow the pages, picking up on the gist of the paragraphs. "So this is—"

"How to perform an exorcism, yes. The good news is you don't need a shopping list of candles or crystals or chemicals."

"So your bag of voodoo?"

Beasey flashes a small smile as he empties his bag. "It's just to help set the scene. Candles and crystals are ambient and relaxing, even to spirits. Not to mention the candles help to contain their energy." He picks up one of the candles and sniffs it. "And I like the smell of pine."

"Wow. I didn't think you had it in you."

"What? A taste for décor?"

"Compassion, actually." I pick up one of his candles and smell it. "Rosemary is good, too."

"See, I'm not a witch. And you don't really think a sprinkle of sodium chloride is going to deter a spirit of the deceased, do you? Next you'll be telling me that ghost hauntings are restricted to local council property boundaries." He chuckles to himself before looking at my blank expression. "*Salt*." Beasey sighs. "Don't they teach you anything at this place?"

I shake my head. "Whatever. So why do words work?"

"We assume it's because words carry emotion, and emotion is energy. If someone keeps telling you how pretty you look you will feel uplifted somewhat, right? The same concept applies. Ghosts are very susceptible to emotional energy, and as Communicators we have the gift of communicating energy to a higher level— for better or worse. So knowing these words will help keep you safe."

Shit. Maybe I was wrong about Beasey, after all. Maybe he does just want to help the dead by helping me.

"There is a lot to learn. Starting with ridding the unwanted."

"You mean exorcisms?"

Beasey looks at me sternly. "Yes."

"Seems easy enough."

"I'll hold you to that. Now, from the top, repeat after me."

It takes me numerous attempts to finish the scripture and get the tones right. When my words start to slur over one another, Beasey calls it a day and promises I'll get used to the new tongue positions and pronunciations. Just as I close the book in relief, Vanessa appears. My mouth drops in shock, Vanessa so casually treading in shark-infested waters, clearly not knowing how lucky she is to not be caught in an exorcism to the afterlife right now.

"Vanessa! What are you doing here?"

"Vanessa, pleased to finally meet you."

"Oh, yay, the other weird one. And of course it's the crazy janitor. Take a good look, Durane, that's your future."

My mouth hangs open at her words. I mean, sure, he's Beasey. And sure, I throw a bit of an attitude his way; he deserves it. But Vanessa is just downright rude.

"I need to talk to you." She says to me before looking at Beasey. "*Alone.*"

I look at Beasey, fully expecting an exorcism practice to take place. He remains unfazed, however.

"Well, you heard the lass. Better get going."

I give him another look, one more apologetic this time.

"Okay."

"And the other one? Caine, is it? Am I going to expect him to show up, too?"

I don't bother correcting him as I leave. "Working on it."

I walk down the hallway and enter an empty classroom. Vanessa appears in front of me.

"So what is it this time, Vanessa?" I ask with a very forced politeness.

"Did you talk to Jordan?"

"I did. There's nothing to say. He was talking to scouts and then he drove to the afterparty at Stephanie's house. He did, however, receive a message from you saying you were going to see Dylan."

"That can't be right."

"Ryan saw the message himself."

Vanessa shakes her head. "Something doesn't add up."

"So what if it doesn't? The point still stands, you got caught up on the bleachers and drank yourself to death. You need to accept that and move on now."

Vanessa scowls my way. "You would like that, wouldn't you?"

Well, yes, but I don't say it outright. Instead I sigh. "Do you know where your cellphone is? If I can get it and check myself—"

"It's broken," Vanessa glowers. "I must have dropped it in a puddle or something because it got water damaged."

"Look, you obviously had something planned, whether it was with Dylan or not. Maybe it was getting the flag blood, or checking on your *Peony*, or meeting another boyfriend, perhaps?"

Vanessa ignores me, her mind elsewhere. "I see Jordan's face. It's faint . . . I'm not sure. I think we had an argument. He told me it's my fault."

"That doesn't surprise me," I mutter.

"I heard that." Her energy dims—which, in this dark and quiet setting, puts me on edge. She huffs, and with a hostile glare she says, "To think I actually felt sorry for you, being a weirdo needing to be babysat by Cole all the time . . ."

I stop listening because I've heard enough of Vanessa's mouth for a lifetime. My recollection of words spoken not long before is still fresh in my mind, and since we're clearly not making progress there is only one way this is going to end.

"You know, I've had just about enough of you, Vanessa."

It's just meant to be quick, a scare tactic to put her in her place. But it's weird yet oddly thrilling feeling myself have so much power. I mean, it's not every day you yield the portal to the afterlife. Yet here I am, doing just that.

"What, what are you doing?"

I can't help but smirk at her sudden change in mood. "Oh, just something I've been wanting to see happen for a while now."

I watch the haze form out of nowhere, creeping up her legs as she struggles to trudge free from it. She doesn't scream or wail, however. She instead looks straight at me and mutters, "Bitch."

"Charlotte?"

I don't notice Cole at first. But then he's in front of me, looking me in the eyes. I stop as the haze attracts to him.

"What the hell are you doing?" He figures it out, shaking his head in disapproval. "I thought you were better than him."

"Cole!" Vanessa clasps herself on him and starts whimpering into his chest.

"Cole . . . I wasn't really . . ." I try to find my words as I watch Vanessa cower close to him. Boy, she could have won Oscars. "I was just trying to scare her away."

"Let's go, Vanessa." Cole puts his arm around her then looks back to me. "I'm disappointed in you, Charlotte."

I huff. It's not like they're around to hear, however, because they have already left. Together.

∞∞∞∞∞

It is dark by the time I get home thanks to a ghost needing to accept that a motorcycle will always lose out against a truck. In the end I guide him to Beasey to deal with. I look on while I finish off the last of the cupboard supplies, my excuse to stay and watch. Because, okay, I'm admittedly a little curious about the process. And yes, it is quick and efficient like Beasey claims. Being right doesn't mean being the best, however. I still believe in good old-fashioned compassion. But if that doesn't work, well, I guess it's always good to have a backup.

Dad leaves a message that he'll be finishing late from work at the diner, so it's leftovers for dinner for me. Once I get home I wash up and let Pippi out for an evening stretch when Vanessa suddenly appears across the living room.

"Vanessa, what the hell are you doing here?" I seethe after a startle, prepared to tell her to bugger off with whatever level of cursing is required.

"He's a very good kisser, you know."

Her words stun me still. "W-what?"

She places her hand over her mouth. "Oh, I'm sorry, *do* you know? Oh, that's right. Just best friends. I don't know what I like more: his lips or the way he sighs ever so quietly as he succumbs to temptation."

I bite down on the inside of my lip. It's all my body can do to remain calm and collected, creating the physical pain to distract me from the emotional tsunami within me.

She smirks, taking full pleasure in the hurt I cannot hide, before disappearing.

Pippi barks twice as she leaves because Cole appears only seconds later.

"Oh," he says impetuously. "Is Vanessa here?"

I turn to Cole, fighting to keep my voice calm. "You . . . you kissed Vanessa?"

His eyebrows furrow slightly, his mind clearly debating if I want to know the answer. But he doesn't need to reply, I realize. His silence is enough.

I huff. "Of all the people, of all the ghosts, you have to get with *her*?"

"Let me explain—"

"No." I slam the backdoor shut then storm upstairs. "I don't want to know."

"It's not like that. C'mon, you know me—"

"Do I?" I turn and snap back. "I don't know anymore, Cole. Who are you? Why don't you tell me about yourself? Like, oh, I dunno, your full name or how you died?"

Cole's face stiffens. When he doesn't reply I roll my eyes. "Exactly what I thought."

I don't wait for a response; I know I won't get one. I close my bedroom door behind me, the only small satisfaction being that this time it is *me* who leaves *him* standing alone for a change. Only he won't be alone because he'll go after Vanessa.

As I go to bed, Beasey's words replay in my mind about what I'd do when Cole isn't around. Only I didn't think it would be so soon, and certainly not like this.

I guess the wake-up call had to come sometime.

I don't like days like today. It's crazy how many 'special days' a person's death carries with them. It's not just their birthday, but their anniversary, their funeral date, even Christmas. I just feel that every day without them carries the same impact, which makes the special days ultimately amount to nothing. It's just a day, and a day shouldn't define them.

But it means something to Dad, which is why he is standing in front of the large brick mantelpiece in the living room, looking at the framed photograph of Mom and the sonogram of my brother who died on this day ten years ago.

I notice one candle is already lit.

"Hey, Dad."

His back is turned to me but I see him move his arm across his face, a quick wiping away of emotion no doubt, before turning to say hello. "Ten years. Ten."

He hands me the lighter. I know the routine: Dad lights one candle and I light the other. He'll probably go visit her grave today to place some flowers. I won't, though. She's not there; she never has been. Not really.

"I'm sure little Billy's keeping Mom on her toes up there."

My parents had a rule: if the baby was a girl, Mom would choose the name, but if the baby was a boy then Dad would get naming rights. I was named after my mother's favorite children's book, *Charlotte's Web*. She used to read a bit to me every night, and when she finished it we'd just start from the beginning again, like a television rerun. My baby brother never got a name because Dad was going to let Mom decide anyway, since she "did such a good job the first time". She never got that chance though, so we refer to him as Billy, after Dad.

I don't hold faith in what I say, but Dad smiles at the idea, and that's the important thing.

"If he's anything like you, I'm sure of it."

He means it as a joke, but it's definitely no understatement. I mean, poor Dad. I'm sure he expected a normal Christian daughter, but instead he got me, and that's no easy feat.

I ponder if Billy would have been like me. Probably not, considering that (as far as I know) what I can do isn't hereditary. If it is, I'm sure the family dynamics would have been a lot different. But it would have been cool to have someone close who understood me; a little sidekick, even.

"I have to get going," I say, noticing the time. "Will you be okay?"

Dad nods which will have to do because I know he won't let me miss school on his account. With a swipe of an apple and my earphones from the kitchen counter on my way out, I say bye to Dad as I slump my bag over my shoulder and head for school.

Cole doesn't appear, but I'm not surprised since I have my earphones on and music up loud, a telltale sign I'm not up for chatter. Not that I want to face him, because after last night I have nothing to say. I wonder how long he'll be off in the spiritverse for this time. Probably a while since he's now got Vanessa for company.

I shudder at the thought, my stomach now feeling queasy.

Now that Cole and Vanessa seem to be a thing I guess there'll be lots of queasy feelings, not to mention changes. Like him spending less time with me. I'll probably have to be careful what I say around him, too. Maybe I should consider him as a de facto member of The Squad. She'll be around a lot longer, too, maybe indefinitely. And when he turns into Vanessa's other half, as a best friend I will have to be supportive without succumbing to the desire to exorcise them both.

I don't like these thoughts, but I'm so into them I don't even notice I've arrived at school and Ryan is saying my name until he tugs on my arm.

"Oh, hey," I say to Ryan as I pull out an earbud.

"What are you listening to?"

I don't even know.

"Just something loud," I reply. Which is true. The underworld could have risen from the pits of Hell and I wouldn't have heard the commotion. I probably wouldn't have cared, either.

"You look like you want to hit someone hard."

"That wouldn't be wrong."

"Not me I hope. Although if you want to let it out I'm pretty well built to take a hit."

I smile. "Don't worry, I'll just do what most other people do and binge on chocolate brownie later while verbally venting it all out to my dog."

Ryan lets out a laugh. "Your poor dog."

"She's used to it by now." I swing my locker open. "What do you have today?"

"Nothing exciting. Health, Spanish, calculus. I think we have economics today." He opens his locker and crams a couple of books inside. "Why? Anything good happening?"

"Let's skip class," I suggest.

Ryan raises his eyebrows. "Woah. Did I just hear that correctly? You want to ditch school?"

"Yeah. Why not?"

Ryan smirks. "I just didn't think you had it in you." He leans against his locker, one leg curling around the other. Two passing junior girls say hello to him. He replies with a wink, and that's enough to set them off giggling.

Just as I scowl at them Ryan turns back to me. "What did you have in mind?"

What did I have in mind? I don't know, but does it matter? After all, it's not like today will be some life-defining day because I skipped a class analyzing the Boston Tea Party or what Othello should have said to Desdemona on her deathbed.

"I've heard of a place," I say, "about thirty miles from here."

"Road trip, eh? I may be down for that."

"We could pick up brownies on the way."

"Fair game," Ryan chuckles.

"Got your swimming gear in that locker?"

"Right here." He pulls out the drawstring bag next to him. "Why?"

"You might just need it," I reply with a smirk.

"Now I'm definitely down." He turns to Liam. "Hey, Liam, cover for me."

Liam stands there raising his arms with an exasperated shrug. I don't see his complaint, though, because Ryan has suddenly got his arm around my shoulder, leading me outside.

He stops me by his car door. "You sure about this? I didn't think you liked detention with the janitor all that much."

To be fair, considering what I'm actually doing during that time I consider it the most important period of the day. Although I don't say that, of course.

"I'm sure," I say instead.

We hop in and head out while everyone else heads in. With a quick fuel stop at a gas station we'll soon be on our way to Winston Watermill.

Cole appears in the empty driver's seat.

"Charlotte." There's a heaviness in his voice but I don't look. I don't even care. "How are you?"

I chew on the gum in my mouth before replying, "Same as always."

"Where are you going?"

"Out."

"You'll miss class."

I blow a bubble of gum from my mouth until it bursts. "So?"

"Charlotte . . ." he starts, but he doesn't continue. He's been here before. He knows he won't get anything out of me today. I have nothing to give.

"Ryan's coming, better move."

"I'm so sorry," he whispers.

Sorry isn't good enough right now.

Ryan then opens the door and Cole's gone.

"I'm back. And look at what they're selling."

My face gleams at the brownie he presents in his hands. "You got brownie!"

I affirm his gesture by placing my lips on his. I don't know why, I just feel like it. And on a day like today I find the distraction nice. He seems to like it, too, because he continues for more, only stopping when the car waiting behind toots.

He rolls his eyes and drives out. "Alright. Where to?"

I guide Ryan with my phone's directions out through the countryside until we arrive. Usually places like this would become crowded over time. Not this place, though. It looks almost untouched, unburdened with human interaction. Maybe it is forgotten. Or maybe it is intentional, a rare little secret spot only the locals know of.

Either way, we are alone.

I don't know what I expected to find. I mean, it's not like I am going to see Cole here in the flesh or a plaque with his name on it. Nonetheless, I have a look around, going over the names carved in hearts on the big oak tree (no Cole, but a few Cs have my unwanted curiosity) and peer into the foundations of what is left of the watermill, although I don't tread farther, deciding to adhere to the caution signs around it.

Ryan goes for a quick swim. I didn't bring a bikini with me, and while Ryan was almost successful in persuading me to go in my underwear since "it's the same thing anyway," I settle for getting an early summer tan on instead. Which is fine because I need it. I may live in the South, but I certainly don't look like it.

"This was a great idea, Lottie." Ryan takes another bite of my brownie. I mean, technically he paid for it. I don't want it anymore, anyway. "I didn't think you had it in you."

He smiles my way, leaning forward to me on his towel.

He doesn't initiate making out now. Well, I guess he never really did. He just chooses a spot and goes for it. Like right now my neck seems to have taken his appetite more than my (his?)

brownie. I mean, whatever. It feels nice. I place my hand on his face, holding his mouth where pleasurable sensations start emitting through my body.

"Charlotte." Cole appears. He stops at the sight of Ryan—shirtless—in the process of trying to get me shirtless, too. But then his head slowly turns, taking the scene around him in before fixating on the ground nearby.

This is it.

This is the place from his memories, I'm sure.

Ryan continues making out with me, but I am totally distracted by Cole. I don't even know why his energy darkens, but it does. He doesn't move, his face twitching an array of mixed emotions marbling his aura with shades of gray. He looks winded, as if the breath he doesn't have escapes him. Then he disappears, the space he stood on as untouched as before, his secrets gone with him.

"Are you crying?"

I didn't realize Ryan had stopped kissing my neck. I didn't realize a tear had left my eye, either.

"Sorry," I say, quickly wiping my eye with the back of my hand. "Today's a minefield of a day."

"Oh?"

"Yeah, uh, my mom and brother passed away ten years ago today."

"Shit, Lottie. No wonder you wanted some time out." He strokes my cheek. "Let me kiss you better."

I feel my face crinkle as he continues kissing down my neck. Not quite the kiss I was expecting. Nor the reaction.

Not that I expect him to understand, I guess. I mean, his grandfather was eighty, there's a difference between grieving lives lived long versus lives cut short.

I feel Ryan tugging on my bra strap. I wonder what my mom was up to when she was my age. Probably in class, for a start. Probably not tanning either, since all the photographs I have of her show her fair skin. But she had me at twenty-three, which means she was definitely doing things like this when she was twenty-two, probably earlier. I stare up at the sky, a stark difference to yesterday, and squint at the bright blue. I wonder what she would be thinking right now, watching down on me. Would she advise me to live young while I can, or would she be disappointed in me?

It's probably for the best I won't ever know.

"We should head back," I say as I gently push Ryan away. "Got a test next period. Totally forgot."

"Fair enough." He casually slides off his car first then I follow, rolling my shirt back down.

We drive back to school, the country radio filling the lack of talk between us. Maybe he can tell I have a lot on my mind and don't want to be interrupted. When we arrive, Ryan pulls into the parking lot and turns off the engine. We both sit there, neither of us in any rush to go inside. I wonder if the school has called Dad and sent out a search party, but considering the lack of calls or messages on my phone I doubt it. Or maybe he's just pulling a cool Dad card and letting it slide considering what day it is.

"Thanks for coming."

"Was worth it." He winks. I wonder how many girls he does that wink to. He seems to have mastered it, with that slight head tilt and angled smile. No wonder he bagged the bridesmaid. I can't imagine there was much talk beforehand, just eye contact across the aisle, then a wink.

We suddenly aren't alone.

I scowl at Vanessa who is standing in front of Ryan's car, her arms crossed, looking peeved as per her usual greeting.

"Yeah, class makes me feel that way, too." Ryan must have noticed my sudden change of expression.

"Yeah, but we must face it eventually. I guess."

School. Vanessa. Cole. Life.

"Are you still up for tomorrow?"

I open the door. "Tomorrow?"

"The party, remember?"

"Yes, the party. I remember. I've got my dress sorted."

"Nice."

"I need to talk to you!" Vanessa nags, her foot tapping on the ground as if she has places to be, things to do, and I was halting her plans.

"Sorry," I say to Ryan. "Gotta go."

"See you around."

I wait until I know Ryan is out of earshot and heading the other way until I seethe at Vanessa through my clenched teeth. "What?"

"Geez, cool it, bitch breath."

"Don't test me today, Vanessa. I'm warning you."

"For your sake I hope you know that Ryan has motives for his flirting."

"What do you care? Aren't you supposed to be busy hooking up with Cole?"

"Yeah, that's why I'm here. He's, like, not himself."

"What?"

"Yeah, he went to check up on you and now he's, like, dark and moody."

"Why?"

"You tell me."

"I don't know why." The bell rings and students start emerging from the classrooms. "Why don't *you* ask him since you're so close now."

Vanessa rolls her eyes. "Well, I tried. But he wants to be left alone."

"So leave him alone."

She twists to face me, arm on her hip, eyes narrow and sharp. "You're useless, you know that?"

She disappears before I tell her to, along with a few other words I have in my mind.

I make haste inside to get to the classroom on time. And I do. Except Vanessa's words play in my mind, along with the way Cole looked. Just as I reach for the door handle I pause, then with a sigh I head back the way I came to the janitor's room at the end of the hallway.

"Beasey." I don't knock. I know he's there from the indistinguishable hazy glow dissipating out from under the door.

"Charlotte." I've distracted him, but it's over, the last of the haze evaporating with whatever spirit had been standing there. "Ever heard of knocking?"

"You should probably lock the door when you do that stuff."

"No student—except you—has ever had any intention of spending time in here. Don't you have class?"

"Yes."

"This must be important, then." He gestures to the chair beside him and opens the latch of the small window, the smell of pine prominent.

"Something's up with Cole."

"Oh?"

"I think it's that trauma stuff you were mentioning. His mood is off."

"In what way?"

"I'm not really sure." I sigh as I sit down. "Sad, angsty. I went to a place he may have had a connection to back when he was alive. I think it set him on edge. Vanessa said he wants to be left alone."

"He's remembering."

"Remembering?"

"His life trauma."

"I don't think he wants to, though."

"He has to."

"Why?"

"Charlotte, ghosts can be held up in their trauma for decades, centuries even. And the longer they are dead, and their impact in the world fades, the more they forget who they are and how lost they have become."

I shudder at the thought.

Beasey blows out the last of his candles. It becomes slightly darker but the seriousness in his eyes is still visible as he continues, "What I am saying is, if you truly care for him, you will help him get through whatever life trauma he has so that he can finally make peace with himself and cross over.”

I swallow, feeling tears welling in my eyes.

“I know it’s hard, but you have to let him go.”

I shake my head. I can’t hear this, not today.

“You need to understand we aren’t here to be their friends. We are here to help them rest in peace.” He pauses for a moment before adding, “Charlotte, we help them *die*.”

His words cause my heart to sink. This is my fault. I just wanted him to open up to me, not suffer emotional trauma. The more I have dug in, the worse things have become between us. And now I’m supposed to ensure his suffering so that he can leave, *forever*?

Yes.

Because I love him.

It’s just a day.

“Charlotte, call me the devil’s advocate here, but as infatuated with that spirit as you are, he had his own life once. Maybe he has other people he cares about that are anchoring him here, like a family perhaps?”

His words make me freeze. I always figured if he does, he would have begged me to pass on a message or two, or at least talked about them. So why hasn’t he?

A chill falls down my spine. Perhaps he wasn’t the only one to pass away when he did. Maybe he was part of a larger tragedy, one also involving his family. He had a relationship with at least one other person. What if he’s with her (or them) when he’s not with me? Could he be some heartbroken Romeo pining over his Juliet, bound apart by life and death?

I stop my mind getting ahead of itself.

“Maybe,” I reply.

“I would still like to talk to him. He knows where to find me, I’m sure.”

I stand and swing my bag over my shoulder. “Well, thanks for the consult. Better get going, though. If people see me here they might start thinking I enjoy cleaning duty.”

I leave him to laugh that off as I scoot to class. Only I’m not laughing. In fact, I'm doing my utmost to not burst out crying over what Beasey just said. To think Vanessa was my biggest worry. Now, today of all days, I am faced with the sobering realization that I have to help Cole bring up whatever it is he's hiding so that he too will leave me.

It's just a day.

∞∞∞∞

Yes, I got told off for being late—again—but I couldn't care less. And yes, the school did notify Dad of my absence, and he was less than impressed when he got back from work. He would have grounded me, but it's not like I'd suffer from being homebound. He knows this, to the point that me going out tomorrow night like a normal teenager is more reason to not ground me. So instead I'm on house cleaning duty. Whatever. It's not like it's any different from what I do after school anyway.

It's just a day.

I've just about finished doing a deep clean of the oven when I hear Pippi bark once from the living room. I walk over. It's dark; Dad retired early for the night so it's just the kitchen lights on and my music for distraction.

I pull my earbuds out. "Cole?"

"Why?"

I have to squint to see Cole. His head is lowered, his aura barely visible in the surrounding dark.

"Why what?"

"Why were you at the watermill?"

"What?"

"The watermill!" he bellows. "Why were you there?"

"Oh. I was just hanging out with Ryan." I probably shouldn't lie, but it's late and I don't think he can take much more today. Nor can I.

"He's bad news," he says, his tone almost condescending.

"No worse than Vanessa," I mutter.

∞ 126 ∞

"You're fooling yourself." His voice is strong and irate. My jaw drops, my emotions boiling up to heat on my cheeks. I begin to form a snappy reply when he suddenly continues, "I want to protect you. But I can't."

I cross my arms. "Cole, what are you saying?"

"You shouldn't be with Tristan!"

"Tristan?"

Cole places his hand on his forehead and squints his eyes shut. "*Ryan*. You shouldn't be with Ryan."

"Cole—"

"What?!" he shouts, before looking my way. "I'm sorry."

He shakes his head and then slumps down against the wall with an incoherent groan. If Cole wasn't dead I would assume he's drunk.

"It's okay."

"No, it's not okay. It will never be okay, never be enough. I will never be enough." His face crumbles before he whimpers, "Never amount to anything."

I take a step closer to get a better look at him. He tilts his face away from me, but I see enough to know there are tears in his eyes, something I've never seen from him before.

"Cole, I don't know what's going on with you right now, but I'm here for you. You can tell me."

He laughs at this. It's short, almost manic, before sinking into himself even more.

"You, here for *me*? How blessed I am."

His words are reassuring, if not concerning.

"I don't know what to do." His voice is now jittery, his body trembling. "How can I help her?"

"Help who, Cole?"

"She's so alone. So sad."

"Is someone in danger?" I hold him by the shoulders. "Who, Cole? Answer me."

Cole looks up at me, his eyes as dark as the night around us. "You, Lolly."

Okay, I wasn't expecting that.

I let go of him and take a step back. Cole hasn't called me Lolly since I was a child. I wonder if I'm the sad and alone person he's referring to, and if so, why is he referring to me as if I am not here?

Then it hits me.

Just as Beasey said, he's remembering his trauma, the safety valve opening to the suppressed memories he's kept locked up inside himself. Which means he's not just thinking them.

He's reliving them.

He suddenly twists his head uncomfortably, his eyes squeeze shut, struggling with the nightmare he's in. "Nobody cares. Nobody cares!"

I lean in close to comfort him. "I care, Cole. Let me help you."

"No!" Cole jolts up. "You cannot have my pain!"

He staggers away from me to the window seat, the moonlight illuminating the dark shroud of him.

My throat closes as I watch him flinch and struggle through his memories. I can't stand seeing Cole so distressed. I've seen a lot of emotional spirits, and for the most part I can stay composed. But it really shreds me to pieces seeing Cole suffer like this.

"It's different, being dead," he pensively says as he places his hand out, watching the energy of him move as he waves his fingers. "Everything feels lighter. But it's still dark in here." His voice dithers at the words, his eyes twinkling with fresh tears. "Everyone lives. Everyone sleeps. I do neither." He then frowns and looks up, shouting out to the night sky, "It's what you wanted, right? What you wanted!"

I silently clasp my hand over my mouth to hold back the emotion within me. As subtle as it is, two lines of tears stream down my cheeks. This is a side of Cole I have never seen before. In fact, in all the years I have known him I have never seen him look this broken.

Cole clearly has some trauma of his life to get through, a Pandora's box he doesn't want to open. And I don't know what to do to help him except do what I do for other spirits who come to me for help.

I can't communicate with my mom, but if I can give Cole the opportunity to communicate with his, that would count for something today.

"I know it's hard to move on from the people you love," I say gently, aware of his newfound vulnerability. "But I can help you. Is there anyone I can talk to, like your parents or—"

"My parents?" his eyebrows shoot up, his shoulders tense as he turns to face me, his thoughts from before suppressed as he asks with a raised voice, "Why do you ask? Is this why you keep asking me questions, digging into my life? Why you were at the watermill? Did Beasey put you up to this?"

"No." I hesitate. "He just made a few points about your wellbeing."

Cole rolls his eyes. "Because Beasey knows what's best, huh?" He stands, his fists clench in frustration. Any closeness I thought we shared is now clearly gone.

"He's just concerned about you. And so am I."

"Is this about that research thing he wants? For that book of his? Wants me to be his lab bunny?"

"No. He just wants to talk. See if he can help."

"Help with what?"

"With getting rid of your negative karma."

"My what?"

"The trauma from your life that's holding you back."

Cole opens his mouth but immediately closes it tight. He tries again, choosing his words carefully as he looks back to the night sky. "Maybe I'm exactly where I'm supposed to be."

"And I'm glad you feel that way. But can you just try it, please?" I ask softly. "For me, at least."

His eyes narrow. "Fine. I'll go."

I blink. "You will?"

"Yeah. Tomorrow. Noon. Tell him."

He disappears without another word, leaving me standing in the dark and quiet with the sobering feeling of how broken we both really are.

It's just a day.

Ten

"Knock-knock."

The sound comes from my bedroom door, Cole's codeword for permission to enter since knocking won't have any actual effect for him.

"Don't worry, I'm clothed," I reply.

He appears across my room, hands hidden in his pockets, hunched slightly forward. His energy is near enough to normal, but I can tell there's a heaviness about him he's clearly trying to hide. He has done so well to hide it, but not anymore.

I don't bring it up, though. Instead, I wait for him to speak. I haven't seen him all day and can't help but wonder how his meeting with Beasey went. I spent most of the day cleaning the house while trying to decipher what happened the night before with no avail. I also researched Winston Watermill, looking for any deaths or events related to the area. Disappointingly, apart from being cordoned off for a couple of months one summer six years ago due to an algae outbreak I found nothing.

I meet his eyes through my vanity mirror.

"You look . . ." he clears his throat subtly before saying, "different."

Different. Not the word I was hoping for yet not wrong, either. The past couple of hours have been dedicated to straightening my hair and applying makeup to match my dress. Eyeliner isn't something I'm overly used to, but I think I have it right. I even have a little curl up in the corners with thick mascara to match.

I tug awkwardly on my dress. I thought I looked alright. Now I glance at myself in the mirror again and feel ridiculous.

"How was the funeral?" I dare to steer the conversation as I subtly wipe off some of the blush. I didn't go to Vanessa's funeral, of course. The school service was enough for me, not to mention the funeral makes no difference to me since I know the truth that Vanessa is still far from leaving this world.

"It was touching," he replies quite solemnly. "She will be missed by many."

I bite my tongue. "And how was your session with Beasey?"

"It was alright." His arms are now crossed and I can feel that he doesn't care to talk more about it, like with everything else.

"Well," I start, unable to hide my annoyance at his stubborn refusal to address what is going on with him, "I'm glad he is able to help. It must be nice being able to open up to someone."

He doesn't reply. Instead he eventually mentions, "I'll be with Vanessa this evening."

I don't cringe. Not externally, at least.

"I'll be with Ryan this evening."

"Have fun then," he replies.

Our eyes meet through the mirror once more, then he's gone.

"I will," I reply to a now empty room.

I look at myself in the mirror and sigh. I hear the sound of Ryan's car coming up the driveway so I reach for my jacket and head downstairs before I change my mind.

"Aren't you hot in that jacket?" Dad asks as I pace to the door.

"No," I lie. "Nights are still cold."

"Well, you be careful now. Call me if you need me." He notices Ryan approaching the door. "And be home by eleven."

"Mr. Durane." Ryan nods.

"Bye, Dad," I say with a quick kiss on his cheek before hustling Ryan by the arm to his car.

Once we're on the road I sigh and unzip my jacket.

"Dang, Lottie," Ryan says. "I need to roll down the windows as it just got steamy in here."

I look down at my dress and blush. It was an impulse purchase from when I was on holiday in Florida last year. I didn't see a need for it and cocktail dresses aren't really my style, but the silver sequin pattern down to the way the fabric flows out in black ruffles had me sold in a moment of girly weakness. I don't know whether tonight is more after-funeral or party, but aside from the slight cleavage the dress luckily works for both.

He pulls over, and before I can even ask if everything's okay he leans over and kisses me, then and there, before driving on.

"I like it," he simply concludes.

I smile back. "I can tell."

Ryan explains to me that this is the first party since Vanessa's passing so he assumes it will be a bit awkward, or at least a bit more low-key. But alas, apparently the party must go on.

He pulls into a driveway that's already full of cars. I suddenly cringe, feeling like a sheep entering the lions' den. Ryan picks up a box of beer from the seat behind him and we make our way to the front door where Liam is already waiting.

"You took too long so we ordered pizza without you." Liam then turns to me and blinks. "Charlotte?"

"Hi," I say awkwardly.

"Told you I was bringing her," Ryan says as he hands over his beer to Liam.

"Yeah, just . . ." he doesn't finish the sentence, but I feel his eyes still fixed on me as we walk in.

"Shit, Charlotte." Sven eyes me up and down, suddenly distracted from Stephanie fawning over him. "Check you out."

I bite my lip nervously and smile. Stephanie's eyes narrow, but she's also looking at me until we enter the living room. Or, at least I think it is the living room; this house seems big enough to have several living rooms.

"Beer's up." Liam follows behind us and starts passing bottles around. He throws Ryan two beers, one after the other, and Ryan catches them flawlessly even though they're wet with condensation. He opens one and passes it to me.

I take a seat on the couch and look around the room. Ryan starts explaining that Liam's family owns a small restaurant chain, which is why they're out of town for the weekend. Business is clearly doing well for them considering the house they own, but then again, looks can be deceiving.

"Where's Dylan?" I ask.

"Busy," Ryan chuckles. He points to the people not from our school. "That guy is Sven's cousin. Forgot his name. And Joanne over there is Liam's new girlfriend, but she goes to Fairview High. They exchanged numbers after the game, and, well, the school competition is there, but they're already pretty tight. Dunno if that'll be the case if we lose a game, though." Ryan snickers to himself as he takes a sip of beer. "Oh, geez. Here we go."

"Oh look, Charlotte came." Gwen comes over and makes herself known.

"Hello, Gwen," I say tensely.

"I almost didn't recognize you, Durane. Look at you all gussied up. It's like you're trying to look cool or something."

Ryan hits back, "Knock it off, Gwen. Someone's getting more attention than you. Ice is over there for that bruised ego of yours, otherwise deal with it."

I can't help but smile as Gwen huffs back to the pool table. If only Vanessa could see me now. I smirk at the thought until I realize whatever she is doing with Cole right now seems to be more important than being here.

"Hey," Mandy says as she takes a seat opposite me. Mandy is the tamest member of The Squad, and if she weren't so attached to Gwen and Stephanie she would probably be well respected.

"Hey, Mandy," Ryan responds. "I thought it was low-key tonight."

"Yeah, well, you know Gwen. She loves being the new Vanessa." She glances over to Gwen by the pool table who's making a point of Jordan's biceps. "Which means all the attention she can get."

"You're too good for her," Ryan says before taking a swig of his beer.

"Don't let her know that," she replies before turning to me. "Looking fab, Charlotte."

"Thanks." I smile back. "So I'm not the only one who's noticed Gwen is a bit different nowadays?"

Mandy rolls her eyes. "Oh, no. It's not just you. Vanessa—may she rest in peace—is, like, the bar she's trying to beat. Which is not cool, you know? Things have been, like, pretty mellow without Vanessa, no offense to her. But now Gwen's trying to *be* Vanessa."

She hands her beer over for Ryan to open. Which he does. Effortlessly. With his bare hands.

I grimace. "As they say, imitation is the sincerest form of flattery."

"Except she never even liked Vanessa."

"What? I thought they were besties?"

"Duh. So of course they hated each other. Everything had to be a competition between them. Grades. Boys. Parties. I bet Gwen's even jealous of the attention Vanessa got being buried today." She halts at this, the realization still clearly paining her. "This party was planned by Gwen and Jordan. The rest of us thought it was too soon, but they insisted." She holds up her beer before adding, "To Vanessa, I guess."

"To Vanessa," Ryan and I say in unison.

Our bottles clink and I take a long sip of my beer. I thought drinking to reflect on the life of someone who died from drinking seemed rather morbid, and I'm glad to know I'm not alone in thinking this. This is definitely a new low for The Squad. At least Ryan and Mandy are above the rest.

"Pizza's here!" Liam declares loudly. Everyone cheers as he places three boxes on the nearby table.

The night actually hits off pretty well. Between Mandy and Ryan with pizza and beer I remain involved, and when Ryan takes on Jordan at a game of billiards I get to know Sven and meet his cousin Bryn. It turns out Sven is into politics and is impressed with my knowledge on the planned residential subdivision on the protected forest land (although I don't let on how I acquired that knowledge).

They've started telling me stories about their annual family holiday to The Keys when Ryan comes over. He passes the cue sticks to Bryn and Sven who declare billiards war on Jordan and Liam, and then Ryan passes me a drink. I sniff it cautiously. Wine. And something else. I take a sip. Definitely something else.

Ryan notices my reaction. "We all donate a little something to the mix." He nods towards a big goblet on the table next to the near-empty pizza boxes.

I chuckle. Here I am, partying with The Squad, drinking who-knows-what.

Ryan takes my arm and leads me to the foyer.

"Enjoying the party?" he asks as he leans in next to me, his face mere inches from mine.

"Uh-huh." I take another sip.

Ryan glances down at my neck, a smirk forms. "You look so hot in this dress."

I smile nervously, wondering how much cleavage is visible at such an angle. His hand rests on my leg above my knee, his fingers fumbling with the hem of my dress which suddenly feels too short.

"Cool music." I force a grin.

Ryan shrugs. "It's alright, I guess."

I wonder what else to say. I fail to remember what we have in common. What do we have in common? Do we even have anything in common?

And then he does it again. His lips, on mine. No warmup, no signal. Just *bam*, now we're kissing. I quickly feel for the table counter to place my drink on so it doesn't tip over.

He pushes for more, his hands now on my waist as his tongue explores my mouth. He tastes like beer. Beer and hot sauce, an interesting combination. It's not bad, I guess. If I were to appraise I'd say the flavors balance each other well.

Just as I start to ponder if I have a future in the culinary industry, Gwen makes herself known.

"Gross. Save it for truth or dare, at least."

Embarrassed, I recoil at her voice, but Ryan simply mutters back to her between breaths, "Jordan's in the next room."

Liam passes by with a wolf whistle. This seems to please Ryan as he smiles, holding me a little higher than before. I see Gwen roll her eyes out of the corner of my eye, which may have been open in surprise as Ryan goes in for another round.

"We'll be in the other room when you're done," Stephanie adds as they walk past.

Ryan doesn't seem to care, however, because he's still making moves on me. Most other girls at school would be jealous if they saw us right now. I should be swooning, I should be encouraging his hands to explore further, to take things further.

So why aren't I?

And then the answer comes, one syllable, the quiet reminder in my mind: Cole.

I squeeze my eyes shut and force the thought away. Cole doesn't have feelings for me. Cole is with Vanessa. Cole has a whole secret past I don't know about.

At least Ryan thinks I look good. I place my hands on his shoulders. I'm not going to lie, the feel of his toned body through his shirt feels nice. Ryan seems to agree because he pushes in closer to me. One of his hands goes lower while the other draws up my torso, finding its way to—

I shudder as his fingers gently squeeze my bra. The sensation sends triggers through my body, signals of intimacy that feel both pleasurable yet somewhat uncomfortable.

Ryan soon notices my lack of requite and stops, his eyebrows low. "Alright, I guess the others are waiting."

With a small sigh he takes my hand and leads me through to the next room where the others have gathered, and suddenly it's as if the past couple of minutes never even happened, as if making out like that is perfectly normal.

Maybe it is.

"About time," Stephanie mutters overtly.

"Nice of you to finally join us," Mandy says as Ryan and I sit on the space left for us on the floor. She passes the goblet to Ryan who reaches for a nearby glass and pours me another drink of mystery wine.

"Guys, girls. It's that time of night. Truth or dare," Gwen announces as she places an empty bottle into the center of the circle we sit around.

Everyone jeers, but the excitement glints in their eyes.

"You know the rules: what happens tonight stays with tonight," Gwen continues. "And, as tradition, our host goes first. Liam?"

It doesn't take him long to decide. "Dare."

Whispers begin among the group. Everyone quickly agrees on a suggestion, and Gwen declares that for every dare act taken he has to take a sip from the goblet.

Some hit their legs in a drumroll as Liam spins the bottle. It points towards Jordan.

"Truth or dare?" Liam asks.

"Double dare," he quickly replies. "Electing Gwen."

Gwen shrieks lightly, but she seems more excited than fearful. The rest of us lean over and decide on an appropriate dare for them both, and it concludes with Liam telling both of them that for every time they accidentally talk to each other they have to remove a piece of clothing.

"Hey, no fair, she has extra layers."

"You're wearing socks—oops!" Gwen giggles as she takes her tights off.

"Not anymore," Jordan mutters as he flings his socks to the wall.

Drumroll leads again as Jordan spins the bottle. All eyes follow the bottle as it slows to a stop.

At me.

"So, what'll it be, Durane?" Gwen asks smugly. "Truth? Or dare?"

I remember what Gwen said as she passed by when Ryan and I were making out, about saving it for truth or dare. Whatever 'it' is.

I swallow.

"Truth," I hesitate.

Gwen and Jordan eye each other before looking back at me. The others lean in slightly, and I could have sworn even the background music beats went down a few bars of volume.

Jordan frowns, his icy blue eyes almost glowing in the dimly lit room, and says the words, "Do you see dead people?"

Oddly enough, I laugh. Not because I find the situation humorous, because I don't. Not at all. In fact, this is probably the least desirable situation I could imagine for the night, even more than what saying "dare" would have entailed. I laugh because I'm nervous. And probably a bit drunk.

"What are you on about?" I laugh again, taking a sip of mystery wine.

"Come on," Gwen starts. "You're always talking to thin air. Everyone sees it. Not even Ryan could deny it."

I give Ryan a look. It's a look of shock, and a little bit of confusion, but not betrayal. That I hold inside.

He shrugs back sheepishly. "It's not like it's a secret, Lottie. Everyone kinda assumes anyway."

I don't like what he says. I take another sip of mystery wine to hold my tongue, except the sip continues into a mouthful.

Gwen adds, "You're either talking to dead people or you imagine you see dead people, in which case you're schitzo and need meds or something."

"Wait, what?" Bryn asks, confused. He looks at Sven who shrugs.

"Charlotte's a schitzo?" Joanne asks worriedly. Liam whispers to Joanne something about filling in the details later.

"I am not schizophrenic," I mutter through clenched teeth.

"So, can you? Can you see them?" Gwen persists.

"You can talk to them too, right?" Mandy adds.

"Yeah, do you need, like, a séance board or something?" Liam asks before turning to Gwen. "Knew we should've ordered one."

I snicker. Of course. All this pretend being nice act is because they just want to see if they can use me to get to Vanessa. That's why I'm here. And like a sheep I walked right into the lions' den, just as I feared.

"Yeah. Yeah, I see dead people." Lamb to the slaughter. "But Vanessa isn't here. She's elsewhere."

With Cole.

Eyes glance at one another. I look at my glass. Where did all my mystery wine go? I suddenly wonder if this is how Vanessa felt before she died.

"So . . . Dylan definitely didn't kill her?" Mandy asks.

"Kill?" Joanne squeaks.

"Dylan was cleared by the police," I assure them. "And he loved her very much."

There's a moment of silence before Gwen scowls at me to say, "You're full of shit, Durane."

I blink. "Excuse me?"

"Well that can't be true," she says matter-of-factly. "Because Dylan's gay."

I blink again. "*Gay?*"

"Yeah," Ryan says. "Came out when police questioned him. Apparently his alibi at game night was at some LGBTQ-whatever meetup with his *college boyfriend.*"

I can't tell if the college or boyfriend part shocked Ryan more. "Seriously?"

"Yeah. I mean, whatever, at least he didn't kill Vanessa. Not that we thought he could be capable of that."

I glance at the eyes in the room. Not all of them waver, but some do.

He adds, "Obviously his devoutly Christian family weren't impressed finding out, though."

"But . . . she never said . . ." I stop in my tracks and frown.

"Dylan admitted she knew," Mandy fills in for me. "She was in on it too, their fake relationship."

"Yeah, but why?" Sven wonders out loud.

His question is ignored, however, as Jordan leans over to Ryan. "You owe me twenty bucks."

"And me," Liam adds.

"Sorry, what?" I ask.

"Nothing," Ryan quickly replies.

"See, some of us had this disagreement going," Liam starts. "Ryan thought you would be able to conjure up Vanessa's spirit to shed some light on what happened to her, and if she's all, you know, okay and stuff."

"I called bull," Jordan interjects.

"You're, like, one of those people that lie because you crave attention or something," Gwen accuses.

"You're weird, Durane. Just like the janitor," Stephanie adds her two cents.

The lions attack. And just like that it all comes full circle. Ryan's interest in me. The Squad playing nice. Me being here. To think I fell for it. To think I wanted it.

"I need to use the bathroom."

I stand up and leave without another word, doing everything in my power to prevent myself from losing my cool, because if I do I know I will start crying in front of everyone. I hear Ryan behind me but I don't look back. I think I stood up too fast because I have to hold onto the wall for balance as I make my way to somewhere I can be alone.

"Lottie, wait up," he calls as he catches up to me.

I dislike that name, I really do.

"You betted on me." I try to not make it sound like it hurts, but it does, which is why I don't want to look at him as I open the door to an empty room. Not a bathroom, but it'll do.

"It's not like that," he says, pulling back on my arm.

"So what is it like, Ryan?" I ask through tight-pressed lips as I pull my arm back. The lights aren't on but I can still see him well enough.

"I'm sorry, alright? I thought you'd be able to help, like you tried to with my gramps. Everyone misses her."

"That's really low of you, Ryan. Did you try just asking?"

"Yeah, you're right. It just didn't seem like you were all too keen on talking to Vanessa the first time . . ."

Okay, fair enough. Dealing with the dead is not an open service of mine. Except I just announced it, to The Squad of all people. I'm going to regret tonight for the rest of my life, I'm sure.

"I wasn't told Dylan is gay," I sigh.

"Nobody was told. We only found out today through gossip at

the funeral service."

"Geez," I pinch my forehead with my thumb and finger. "I didn't know Dylan was gay because *she* didn't say Dylan was gay."

"Well, yeah. It was a bit of a shock to everyone. Except Gwen. You know, she's been suspicious since ninth grade, but kept it on the low since Vanessa started dating him." He snickers. "Boy, was she smug when the truth came out."

I roll my eyes and snap, "That's not what I mean!" I pull Ryan through the door and close it behind me. It's suddenly a lot darker but the window reflects enough light from outside to see his features. While I know I really should stop talking at this point, part of me just wants to release these words, and the intoxicated part of me is all for it. "I didn't know Dylan was gay because Vanessa didn't tell me. *Posthumous* Vanessa, that is. Vanessa of the damned."

Ryan raises an eyebrow. "You're drunk."

"Maybe I am," I admit. Okay, I know I am. "And Vanessa didn't say anything about Dylan, but come to think of it, she probably didn't just to spite me." I feel like hurling but swallow it down. "And let me be the one to tell you: dead Vanessa is as much of a bitch as alive Vanessa was."

Ryan snorts back a laugh. "Lottie, you're funny. Seriously. You should write comics or something. But the joke's over."

Funny? Joke? Is that how he sees this? He's stupid. Ryan Hill is fucking stupid.

Then again, here I am. I guess I'm the stupid one. I mean, he doesn't *not* believe me. I think. Maybe we are a good match, after all. We're both human, we both struggle through economics class. And looking at Ryan even with only the reflection of the outside light, he admittedly is good looking. I make him laugh, too. That counts for something, right? Maybe someone like Ryan Hill is the best I can do.

"Hey," he chimes in a soothing voice as he lifts my hand and cups it with his own. "Let's forget all this silly ghost stuff and stay here a bit longer."

"I don't care to go back to that, Ryan."

"I don't, either." His hands vine down to my waist and suddenly I'm being drawn into him. "It's a stupid game, anyway. All Gwen wants is the opportunity to strip and make out with Jordan."

He then kisses me, his hands quickly trying to resume from where they were earlier. And, okay, it does distract me from my emotions. But the more he grinds up against me, his hard-on now very noticeable against my navel, Vanessa's words come through the drunkenness of my mind. And as much as I don't want to admit such a thing with the core of my being, she is right.

Ryan doesn't do friends.

Only flings.

"I need some air." I push him aside and head to the door. I hear a sigh of frustration, but I don't care. I don't want to be here. Where's Cole? My head's starting to hurt. "I'll message my dad to pick me up."

"No, I'll take you back. I said I would."

I may be drunk but I'm not stupid. "You were drinking, Ryan."

"*One* beer. Like an hour ago."

I look at the clock by the door. Half-past nine. I would agree if I knew that was the truth. If I trusted him.

But I don't.

"My dad can be here in ten minutes," I say instead. "I don't want you to miss out on the night by playing chauffeur."

He agrees, to my surprise, and I take out my phone and message Dad while heading outside. The night air is reassuring to my mind as I lean on the large clay pot by Liam's front door. It helps with the swaying, but the headache—which I don't think is a side-effect of the mystery wine or the dubstep, at least—stays.

"Everything alright out there?" Liam comes to check on me.

"Just had too much to drink." I force a smile. "I am *such* a lightweight. Can barely stand! So I'm gonna shamefully call it a night."

"Yeah, whatever," he replies and goes back inside, clearly less interested in me now that I am not summoning the departed with a glass orb or séance board.

Ryan comes out as I notice the lights of Dad's truck approach.

"I still think you're kinda cool," he adds before giving my dad a quick wave of acknowledgement.

Kinda cool. Just like my windchimes are *kinda* cool. Well, it matches that I think he's *kinda* crass.

"Thanks," I say. I stand, zipping up my jacket, and walk as straight as I can to Dad's truck.

He calls back, "See you around at school, I guess."

"Yeah." I guess.

"And remember to drink water before sleeping."

The drive back was easier than I thought it would be. I expected some Coach Dad talk about drinking or boys, and was surprised he didn't go there. Maybe he trusts me more than I realize, but he is probably just glad his daughter called and is home safe and early.

Dad goes up to bed first while I adhere to the only smart thing I've heard Ryan say and drink some water.

"Deep in thought?"

I don't even look at Cole standing by the refrigerator. As supportive as I want to be for him, all I can think about right now is how much of a mess everything is for me.

"No."

"How was your evening?"

"Eventful." I put the empty glass in the sink and make my way upstairs.

"No goodnight smooch from Ryan?"

I shoot him a warning look. "I'm not in the mood for this tonight, Cole."

"What? Friends, makeup, clothes. Check, check, check. Ordinary *is* what you wanted, remember?"

"Silly me."

Yes, silly me. Silly me for thinking I could be ordinary. Silly me for thinking I could at least be seen as normal, for letting my guard down, for thinking Ryan liked me, and for thinking Cole could like me.

"Things didn't go all lovey-dovey with Ryan, then?" he asks behind me, but is already in my bedroom as I open the door.

I drop my bag on the ground and close the door behind me. "Turns out Ryan and I misunderstand each other."

"Good," Cole mutters quietly.

Whether he meant for me to hear that or not I don't know, but it hurts nonetheless. Along with everything else tonight.

"Wow. Thanks for your kind words," I snap back, probably a bit louder than I should have. I wobble as I take off my heels, one after the other, and fling them to the side.

"Are you drunk?"

The thing is, I'm not *that* drunk. Tipsy, yes. But not swaying-room-hurling-into-the-toilet-blackout-level drunk. More like speak-my-mind-and-don't-care-level drunk.

So I have no inhibitions holding me back when I reply, "Maybe. Maybe not. Maybe I just don't want to talk to you about it. I mean, I don't have to. There's no commandment set in stone given unto you saying I have to, right? Maybe I'll talk it over with Beasey."

Cole raises an eyebrow at me. "Charlotte, are you okay?"

"I'm great, Cole. Just great. But enough about me, how did your date with Vanessa go?" I take my earrings off with more force than my ears deserve. "Do ghosts even do that? Date? Do they have ghost functions at ghost bars where they order ghost beers and nibble on stale ghost peanuts?"

"We mostly talked if you really want to know," he replies, dodging the jacket I throw to the chair behind him.

"Ah, yes. *Talking.* You both seem to do that a lot, among other things, I'm sure. She must have a lot to say. Lots of important, useful things we could know about, like her gay boyfriend, am I right?"

"What?" Cole shakes his head. "Is this about the kiss? She got caught up in the moment. She apologized."

I snort, "Oh, I'm sure she did."

"She's had a big day today in case you forgot. Besides, she's actually kinda cool, I think you should give her more credit."

I huff in speechless protest as I take off my bracelet. "Well, by all means, don't let me interrupt. And feel free to reminisce over all the times she made me cry behind the gymnasium during lunch break while you're both *talking* so much."

"People change, Charlotte."

"Not people like *her*."

Cole is exasperated. "She's learning to come to terms with leaving her life behind, with finding her peace."

"Yeah, so you keep saying. But I'm over it."

"You know, not everything's about you, Charlotte."

I open my mouth but then press my lips together tightly.

"Leave."

"Charlotte—"

"Now!"

There's silence, a test of the atmosphere between us. Usually I'd cave in, but the daggers in my eyes aren't lowering. He opens his mouth to say something but hesitates. Then he's gone.

It's the first time I've kicked Cole out of the house, and the first time since he came into my life that I don't want him around. But with everything that's going on, Cole not being around is something I may just get. Which is why, for the first time since he came into my life, I feel lost and alone.

Eleven

Dad knows I don't do Sunday mornings. He tries to get me to go to church with him, and sometimes he succeeds (the persuasion of Waffle House afterwards doesn't work on me like when I was younger, even though his parental efforts still do. And Waffle House is still good). But he knows he'd only get my Sunday morning moods.

He must know today is one of those days, because when I eventually wake up I feel terrible, only I don't know if it's the hangover that's making me feel this way or the recollection of what happened the night before.

The party.

The bet.

Ryan.

Cole.

I pull my pillow over my head and punch into the mattress, harder with each wave of recollection that comes back to me.

I decide to stay in bed all day and just drown my mind away with a movie marathon, but bladder and hunger pangs eventually call so I have a long hot shower and then make my way downstairs. Some part of me expects Cole to be standing there, waiting for me, wanting to "talk".

Except he's not.

Good, I decide. I live here after all, and I shouldn't have to feel cornered in my own home.

I go through the usual breakfast motions and fry up some eggs for a hangover buster. While eating, I pick up the newspaper and scroll to the horoscope section. I don't really believe in horoscopes, but if there's anything I've come to learn in life it's that the line between the believable and unbelievable is incredibly gray. I read under Cancer:

This is a time for deliberation: when tested by certain people it's better to act purposefully than quickly, better to admit what you really mean, even if that takes some time.

I huff and place it back down. I don't like it when the witch doctors who write this stuff sound more reasonable than me. At least Roy the caregiver has made the crime headlines.

"Morning," Dad enters through the front door. "Or should I say afternoon?"

I glance at the clock. Both hands have just passed twelve.

"One of those days, Dad. One of those days."

Dad pours himself a glass of water. "Nothing like experience to learn the limits of drinking. I'm glad you're socializing with," he pauses before saying, "kids from school. But don't get into the habit of partying every weekend. You're still seventeen. That Stalinski girl is a sad reminder of how easily things can go wrong."

"Don't worry, Dad. I won't be doing that again anytime soon."

He shoots me a concerned parent look before putting his glass in the dishwasher. "You got any plans for the rest of the day?"

I want to say chores and a movie or two with Pippi on my lap. I'm sure Pippi would want me to say that too, but I'm still holding onto the emotions from last night. And I need to clean up the mess I have found myself in.

So instead, I even surprise myself when I say, "Church."

This makes Dad's eyebrows rise. "Oh?"

"Yeah." I speak over a mouthful of egg. "So don't say I never go."

Dad eyes me suspiciously. "Charlotte, did something happen last night that I need to know about? With that Ryan kid?" He rubs his chin. "I don't need to remind you of the importance of chastity—"

"Nothing happened," I quickly reply. I gobble up the last of my breakfast, now wanting to get going before this conversation takes an uncomfortable turn. "I just haven't been in for a while. And since you let me sleep in this morning—which I appreciate, by the way—I figure I'll make up for it now."

"Okay, then." He seems relieved at my decision. Or maybe it's the confirmation that I'm still his innocent little girl.

I put my plate and fork in the dishwasher then grab my bag off the counter. "Can I borrow the truck? I'll be back later."

"Will you be back for dinner? I'm thinking I might try my hands at a fish casserole."

I squirm. "Eat without me."

I grab the keys and set off. It's odd that I find myself willingly going to church, but while I fully intend to use this as a reason to put off having to go for a while, the sinner within me may have brushed over the actual reasoning for going.

"Beasey."

Beasey looks up from the cupboard he's rummaging in, looking briefly surprised through his usual half-frown.

"Charlotte," he says. "I can't say I was expecting to see you here, at least on a Sunday afternoon."

"Yeah. Me neither."

I look around the maintenance room, except it's more of a staff room. Shelves of cleaning products and equipment align the wall from the door, but across the room, lit up by the small windowpane along the top of the wall, there's a washing machine, kitchenette, a table, and a couple of chairs. There's even a foosball table in the center of the room and a small television on top of the refrigerator.

Beasey notices my gaze. "One of the finer church maintenance rooms I've been in."

"Are you even a Protestant?"

"I'm here for the spirits, Charlotte, not the sermons. I serve God under all branches of religion." He finds what he's looking for and takes it out of the cupboard. "You, however, look like you need some guidance from the Lord. Is there something on your mind, child?"

I snort. There's no way I'm going to tell Beasey all my dramas, especially when guys are in the mix. To be honest I'm not entirely sure why I'm here. I thought the drive and the quiet would clear my mind, but I can't seem to shake off my frustrations. Maybe I do need the Lord's guidance, after all.

"I just feel like I can't be myself. I'm fed up with being regarded as a freak. I'm fed up with being different. I'm fed up with having to hide who I am."

I don't move beyond leaning against the doorway to cross my arms. I don't want to sit down. Once I sit down I know I'll be pouring my mind out for hours. Or fall into a hangover nap. Maybe both.

"A smart intention doesn't make for a smart action, Charlotte. You are still your own person and must put yourself first. You won't be effective in carrying out the duty God has given you if you are not yourself. But showing off to the world will garner a lot of reactions which you clearly would be vulnerable to."

He passes me a mop. Of course. With a huff of protest I start on the floor. But he's right; if I can barely get through the school day without awkward looks or comments, how would I face the rest of the world as an open book?

"The world isn't really open to people like us," I complain. "Which is ironic if you ask me, because it's the judgmental ones who usually end up carrying the most negative karma from their lives and needing my help. Not to mention it's a bit hard to be living happily when you have to deal with so much turmoil and death."

"You see ghosts because you're sensitive to their energy. And energy transmits, Charlotte. What they emit you receive. You have to train yourself to be aware of your emotions as well as theirs, and to keep them separate. The same applies for the living, too."

"Is that why you're always a buzzkill?"

Ignoring me he continues, "You're a Communicator. It's in your nature to feel the urge to help others, to feel empathy."

"That doesn't make things easier."

"Why should it make things easier?" He pours some drain cleaner into the sink. "It's not that you don't want to help them, it's that you want to help them *your* way, which won't always be the *right* way. When you go to confession or confide in someone, do you expect them to solve your problem for you? No. We are only the guides. It's not our place to judge." He peers down the drain. "Don't hold onto the mess others leave behind."

"So what you are saying is . . .?"

"You can't help them all, Charlotte, and you shouldn't have to compensate yourself for trying to. It's their karma to sort through, not yours."

I nod. Once again Beasey is right. Sure, being able to see ghosts is something I should feel at least somewhat special about. So why does it feel like such a punishment, like I can't do anything right?

"It's a thankless duty being a Communicator. Sometimes it can be difficult, and sometimes you can be tested. But it's all part of a greater purpose we have to entrust to the Lord."

I huff, mopping over a stain on the floor that won't go. "Bullshit."

"I don't think that regarding your gift as bovine excrement is going to help you see past your strife, Charlotte."

"It's not a gift."

Why won't the stain go?

"But we have a gift from God—"

I throw the mop onto the floor. "Stop calling it a gift, it is not a gift!"

Beasey doesn't flinch. "But of course it is a gift."

I snort at the ridiculousness of what I hear. "Gift, right. The gift that had me terrified of the dark and too afraid to sleep every night? The gift that crippled me with anxiety? The gift that had me in more psychiatrists' offices than I'd like to remember? Not to mention the pills, the dejection from my father, priests fearing

I'm demonic, the social exclusion at school? Yep, it sure is the gift that keeps on giving!" I feel myself practically shouting now, energy I need to exert. Tears dwell in my eyes but I can't stop.

"Do you know what hurts me more than all of that put together? Of all the ghosts I've come across all these years, I've not yet come across the one person in existence I actually want to see." I sniff. "Why isn't she here? She *knew* I could see them. She could still be here for me. So where is she?"

"Charlotte, I—"

"Did you take her from me? Or someone like you?"

"Charlotte—"

"I was seven years old! She only went to pick up a crib. She wasn't even at fault; the other driver didn't stop. It's not fair."

Beasey stays silent until I've calmed down. I wonder if he's a parent. He would either be very good or very bad at being a dad, I can't figure out which.

"You will never get anywhere trying to fight what you can't," he eventually says. "Like the ghosts we deal with, we have to accept our circumstances and move on. Don't wait for death to reach you to learn that life lesson."

Suddenly we're not alone.

"I would ask if this is the right place, but since you're looking at me I assume it is." The man, who I'm guessing is in his early twenties, takes his hat off once he notices me. "Ma'am."

I blink. I haven't been called "ma'am" before, but considering no guy would willingly wear suspenders and cap-toe leather shoes—at least not guys from this century, anyway—I can't help but nod and blush at his old-school chivalry.

"Ah, yes. My one o'clock is here."

I cringe at Beasey's casual tone, alluding the passing of those gone to a trivial appointment, especially with this guy who has clearly been around for a while.

"Care to watch? Or even join in? Charlie won't mind, right?"

Charlie awkwardly blushes. I highly doubt he was expecting a young *ma'am* to watch on as an audience.

I save him a reply. "I'll pass. There's someone I need to pay a visit to." I put the mop aside then smile and nod to Charlie who scrunches his hat and nods back awkwardly, grateful for my exit.

"Suit yourself." Beasey nods. "God gave you a gift, Charlotte. Remember that."

While I still have trouble seeing my ability as a gift, I accept that it's worth trying to view the concept differently. I mean, I can communicate with the dead. I change lives, for the better. Heck, I could probably have my own talk show and be famous (not that I want that publicity, but I imagine there'd be a fair number of digits in those paychecks if I did). And then there's Cole, the best thing that's ever happened to me, even after all that's going on between us right now.

I sigh as I turn on my right turn signal and pull into Hamston Drive. Hamston Drive is one of those new subdivision roads with mini mansions and manicured lawns that are far too big and a waste of space if you ask me. Of course Vanessa lived on such a road.

Feeling out of place with my dad's old truck, I decide to park on the curb and walk the rest of the way. This is also because Cole may be here with Vanessa and would hear the recognizable sound of the truck approaching, and I don't want to face him right now. So discrete approach it is.

I hear her before I see her, having one of her tantrums. Cole obviously isn't with her since she's supposedly such an angel around him. Usually her energy would intimidate me, but she's up against energy to match her own this time.

I pace to mailbox number five, and her house comes into view. The teddy bears and flowers on the berm that were displayed on the front page of the local newspaper have all since gone, save for one lone orange ribbon entangled in the hedge.

Vanessa stands at the head of her family's driveway, her eyes fixated on her ice-blue BMW. She notices my reflection in the car window because she glances back at me, only I don't seem to hold her interest as she ignores me and turns back to her car.

"Vanessa!" I seethe through clenched teeth so as to avoid the neighbors' attention. She doesn't flinch, though. She doesn't even look my way.

"It's Sunday afternoon. I always pick Adrienne up from dance class on Sunday afternoon." She slowly paces around her car, her hand stroking along the frame of the driver's door. "I hate having to pick her up every weekend; I have other plans, but I have to say, 'oh, sorry I can't hang out' or, 'raincheck on cheerleading practice because I've got to pick up my little sister'. And I complain when there's traffic and I complain more if she finishes late."

She pulls at the car door handle, but of course nothing happens. "I always do it, though. Every Sunday afternoon I take the trip to the city, I sit in traffic, and I wait for her, even if she finishes late. And then we go and get ice cream, and she always chooses the strawberry cheesecake flavor and I order chocolate fudge brownie flavor, even though I'm supposed to be on a no-sugar diet, because it's my secret guilty pleasure."

A neighborhood kid passes by on his bike, slowing down to stare at the house. He notices me, then quickly peddles away.

"But I'm still here. It's still me. I want to sit in traffic again, I want to eat chocolate fudge brownie ice cream again. I want to pick up my little sister from dance class!"

She kicks the car, her leg going straight through. She pulls her hair and screams in frustration.

"Vanessa—"

"*Don't*. Tell. Me," she hisses. She turns sharply to face me, her energy pulsating dark through her. "I can't do that anymore, can I?" She hunches forward, her voice cracking to the sorrow dwelling in her eyes as she says, "Because I'm dead."

I take a deep breath in and clench my fists, feeling all the rage inside me I've been holding in wanting to burst out.

But all I can say is, "I'm sorry."

There are a few wails and a lot more cursing, but she soon exhausts herself enough to be approachable, her dark drained to a dull, faint gray.

"She said a prayer before bed last night," her voice dies into a whimper as she slumps to the ground in defeat. "We're not overly religious, but she did so anyway. She asked for me to be there to pick her up."

Vanessa turns to me, and I have to say I'm a bit stunned. I have never seen her looking so . . . *vulnerable.*

Which is why, again, all I can say is, "I'm sorry."

"She's expecting me."

Kids play across the street on their BMX bikes, clueless to the meltdown just performed by their ghostly neighbor. I wonder how I would have looked at that age, talking to the air around me.

"Can I help you?"

I turn and face the woman standing at the front door.

"That's my mom," Vanessa mutters. "Just say you're here to pay your respects, she'll leave you alone."

It's hard to assume the woman is Vanessa's mother. She looks more like an older sister with the same blond hair and sense of fashion. Looking closely I can see Botox has done a lot of the work, but young and in style is definitely a trait of the family.

"Actually, yes." I tap the car. "I have a request to make."

∞∞∞∞∞

Just as Vanessa described, there is traffic. But just as she also described, we aren't late because her class is running overtime.

I sneak through the door to the small theater and take a seat along the back row, careful not to make heads turn.

"That's her, second from the left. Isn't she great?" Vanessa smiles—probably the first genuine smile I've seen from her without Cole present—as she watches her sister on stage.

"Yeah," I agree.

It isn't a lie, either. I look at Vanessa and her aura is the brightest I've seen on her. We watch the end of the dance rehearsal and on Vanessa's signal I walk up to her.

"Adrienne?" I wave awkwardly. "Hi, you don't know me, but I'm Charlotte. I knew your sister . . . we had some classes together."

Adrienne raises an eyebrow suspiciously. Vanessa said she was determined to keep up practice even though her parents told her to take a few weeks off, but also warned she has become pretty closed off and moody.

"Vanessa told me about how she'd pick you up every Sunday after dance class and then get ice cream. Well, since she really enjoyed it I thought I'd do it on her behalf today. Your mom said it's okay; she called your dance teacher to let her know."

"She said that?"

"Yes. You can call her to confirm if you want." I take out my phone but she holds her hand up.

"No, not Mom. Vanessa. She said she enjoyed picking me up? You're lying." She takes a seat to change shoes. "Vanessa hated picking me up and she hated me."

I glance at Vanessa who rolls her eyes.

"I'm sure she didn't mean that. Siblings have . . . unusual ways of expressing how they really feel."

"Do you have any siblings?"

"Not . . . exactly."

"Then how would you know?"

I crouch down next to her, helping with her shoelaces. "I had a baby brother. He died. I wish I could have been a big sister to him, but now I have to be the best I can be for both of us."

"Shit, Charlotte. Cut deeper, why don't you?" Vanessa remarks by my side.

Ignoring Vanessa I continue, "Your sister might have been a, uhm, *handful*, and it sucks that she's gone, but you have to carry on and live the best life you can for both of you."

Adrienne pouts, in the way a child doesn't want to hear what they're being told.

"You know what you need? Ice cream." I stand up. "And I'm buying."

Without reply, she seems to agree to this. The walk to the ice cream parlor only takes a few minutes, but it's long enough for Adrienne to tell me about her passion for dance. It's clearly the only thing that takes her mind off things, and from my experience with my fair share of therapy it is good to have a healthy vocation that encourages physical activity and communication. Come to think of it, it's probably the reason Dad started on the garden, because I certainly wasn't going out dancing, or even going out at all.

Adrienne goes straight to the window seat which I assume is the same one she always goes to while I get the ice cream.

"Vanessa always ordered chocolate fudge brownie," she remarks as she digs straight into the strawberry cheesecake scoop I pass to her. "I guess you're not Vanessa, though."

The ice cream parlor is buzzing with noise and happy kids, but I still hear Adrienne's disappointment. I guiltily look down at my scoop of mango sorbet, wondering if I should change it.

"Tell her I'm here," Vanessa orders.

I narrow my eyes at her before turning to Adrienne and sighing. "She's here," I whisper loud enough for her to hear through the surrounding chatter.

Adrienne perks up. "Where?" she asks, looking around.

"In spirit, I mean. When you dance, or when you eat strawberry cheesecake ice cream. In the annoying way Vanessa is."

Adrienne giggles.

"Tell her she danced well today. And that she should keep at it."

"I'm sure that right now she's saying you danced very well today, and to keep doing it. And that she's proud of you."

Adrienne scowls. "You're lying. She wouldn't say that."

"Tell her to stick Mr. Sparkles up her butt," Vanessa snaps back.

"She did indeed say that. And, uhm, to stick Mr. Sparkles up your, er, butt."

Adrienne's eyes widen. "She told you about Mr. Sparkles? The bitch."

"Language!" Vanessa and I warn in unison.

"Sorry," Adrienne retorts with that pre-teen attitude, the one that tests boundaries. I'm suddenly glad I won't have to see her in high school; sass also seems to be a trait of the Stalinskis.

Adrienne takes the last spoonful of ice cream and sighs as she crumples the paper bowl between her fingers. "I wish I wasn't angry at her before she died. She was trying to throw Mr. Sparkles into the trash."

"That bloody unicorn plushie," Vanessa chimes in as if she's there, remembering and reliving. "I won that thing at a carnival when I was her age."

"She told me she won Mr. Sparkles at a carnival, when she was about your age," I relay.

"How'd she win it?"

"Kissed a guy for it."

I shoot Vanessa a look.

"What? He was a cute eighth grader, the unicorn was cute. Was a winning first kiss in my opinion."

"Ring toss," I say instead.

"I only owned it for about five minutes. Adrienne wanted it so badly as soon as she saw it, I gave it to her just to shut her up."

"She won it for you," I add, looking at Adrienne. "You must have been only four years old."

"Three-and-a-half," Vanessa fills in.

"Three-and-a-half," I correct myself.

Adrienne smiles, but it dies quickly. "The last time I saw her I shouted at her to get out of my room."

My chest sinks as I think back to last night, the way I told Cole to leave.

"We all say things we don't mean," I admit.

Vanessa tuts. "Yeah, duh, we're sisters, Adrienne. It's how we're meant to communicate."

"Sisterly love, think nothing of it," I reassure Adrienne with a light grip on her arm.

We're all quiet, a moment to reflect on what we've said, what we've done.

"Well, I better get you home," I eventually say. "Traffic out of here this time of day is a b—I mean, *bummer*."

"Yeah," Adrienne says. "Thanks for the ice cream."

"Come on," I say, reaching for my bag. "You can tell me all about Mr. Sparkles on the way back."

The drive back was quicker than expected, which was a slight shame because I was enjoying hearing about Vanessa through Adrienne's stories. Or maybe I just enjoyed seeing Vanessa cringe in the back seat. Either way, it was a welcoming change to see a lighter, more normal side of Vanessa I didn't know existed until now.

Driving her BMW was pretty sweet, too.

"I wish I ate more chocolate fudge brownie ice cream." Vanessa and I stand on the curb by her house after dropping Adrienne off. "Stupid diets. Fat lot of good they were—pun intended."

"I'll remember that the next time I'm on my period and want to eat a tub of M&M's with a romcom."

"Girl, all the way."

It's an unusual moment, as if Vanessa and I have reached some sort of neutral territory over the sisterhood bonding of menstruation and chocolate cravings. Not that it lasts, however.

"Why did you even come here anyway? Weren't you busy with Ryan?"

I sigh as the dramas I'd rather not think about come flooding back.

"It doesn't matter anymore. You just never said that Dylan is gay."

"Was I supposed to? I may be dead but I can still keep a secret."

"But . . . it would have been useful to know, that's all." I idly kick a stone across the path. "Cat's out of the bag now, anyway."

"It was always going to be. Dylan just wanted to be as far away and forgotten about as possible when it did happen. We were going to move to California and get a place together. He was going to meet his boyfriend there and become an architect while I was going to study fashion design and win over the heart of a famous singer or producer."

I can't help but smirk as I picture that. If anyone could make it happen, it would have been Vanessa.

"Why'd you do it? Fake a relationship with him, I mean."

"Dylan and I have been best friends since our first day of elementary school. I was the only one he told; I was the only one who knew him well enough to see the real him. Since girls were crushing over him and Jordan was trailing after me, we agreed to fake a relationship. Dylan would keep his secret and all the girls and Jordan would back off. It was a win-win. And it worked, too, until . . ." She pauses to compose herself. "Poor Dylan. His parents have probably ostracized him by now."

Poor Dylan indeed. Like me, Dylan had built a façade to be normal. And it worked. Until it came crashing down.

I stand up. "I'll look out for him if I see him. Lord knows this town has enough social rejects."

"I know I've been, like, such a drag for you," she says, which is probably the biggest understatement of the year. "It's just hard to come to terms with, you know?"

"I get it," I say, because suddenly I do.

Vanessa is dead. As in *dead*. Gone. Her life—everything she was and had yet to become—is no more. She will never get the chance to experience things like graduating with that fashion design degree she will never obtain, or getting married to her love she will never meet, or holding her children who will never be born, and all the millions of other special little moments in between.

The one thing she wants is to be alive again, but that is never going to happen.

So when I arrive back home and see Cole leaning against the trampoline, hands slouched in his pockets, his mind a million miles away with the evening stars he's looking up at, my heart falters.

He stiffens as I approach. "Look, about last night—"

I don't even think. I wrap my arms tightly around Cole, holding onto the precious life of him that still remains, scared that at any moment he may suddenly be no more.

"Charlotte." He sounds surprised, confused. But then I feel his arms around me, the light embrace of his feather-touch soothing and comforting.

"I'm sorry," I sob.

"Shh, it's okay," he replies softly. His head touches mine, soothing my heartache, his caring and comforting energy healing my pain. "Everything's okay."

We curl up on the trampoline, side by side, watching the night sky as I slowly slip into slumber. Nothing is spoken; no words are needed. I trace the milky way through the light patches of cloud, each and every little speck a world of its own, a different place, a different time, the light of its existence shining all the way down to us, two more specks in the universe of specks. I take comfort in knowing that just like the stars that keep shining, Cole also shines on.

Beasey is right. I do have a gift from God.

That gift is Cole.

Twelve

I wake up at first light, the sun just touching my face through the window. It's already warm, and uncomfortable sweat is sticking to me. I squint and look around. I must have fallen asleep as soon as I went to my room because I'm still in my clothes. I stretch and wash up feeling oddly prepared for the day, which is stupid considering I know it's going to be a shocker.

I make my way to the kitchen and greet Pippi who's expecting breakfast from me. I feed her first and then lazily make myself a peanut butter sandwich. I notice Cole sitting on the water tank, admiring the sunflowers. I pour myself a glass of water and then join him.

"You dreamed of me." He notices me without looking. "You were calling my name. Telling me not to go."

"I don't remember."

He turns to face me and smiles, softly at first, but then his lips form a slight downward turn, concern heavy in his eyes that weigh down on my relaxed morning ambiance.

"I didn't know if you wanted me back here," he says. "But then I heard what happened at the party."

"How—"

"Vanessa told me before you came back. She overheard The Squad talking about it."

I roll my eyes. Of course. Even when dead she still spreads gossip about me.

"I had to make sure you're okay."

"As okay as I'll probably ever be," I mutter. "Besides, it's your home too, Cole."

"I should have been there for you and not been so envious."

"Envious? Of what? Getting drunk? Being ridiculed and used?"

Cole gives me a look, one that's as confusing as he is. He forms a small, tight smile, his dimples wanting to be shown, before glancing away, his face back to being serious. "And I should have supported you better. I'm sorry."

"It's okay."

"No, it's not okay. My behavior . . . I wasn't in the best state of mind."

I see it in him, the heaviness in his eyes, the change in his aura, the same small, subtle reaction to the mention of his past that now seems so clear.

"You can always talk to me about it."

"There's nothing to talk about. Just some bad memories. It won't happen again."

"It's okay if it does, Cole. Nobody's perfect, and there's no shame for admitting it."

"I'm fine," he affirms. He gives a small smile but I can see something is still there, his safety valve sealed shut for now. "Things will be back to how they were before."

"That sounds nice." The old normal never seemed as desirable as it does right now.

Cole gives me a worried look. "Are you sure you're okay, though?"

"I'm fine. Well, I will be, I guess."

"You guess? Charlotte, protection is no guessing matter. If you need to . . . see a doctor . . ."

"What?" I shake my head. "Ryan and I, we didn't actually, you know, sleep together."

"Oh?" Cole chuckles. "Well, prepare yourself for a rumor or two at school, courtesy of The Squad."

I groan and sink into my arms.

Cole pats my back sympathetically. "It's a good thing. Waiting,

I mean. For the right person.”

You're the right person.

I flinch at my thought. Cole thankfully doesn't notice my subtle jerk, because as much as I don't like the following thought, I need to know.

“Do you still love her?”

Cole looks at me. “Who?”

“You said that you had sex before. Do you still love her? Is she holding you back from crossing over?”

Cole's face stiffens. “Charlotte, I had sex, but that doesn't mean I was in love.”

My eyebrow lowers. “So you're lecturing me to do what you didn't when you said to wait for the right person?”

Cole shifts uncomfortably. “I wouldn't call it a lecture. Besides,” he pauses, “it's not the same.”

There's a long silence, stretching into awkwardness increasing with every passing second.

“You're not with Vanessa this morning?” I try changing the subject.

“She's following her family right now. I think she's accepting that they'll start moving on soon. Especially now she's been laid to rest.”

I guess I should be happy. Maybe I will be later, but for now I can only reply with, “Oh.”

“She told me what you did for her, too. I'm proud of you.”

I shrug, keeping my head low. I really don't want to look at Cole when I say, “She's not *that* bad, I guess. I won't hate on you if you want to be with her.”

“What?”

“I mean, I didn't think that blonde and bitchy is your type, but as your best friend I will support your choices. You deserve love, too. Even with her.”

Cole makes a sound, an almost laugh. “You think I've fallen for Vanessa?”

Okay, now I lift my head out of my arms. “Yes?”

“Vanessa kissed me, Charlotte. And, yeah, she's pretty good

at it, I'll give her that. And I didn't pull back straight away. It was a surprise, not to mention something I haven't experienced in a long time. But do you really think I've fallen for *Vanessa* from *The Squad*?"

I shrug. "Yes? I mean, you've spent so much time with her lately, you get along well together, and you're both . . . well, you have a lot in common."

"That doesn't mean I have those types of feelings for her. Vanessa's just someone fun to hang with for a change."

"Geez, sorry."

Cole rakes his hand through his hair and exasperates. "I mean in the ghostly void I'm in. It's different, in a way you don't understand. She does, though. She—"

"Yeah, I get it."

I do. They're a whole different entity on a whole different plane of existence, so of course it's going to be different.

"It's not just Vanessa, though. I'm trying to be there for you, too," I say. "But you keep pushing me away, even though you know everything about me from my favorite movie to the way I make my cereal."

Cole lowers his head.

"I mean, for all I know you could be stealing from old ghost ladies, or hanging out with other Communicators, or bringing ghost girls back to my room."

"You think I would do that?"

"Of course not." I hope not. "The point is, Cole, you're the closest person in my life, yet I know so little about you."

Cole sighs. "You're right. You deserve more. I'm sorry."

"I'm not a little girl anymore," I say. "You can open up to me."

He cups my face in his hands. "You're growing up so fast, I can't keep up." He smiles, that genuine Cole smile that makes me feel tingly inside. It is good to see it again, but it is short-lived because he then glances up at the sky, his lips tight, eyes unsure. It only lasts a second, then he disappears and reappears on the water tank.

"I really wish I could do that," I mutter.

"Being dead has to have some perks," he replies, looking at the sunflowers again. The buds are mostly closed, the smallest tint of yellow poking through. "You're not the only thing growing up so fast."

"They're so early this year."

"I guess they're making the most out of the time they have."

"Live young."

"Die young."

"YOLO."

We both snicker, our normal selves again. Cole studies them a few seconds longer, watching a caterpillar make its way up a stem.

"Danielle."

I look up, confused.

"The girl I slept with." He kneels down, placing a finger on top of the caterpillar as it trails up the plant stem. It wriggles slightly under his touch, then continues on its way. "She lived nearby but we only really started getting close over social gatherings by the old watermill. Like me, she didn't come from the best of households. I guess that's how we bonded. She also had a boyfriend but he was an abusive asshole so we only saw each other when he wasn't around. We would drink whatever, smoke whatever, anything to make the nights last so we didn't have to worry about the days."

Cole quietly chuckles to himself, his mind going through memories I would rather not know.

"She was such a punk, in a cool way. Bold and funny yet caring. She would never see herself as a victim. We often joked about running away together, starting anew in a different state, somewhere by the coast. Just driving away and never looking back. We were so close, too. So close . . ."

"What happened to her?"

"It took a while, but she's okay now." Cole turns back to the caterpillar, surprised at how far it has crawled. "She's twenty-nine now. Married to a decent guy. Has a kid of her own. A boy."

I wonder how he knows that, but then decide some things are

just too personal to ask.

"She survived." Cole chuckles to himself again before muttering, "At least one of us did."

"I'm sorry, Cole."

"My point is, it was only because we needed one other that we found solace in each other. It was nice, but for the wrong reasons." He pauses before continuing, "Sometimes the idea of having someone is enough. Until it's not."

Like with Ryan.

Cole glances back to the caterpillar, now breaching the bud of the young sunflower. "Existence and suffering go hand-in-hand, Charlotte." He turns to look me in the eyes. "But I want you to remember that you will never have to suffer alone. Not while I'm around."

I take in his words with a smile. Not only because he's not actually infatuated with Vanessa, or because his reassuring words are accompanied by the soft, caring eyes of the Cole I know and love. I smile because Cole opened up to me, the first step in what I hope is his recovery through his life trauma, whatever it entails.

He stands up. "You really think blonde and bitchy is my type?"

I titter. Then he does, and the flow of us returns.

Dad then comes out to ask me why I'm not getting ready to go to school and I realize I'm running late. Luckily, he has time to drop me off so for once I make it to class on time.

Cole is already standing at the classroom door waiting for me, a nice touch I can get used to.

"I'm here for you," he reassures me.

I dread what I'm about to walk into, but I force a smile nonetheless, unintentionally directing it to Leslie who approaches me. "Hello, Leslie."

"Hello indeed," she replies. "Been quite the weekend, I hear?"

"If it's about Saturday night then I don't know what you've heard but we didn't do anything. At least not much." I notice Ryan and The Squad coming down the hallway. If they notice me they don't show it.

Just like that, I'm discarded.

"So you're not carrying his babies?"

I shoot Leslie a disapproving look. "No."

"But you're hitting it off with him?"

"No. Not anymore."

I wonder why I'm not upset about that. I guess some feelings—or lack thereof—speak answers like Cole mentioned. Maybe I'm still happy to know that Cole and Vanessa aren't a thing. Heck, I'm just happy that Cole's back by my side.

"Sounds like a drama you'll have to tell me all about later. Ready for the economics test?"

"What economics test?"

"The one we have in about three minutes."

Shit.

I had totally forgotten. "Can't wait."

We enter the classroom just behind Ms. Cassidy and slip into our seats.

"Settle down, class. You know how it goes: silence and blue or black pen only," Ms. Cassidy remarks as everyone else ends their chatter to take their seats.

"You know," Cole has that mischievous smile forming, "I can just look at the answer notes on the teacher's desk and tell you."

"Cole!" I whisper a bit too loudly. Someone turns their head. I duck my head behind my backpack and whisper quieter, "That's cheating!"

"So?"

"That's wrong."

"You deserve a break." He leans back on the desk in front of me, his legs crossed. If he were physical he'd put the likes of Jordan to shame as the coolest guy in school. "Your gift shouldn't be all hard work; you're entitled to some perks here and there."

"You have one hour. Take one and pass the rest back. You may start," Ms. Cassidy calls out as she sits down. She doesn't wait long before taking out her phone.

I take my pen out and put my backpack under my chair.

"Cough twice and I'm at your servitude," Cole chimes.

I look at the paper handed to me and all the numbers and

letters seem to morph into one blur. It might as well be an alien language.

Dammit.

Screw the guilty conscience; Cole is right. I am entitled to a bit of slack here and there.

I cough twice. Cole's smile widens. I nod. With a clap he leaps up and jumps over the desks to the front, not that anyone notices.

"What do we have here, Ms. Cassidy? Don't mind if I take a look."

He reads out the answers one at a time and I can't help but think how sexy he is being such a bad boy.

"Thank you, Ms. Cassidy, you've been a great help!" He bellows each word at her but she doesn't even flinch. He then pulls a weird face as he looks at her phone. "Yeesh, Ms. Cassidy. Online dating sites in class? I'd confiscate your phone if I could."

He walks to my side and I cut my girly gaze.

"Now remember, a smart cheater gets some answers wrong," he says.

I look down then add an extra zero to the answer on the first question, leave a question mark for the last answer, and change the answer for question 5a from option C to option D.

"You're welcome." He bows. "I've got that stupid meeting with Beasey now. Don't worry, I'm just going to tell him I won't be taking part in his research anymore. You hang tight, take a rest. I'll be back shortly." He winks before strolling through the wall.

I can't help but smirk, even as I look down at my test paper. I cheated. On a test. And to be honest, I don't even care. I feel bad, but in a cool kid way. I may have to re-evaluate myself; the temptation has been tasted and it's good. But like Cole said, it's just a stupid test.

I spend the next while debating in my mind where I stand on the morale front of using ghosts for personal gain. Maybe I could be a magician and do tricks like Cole and I used to do for fun. Not that ghosts would want to spend their afterlife being my rabbit in a hat.

I could start up a mafia and hire ghosts for snitching gigs. I wouldn't have to worry about labor laws or unions or pay, and it would be perfectly safe because no one would get hurt. Except for the bad guys when they get arrested. Or the cheaters or abusers or dirty politicians.

Then again, finding morally-sound ghosts willing to do so would be the bigger issue. Not to mention they could cheat or lie themselves, or just decide to cross over in the middle of a mission. I scrap all of the ideas that come to mind, but conclude that there can be some perks to this "duty" of mine the man in the sky gave me. So as far as I'm concerned, this economics test is mine for the A–grade.

Besides, I have far more pressing matters to deal with. Like being there for Cole, who undeniably still has trauma regarding his life. And Dylan, whom I see walking past the classroom door.

I glance at the clock. It's reasonable enough to hand in the test by now, which is what I do. Since that's it for the lesson I am excused. I decide to let Cole find me himself and scoot off after Dylan. I catch him on the bleachers, eyes closed and earbuds in his ears. Like most students at Foxton High School, I always thought he was a troublemaker, not knowing his broody and moody nature was shielding his vulnerability of being different. I guess everyone has their façades, some more well-built than others.

"Hey."

Dylan looks up straight away, eyes squinting at my silhouette as he pulls out his earbuds.

"What do *you* want?" he asks, both confused and annoyed at my presence.

"Just passing by. Seeing how you are."

"Why do you care?"

"I didn't know you're gay."

Dylan sits up, his jaw tight and fists clenched.

"Calm down, terminator. I'm not judging. I'm just making sure you're okay. It can suck being different in these parts." I add softly, "I would know."

This seems to calm Dylan down because he relaxes enough to lean on his elbow.

"How's the family taking it?" I ask.

"In the seven stages of grief they've just entered the territory of anger."

I sit down next to him. "I'm sorry to hear that."

I really am. It hasn't always been easy with Dad, but he was never angry at me. His love for me, like his love for the Lord, is unconditional, and I can't imagine how worse off I'd be if he showed anything less.

"I don't need them, anyway," he replies. I don't quite believe him as he places his phone down with more force than necessary. "Pedro is getting a place. I'll be gone as soon as school graduation is over."

"Not much longer now. Hang in there."

"I heard what happened at the party."

I roll my eyes. "Geez, we didn't have sex!"

Dylan raises his eyebrows. "No, I mean them trying to spook you out with summoning the ghost of Vanessa. They're toxic. I see that now."

"Oh. Yeah, they are."

"Charlotte."

Vanessa's sudden presence startles me, but I'm more surprised that she referred to me by my first name for once. I squint her way, the energy of her lacking the silhouette effect. I just about see concern on her face but her demeanor quickly changes when she sees Dylan.

"Vanessa," I say.

"Dylan!"

"What about her?" Dylan asks warily, seemingly oblivious to her gentle embrace around him.

"Um," I start. "Do you feel her?"

"What?"

"I mean, like, her spirit."

Dylan cautiously sits up straight. He shoots me an icy stare, but it slowly melts into a softer complexion. And just like that, it's like he becomes a different person.

"Sometimes I think I do. But then I remember she's gone. Having such thoughts doesn't do any good."

"I'm here, Dylan!" Vanessa cries at him.

"She wasn't liked by most people, but most people didn't know her like I did. And I miss her," his voice cracks, eyes welling with tears. "For what it's worth, I do miss her."

Maybe it's because I pity him. Maybe it's because we share a mutual territory of being different. Then again, it's probably because Vanessa is at my side nagging me to, but I say, "She says she loves you, too, uh, *boo*."

Dylan looks up at this. His eyebrows raise, his eyes tense yet tearful. He seems conflicted, whether or not to believe me. But he huffs ever so slightly, a settling smile on his lips.

"If she were here," he says cautiously, "I would say only until the sun goes down. Every single day, for the rest of my life."

There must be some secret meaning in the words, something only they share. I'm not going to ask, but I think some part of him knows she is here and knows that's what she needs to hear, because I glance at Vanessa and see her giggle, tears glistening in her eyes, her energy light and glowy.

"If she were here," I reply, subtly wiping my own wet eyes, "she'd be very happy to hear that."

The bell rings and the moment subsides. I clear my throat. "Well, I have to get ready for next period. You going to prom?"

"No way. Got two tickets, but, well, it wouldn't be the same even if I wanted to go."

"You should go. With Pedro."

He looks at me as if he's just seen a ghost (he clearly hasn't, though). "You crazy?"

I tilt a smile. "Maybe."

We exchange phone numbers before heading off to our next classes with a parting smile. I expected Vanessa to follow Dylan, but it's me she's trailing after.

"Why are you here, Vanessa? I have class. You know the rules."

"Don't get me wrong, I'm glad I was here for that," she replies. "But I didn't come here for Dylan."

"Oh. Well Cole's not here."

"I know. That's why I came," she replies nervously. "Cole is being weird again."

∞∞∞∞∞

I had, of course, gone straight to Beasey to find out what went down when Cole went to visit, only I couldn't find him until after lunch break, and Beasey wasn't saying anything, even referring to patient confidentiality clauses from the Health Insurance Portability and Accountability Act. This annoys me, because Beasey now potentially knows more about Cole than I do, and he is being morally righteous in knowing so, something I wouldn't normally associate him with.

This also puts me off paying attention in class, which isn't great when entering the final run of high school. Where is Cole to help me ace this biology worksheet? Not that pairing alleles is more important right now, because if I knew where Cole had disappeared to I would be there and not here.

So I do my best to get through the day, through the shunning of The Squad and Leslie's pandering questions, in the hopes that—against my usual desires—Vanessa will show up and shed light on where he is.

She doesn't, but I find my concern not increasing as much as weaning into annoyance. Cole knows where I am, and I said enough times that he can open up to me. Maybe he doesn't want to disrupt me and is waiting for school to be over. Maybe Beasey just pissed him off. Whatever he's going through, there is nothing else I can do right now, so when the last bell of the day rings I head straight to where I usually go.

"Last detention," I declare as I enter the art classroom. Since I decided to skip school last Friday I get to fulfil the last of my detention duties today. Beasey knows this and is already setting out the wipes and spray bottles, his back turned to me. The classroom is empty except for us, but as with the usual end of day rush in the art department, the paint pots and brushes have been left dumped in the sink. "We've got a lot to get through, I'm sure. So, what'll it be? The truth behind the Bloody Mary curse? How to perform a proper séance? Zombies? Please say zombies."

I pick up his book and flip through the pages, noticing the ripped edges of the spine.

"There are pages missing," I say.

"Confidential," Beasey replies just that one word, probably expecting my curiosity. He would be right.

"Confidential? From what?" I ask, but I don't need a reply. *Me*.

It's confidential from *me*.

"Consider our detention sessions a free trial."

"I thought you said there was no cost to join your little club."

"There isn't. But membership is required. And training. Proper training."

"You don't think I'm ready?"

Beasey now turns around to face me, his expression and voice serious, even condescending. "From what I've seen of the way you do things, no. I'm sorry to say that you've still got a long way to go."

I huff. "Well, I did just fine without you before." I still don't mention the number of scrapes and bruises, close shaves, or times I've ventured on the other side of the law, however.

"You're too emotionally attached. To them."

He stresses the word "them", but I catch on to the undertone of his voice.

"Look, if this is about Cole—"

"You need to let him go, Charlotte," he interrupts. "It will only hurt more if you don't."

I open my mouth to protest, only I don't quite know what I'm arguing. And anything I say could seem selfish, something I don't want Beasey to rightfully point out.

Beasey turns on the faucet with more force than necessary.

Water churns out leaving a splash trail on the counter, not that Beasey seems to care as he squirts some soap into the water and twirls the brushes around hastily. Cole isn't the only one in a weird mood, obviously.

"So how do I get this 'proper training', as you put it?" I ask instead, leaving him to the mess of water he's creating while I start on the sweeping.

"There's a place established for people like us."

"Oh?"

"In Italy."

"Italy?"

"It's a country in Europe."

"I know where Italy is, Beasey," I scowl. "Our education system isn't *that* bad. But aside from one week in Mexico five years ago, I've barely been out of the South. I can't just go and live in *Italy*."

Okay, so going off to live in Italy isn't exactly a death sentence. In fact, it sounds a lot better than anything I've got planned for my future here, which is pretty much nothing. Italy has a rich culture, history, and cuisine to immerse myself into, and I'm sure there would be some hot Mediterranean guys to gawk at, too. But as much as I love the idea of being wooed by an Italian hunk on the Venice canals while dining on prosecco and pizza, there's just too much holding me here.

Like Dad and Pippi. And, okay, Cole as well.

"Why not?" he asks as if *I'm* being the ridiculous one here.

"I don't know Italian."

"L'italiano è una lingua bellissima," Beasey replies, although I only look at him scornfully. "Italian is a beautiful language. You can pick it up in a year." He glances back at me before adding, "Or two."

I cross my arms. "So I'm just supposed to drop everything and run off to Europe to join some ghost club? I have plans, you know. Plans for my future, like further study, get a degree, establish a career."

"You could do further study in Italy, too. There's a well-established Christian university nearby we have, uh, *connections* with. You could get a student visa, a scholarship."

"I can't leave my dad."

I can't leave Cole, either.

"Your father would be proud."

"How do you know that my father would be proud?"

"We've talked. At church. He was quite apologetic for his daughter's reckless behavior last week."

I look away shamefacedly. There wasn't any sign of my fist-on-face contact under his eye anymore, and I had actually forgotten about it.

"He wants the best for you, naturally. Surely you want that for yourself, too?"

I look back to the book, where the missing pages are supposed to be. What did they say that was so important I can't just read now? And what else can I do, can I be? The answers, it seems, await in Italy.

Beasey continues, "You won't be considered different, something you've clearly expressed disdain about. And you won't be alone."

"I'm not alone now," I remind him.

"You and I both know that's not entirely true. And you know what will happen once Cole gets through his, uh, *internal conflicts*."

How could I forget? It's propagating in my mind all the time, slowly filling me with anxiety that the time for him to want to leave is coming closer, especially at times like right now when I know something is up with him.

But even if he chooses to hang around longer, what happens afterwards? Would he even want to be with me? Because it's not like Cole has made a move or even shown any signs of affection beyond our platonic friendship to be something . . . more. I mean, there's no law of the universe saying we can't be something more. I think. Maybe Italy would have some answers on that.

Beasey is studying my face for signs of a reply. Just to tip the scales in my mind further he then adds, "This is about you becoming who you are, Charlotte. It's your sacred duty."

"*Sacred* duty?" I take a step back. I mean, I'm not some *Avengers* character off to save the world. I'm a seventeen-year-old girl from Georgia who can see ghosts. It is just something I can do, and that alone doesn't have to define me as anything sacred or dutiful.

Does it?

"Think about it. That's all I ask."

I nod.

"Well, you run along now."

"But I've only just started cleaning."

"You have a lot of thinking to do. Why don't you find Cole, see what he thinks?"

"Uh, okay," I reply, surprised he finally used Cole's name. I pick up my bag, deciding not to argue about getting out of cleaning duty. I then turn and give Beasey a skeptic look. "Well, it's been educational, and uh . . . fun, I'm sure. But I'm going to enjoy my newfound freedom now. With Cole, if he'll show up."

Beasey nods, but not before leaving me with sobering parting words: "Everyone leaves, Charlotte. Everyone moves on. Eventually."

Thirteen

Cole seems different. Not that he's opening up about it, because he's not. Not that he's even been around to open up about it, because he hasn't.

But now that he has decided to appear, it's clear something is going on with him. His aura is dull, his movements jittery. He avoids eye contact, but in the moments he does look at me it's there, that heavy look in his eyes, the one that shows he's hiding something.

Except not even he can hide it now.

"Morning," I say as I throw my apple up in the air and catch it. I try to sound as casual as possible to not scare him away. He reminds me of a timid cat, wanting to get close but too unsure, taking one step forward before two steps back and then running away. I consider going "psspsspss" at him to see if that entices him, but I don't think he would appreciate such efforts. So instead, I bite into my apple and continue the walk to school.

"Hey." He waits a few paces before asking, "How have you been?"

"Fine. It's been a very uneventful couple of days, actually. No drama from Vanessa, and the only drama at school is about prom tonight, not that I'm going. Oh, and I helped a ghost move on yesterday. Bone cancer. College kid. Nice guy."

"That's good to hear." Cole looks at me. He's smiling, but it's a sad smile, something between pride and sorrow, a reconciliation of sorts. "You're all grown up now. No longer scared of ghosts.

No longer needing me to protect you."

"I wouldn't say all grown up." I stutter a laugh through the concern I'm feeling from his words. "I'm only seventeen. And I'll always need you, Cole."

"Charlotte," he starts. His voice is quiet and tired, and I don't like where this is going.

"You said you'd be here for me, no matter what." My chest sinks but I hold the emotion in, trying to remain as calm and open as possible.

"I did, didn't I? I failed you. Again. I'm sorry."

I cross my arms. "Tell me the truth this time. Where have you been?"

"Places."

"Such as?"

"My grave."

The answer came out from his mouth with no hesitation, no tone of anger or sadness, and now I'm the one with no communication to give. As with most other things about him, Cole has never mentioned his grave before. I didn't even know he was buried.

"Oh." It's all I can think of to say. I don't know if it was an accidental slip-up or a cry for help, so I ask, "Do you want to talk about it?"

"No."

Again, no hesitation, no emotion.

"Okay." I don't push it. I stare down at my feet awkwardly. Even though I've slowed my walk down to an elderly stroll to prolong this time with Cole, I'm nearing school. I don't have much time but I want to get as much out of him as possible.

"I think you're right about Beasey," I say.

Cole visibly frowns at the name.

"He said I should go to Italy. Italy! Can you believe it? Apparently there's a whole group of Communicators over there, and he said it would be good for me to meet others like myself. And get this, he ripped out some pages from his book, and— hello? Are you even listening?"

"You should go to Italy."

I pull back at his assertion. "What? Really? You don't even know the details."

"Beasey told me."

Big mouth Beasey.

"It's the opportunity of a lifetime. You'll get to leave small town America, which is what you want. Not to mention you can meet others like yourself. You'll get to feel ordinary there."

"Maybe ordinary is boring after all. Besides," I stop behind a bus shelter where nobody can see me, but I take out my phone just in case as I look him in the eyes. "I don't need anyone else. I have you."

"What if I wasn't here, though? Would you go then?"

I lower my phone, the weight of the world suddenly heavy on me. Would I go if Cole wasn't here? I honestly don't know. I'm not going to say that, however.

"We're a team, Cole. You and me. Wherever, whenever. Besides, what more do I need to know? I'll never be able to help every ghost in the world."

"I know," he replies, his voice now the familiar caring and compassionate tone I know him by. "But you make a difference, one soul at a time."

Soul. He's never used that word before. Ghost, yes. Spirit, yes. But never *soul.*

The school bell rings in the near distance.

"You'll be late for class. I have to do some things, but I'll be back soon."

"Promise?"

He nods. "Haunt ya later."

We part ways and I dash for class. Ms. Cassidy seems to have given up on commenting on my tardiness. Or maybe it's the A–grade economics test paper she hands me that gets me off the hook.

Now I may have misheard, but when Cole said that he would be back soon, I assumed he meant, well, *soon.* Morning passes, and by lunchtime I give up on him returning. So when the bell for afternoon classes rings and I make my way to the classroom, I do my best to avoid the other ghost in the hallway waiting for me.

"Hey, sweet cheeks," he says in a strong Southern accent, even though I do my best to avoid eye contact. "It's you, isn't it? The one that can see us."

This time I grant him my attention. He couldn't have been older than thirty, although his rough beard was pushing it. He strides up to me with more pride than he should have for someone so unshaven and impudent.

"So it is true. I wasn't told you'd be such a belle, though."

"I'm busy. Go away."

I pace into the classroom and take my seat. The ghost doesn't seem to care that I have class though, since he follows me in, his overhanging belly in my face as he leans over me uncomfortably close.

"Name's Logan, 'case you were wonderin'."

"I wasn't," I mutter under my breath. Where is Cole? "Go away."

"Knocked a beehive. Just a bump. But boy, they kept on coming. I ran and whacked at them but they wouldn't stop."

That's because if bees swarm in attack they're most likely Africanized honeybees. And you don't whack Africanized honeybees; you make a break in a zigzag run for a sealed vehicle or building, otherwise you hope you have enough fitness to outrun them for a quarter-mile dash.

Logan clearly didn't have that fitness level, nor a nearby shelter. I don't feel sorry for him, however, as he places his hand on my shoulder.

"You feel that, huh?" he murmurs. He slowly slides his hand down my chest, resting it where no part of him should be touching. "What's a pretty thing like you gonna do for a ghost like me?"

I jolt up from my seat, the scrape of the desk on the floor getting everyone's attention.

"Not again," someone behind me mutters.

"I need to use the bathroom," I say to Ms. Cassidy as I make my way to the door, feeling the déjà vu of this classroom exit.

"I don't give out hall passes five minutes into class, Miss Durane. That's what lunchtime is for."

"I'm not asking for permission," I retort as I walk out without looking back.

Logan whistles behind me. "She sure looks pissed. You a feisty girl, just like them bees."

I turn back and smirk. "Oh, I'm feisty. Want to see?" I motion him to follow me with my finger.

He seems to like the sound of this and happily follows me down the hallway.

"After you," I say, before closing the door to the janitor's room behind me.

∞∞∞∞∞

"What was that all about?" Leslie finds me in the school bathroom. Being a senior known for being weird I can intimidate the younger students into backing out and using the other bathroom down the hallway, which is good when I want to be alone, especially when I look like the state I'm in right now.

Not Leslie, though. No one intimidates Leslie.

"Nothing," I mutter in reply.

"No way that was nothing. Teacher's livid, you should've seen her face go puffy and red. In fact, I think she's calling your dad right now." She plonks my school bag on the ground beside me. "Here's your stuff, by the way."

"Thanks."

"Are you on drugs?" she asks, looking at me more closely through the mirror plastered across the wall in the one remaining area above the sink that isn't cracked or covered in graffiti hating on various teachers and exes. "More importantly, have you got any for me?"

I look up to see myself again. The drops of water hanging on my face isn't sweat but the tap water I splashed over myself. I have also gained some color back since I last looked, although I still look pale and out of it. Exorcising is exhausting, especially when up against someone of Logan's strength, something Beasey failed to mention. It wasn't as quick as I thought it would be either, and a lot of ghost-on-Communicator wrestling was involved until I got it right enough for the haze to fully take over. I have vomited only twice since.

"I'm not on drugs, Leslie. I just don't feel very well. Low blood sugar."

"Here." Leslie takes a granola bar out from her bag and places it in front of me.

"Thanks." I smile and take it. For the most part, Leslie fulfills her side of our spurious friendship admirably, especially considering I haven't made it an easy ride for her. I'd have to find a way to make it up to her somehow. Does she like books or chocolates? I don't even know anymore.

I take a bite of the granola bar, hoping this is the only side-effect from exorcising I'll have to deal with. Because as emaciated as I feel right now, I also feel buzzed. I don't know how, but conjuring up a power trip on the light energy of heaven or whatever it was has caused quite the serotonin hit. I wonder if this is what being high feels like. Or what dying feels like.

Beasey obviously foresaw this, because even though he only walked in at the last minute, he was so impressed he notified the school nurse on my behalf that I was queasy and brought back a soda.

I hear the bell ring.

"Well, see you around," Leslie says before leaving.

"Yeah," I reply. If I make it until then, that is. Because I'm pretty sure half of me got sucked into the after-void with Logan.

As it turns out, Ms. Cassidy's attempt to discipline me got overruled by the school nurse when she came to check up on me. Dad didn't believe me until I video called him, my face enough evidence he needed to give the school permission to let me go home. And boy, did I sleep when I landed on my bed. Dad made chicken soup thinking I was coming down with the flu. Even though I'm already feeling better, I happily accept his efforts and eat outside on the porch chair.

"Charlotte."

I take a slow sip of my soup before bothering to answer. "Cole."

His energy is gloomy, but I'm still too spent to deal with trying to get him to communicate about it.

"How . . . how was school?" He's jittery again, fidgeting with his fingers.

"Oh, just the usual classes, a few taunts about me being Ryan's side fling here and there, cafeteria food was that bad spaghetti and meatballs again—oh, and I exorcised a ghost."

"What?"

"He was touching me inappropriately. You weren't there. So I took him to the janitor's room and exorcised him."

Cole looks at me intently, a mix of care and concern in his eyes.

"You weren't there," I repeat solidly.

Cole glances down at that very moment. Emotion sweeps across him, something dark, like fear or sorrow or . . . guilt.

It is guilt.

It always has been.

"I'm sorry."

"It's fine. I handled it."

"It's not fine. I'm supposed to protect you."

I stare at Cole, flattered at his declaration of care for my safety. But there's something about the way he says it, and by the way he avoids my eyes he knows it, too.

"What do you mean, you're supposed to protect me?" I put my soup down and fold my arms over my chest, staring at him expectantly for a clear answer I know he won't give.

"You're reckless. Someone has to." He falters over the words, dying to a broken mutter, but the damage is done.

"Reckless? Well, yeah, I've had a few bumps here and there. But I don't have to be reckless anymore now that I can just chant them away.”

“It’s not right.”

“Why not? I think Beasey proves a point here.”

Cole looks at me, his eyebrows furrow low. Then, as if hitting an epiphany, his eyes widen, his nostrils flare. “It’s what he wants.”

He vanishes before I can even summon an answer to that. Not that I have one, because I have no idea what he’s on about.

But what’s new?

∞∞∞∞∞∞

When Vanessa shows up the next afternoon at school I am actually glad to see her for once.

“Ah, nice of you to pop by. Tell me, did you bring anyone else with you today? A few more drugged up party girls, another farmer? Perhaps a dodgy politician or two this time?”

Vanessa glances to her left, then to her right before settling on me. “What?”

“Don’t act ignorant.”

“What are you on about?”

“The other ghosts.”

Vanessa looks over her shoulder again. “If you’re on drugs or having a freak moment, can it wait until later? I want your help with something.”

“You did send them to me, didn’t you?”

“Are you talking about those three drug OD girls? They were cool, and yeah, I recommended you. So what? You should be flattered.”

“What about the pervy redneck farmer?”

“What pervy redneck farmer?”

“Is this some bitch revenge tactic of yours? Because I’m over it, Vanessa, I really am. I may not have finished exorcising you last time, but I’ve had practice since.”

“You know what, I think you like the attention from the dead,

∞ 184 ∞

I really do. It's like your kink or something. But if there was a pervy redneck farmer guy here then *I* certainly wouldn't be here."

"That's because I got rid of him. After *someone* told him about me."

"And you think I did? What the hell Durane, you think I'd even talk to creepy pervs let alone give them directions to you? Are you seriously for real right now? I want you to focus on me, not some hillbilly creepazoid. *Me*," she says, pointing to herself.

Okay, that I can believe.

"So if it wasn't you then who was it?"

"I don't know, and newsflash: I don't care. Now are you going to help me or not? I think I'm remembering things . . ."

I don't listen. Someone clearly sent Logan to me, he said so himself. Did Cole say something? No, Cole wouldn't. Not ever. Which only leaves . . . of course.

Beasey.

How could I have been so stupid?

"You're right. Sorry, Vanessa." Words I never thought I'd say. I swallow, although it's my pride I'm suppressing more than the sick building up in my throat. "You'll have to find me later. There's something I need to sort out."

I leave her reply hanging because I storm straight for the janitor's room. This time there's no exorcism in play, which is probably a good thing because my raging energy might have diverted their ascension to somewhere a lot darker.

"You son of a bitch."

"Good afternoon to you, too."

"You knew he was trouble," I say as soon as I slam the door behind me. "You could have exorcised Logan the moment he stepped foot into Foxton High School. But instead you told him to come to me, didn't you? To get me to exorcise him. To get me to conform to your ways."

He doesn't even try to deny it or look apologetic. "I would put it differently, but yes."

I clench my fists, but I allow that anger to roll back inside me. "How could I have been so stupid?"

"Charlotte, try to understand why I did it. You need to be aware of dangers and how to protect yourself—"

"Stop. Don't make this about training. You manipulated me."

"I wouldn't go that far. It's more of a tough love approach."

"Tough love? Really?"

"A push in the right direction. I'm trying to help you utilize your gift."

"But with you it's not about helping, is it? It's about power."

"That's a little conclusive, don't you think? And this isn't about me."

"You're right. It's about me and Cole, isn't it? You're trying to separate us."

"Charlotte, trust me when I say it's for your own good."

"You don't get to decide what is for my own good!" I snap back. "Or Cole's. You've done something to him, haven't you? He was fine before you got involved. Where is he? What did you say to him?"

"Charlotte—"

"What did you do to him?"

"I only helped him remember. Confront himself."

I reach for the door. "Stay away from me and stay away from Cole."

"Charlotte—"

"Just leave us alone!"

I slam the door behind me, too angry to care about the students looking my way. Not even Gwen succeeds in throwing a snarky comment my way as I head to the library, but I quickly decide that between Beasey and prom excitement I don't even want to be in this building, so I take my free period outside with Leslie. I am surprised to find Dylan come by and join us. I guess we're acquaintances now; Leslie seems to have warmed up to Dylan since he's not so petulant anymore, while Dylan seems to respect Leslie's blunt attitude. If it wasn't so close to the end of high school I could see us three becoming a new little clique.

Between Leslie and Dylan, I manage to forget about everything and feel somewhat normal, but the walk back home with my mind brings everything back with the frustration it carries.

Pippi greets me as soon as I open the door. I don't glance back at Cole standing by the fireplace; I've already noticed his less-than-glowy aura and I certainly don't have anything better to offer him right now.

"Bad day at school?" Patricia notices my mood as she walks into the kitchen.

While she takes me by surprise, it's not the first time I've come home to see Patricia here. I wonder if I'll see her at later hours too, or if Dad will give her a spare key soon. Not that I would mind.

Out of my peripheral vision I notice Cole disappearing, granting me privacy. Pippi lifts her head slightly but settles for a soft bark before curling up on the floor nearby and closing her eyes for a nap.

"You could say that." I drop my school bag on the table and peer into the living room. "You're watching the baseball game? Who's winning?"

Patricia glances back to the television. "Atlanta Braves, of course."

"Dad will be happy."

I can't say I'm a huge fan of sports; it's mostly an excuse to bond with Dad. I find it only fair considering he plays both father and mother that I should pitch in, so to speak, and play son as well as daughter. I think we both secretly know we're doing it, but we let it play out, our own way of bonding with one another.

"He's just washing up upstairs. We're checking out the new sushi place in town."

"Dad? My dad, eating sushi? Really?" I choke back a laugh. "Good luck with that. I've never seen him eat out for anything that doesn't include a chunk of a cow."

Patricia smirks. "I can try. And you don't have to sit through the game. It's recording, don't worry." She winks my way and switches off the television.

I like how Patricia gets me. Even though she is a native to the South, like lots of aspirational youngsters at eighteen, she left small-town living and took off to the skylines of New York City for the bustling corporate life. She landed a career in a software company and apparently was doing pretty well until her husband got sick and her family roots called her back home. She also never had kids, even though she's admitted that she wished she had, which is probably why she's so motherly to me.

"So how is everything at school?"

She follows me into the kitchen as I open the cupboard. I'm sure Dad has filled her in with everything that's happened with me lately so I don't bother denying any of it.

"Good, I guess. Classes are starting to wrap up." I hold up a mug from the cupboard. "Lemonade?"

Patricia shakes her head. "Any decisions on what you'll do next?"

"Not yet. I'm still bouncing ideas around."

I'm not going to mention the Italy proposal to anyone, although admittedly it's certainly loitering in my mind, regardless of the man behind the offer. It's an odd feeling being presented with such an amazing if not unexpected opportunity, and as such it needs a lot of thought. I mean, I take Spanish, not Italian, and even with Leslie's help my grades are only just in the passing percentile. I don't even know any Italians. Not to mention it's half a world away, which is still far even with ease of modern international travel.

That is, of course, if this is all legitimate. I mean, I'd be stupid to jet off to another continent to join some secretive organization on the word of a middle-aged religious janitor who has clearly deceived me more than once and has his own ulterior motives.

Patricia must have heard my sigh. "The world's yours for the taking, Charlotte."

I force a smile.

"And how are things with *them*?"

I pause at the word, but I don't let it linger. Patricia is more open-minded than Dad, especially since I told her some things her late husband wanted to communicate to her, things about accounts and insurances and finances I have no comprehension of. It turns out he was a very forward thinker, but he just didn't get to finish the admin work before the cancer got him so he wanted to make sure that Patricia was properly set up. She appreciated this from both of us, and even though she hasn't brought it up since that day, I know it's stuck with her. But that's okay; she's not one to judge. Which is probably why I like having her around so much.

"Been better, been worse," I admit.

"You seem more anxious than usual. Bill said you weren't feeling too good yesterday and the school called him to let you go home."

"Just a passing stomach bug," I lie.

Patricia gives me a concerned look. She has a natural motherly instinct of knowing when I'm not being fully honest.

I sigh. "There may be this one *friend* I am having trouble *helping*," I say, deciding on giving her something to feed her concern. "He's stressed about something and won't open up about it."

"Sounds rather familiar, doesn't it?" she replies as her face dips my way.

"Touché," I admit. "He used to be so cheerful if not cautious. Now it's like he's distant and caught up in the past he wants to escape from but can't."

"Cheerful people usually know what it's like to be sad," Patricia remarks, "which is why they hold on to what joys they can. Unfortunately, that's something you come to realize with age."

I know Patricia's trying, and as insightful as her words are, it doesn't make me feel any better about Cole. Because suddenly the persona of him seems a little clearer, and I wonder just how sad he really is.

"What do I do?"

"There's not much you can do except let him know that you're here for him through the good and the bad," Patricia replies earnestly before giving me another look. "Are you sure *you're* okay?"

"Nothing I can't handle." I smile in reassurance. It's not like she can do much to help beyond giving motherly advice.

"Just remember to put yourself and your health first."

Pippi paws at the back door so I excuse myself to let her out. It's not toilet business she's intending, though. She scampers straight up to Cole on the trampoline for his attention. She tries to lick at his hand, something she does to me when she knows I'm sad, before curling cup on the grass by his side.

I walk up to the trampoline and lean my head back to the sky. By now the sun has gone behind the hillside, but the afternoon warmth still remains. My eyes trail a mosquito, the first of many to come over the next few months.

"Beasey is unbelievable. He sent that sleazebag ghost after me. Can you believe that?" I turn to him. "But you already figured that out, didn't you?"

"Yes," he simply replies. "He hoodwinked us both."

"Maybe tell me next time? It's my fault, though. I said yes to his training. I should have seen it coming."

Cole may be slumped on the ground stroking Pippi's fur, but he's listening intently to every word I say.

"What he did was wrong, but he does have your best interests at heart. Which is why I think you should listen to him."

I shoot Cole a look, one that hopefully shows how dumbfounded I am at his words.

"Are you serious? Look at yourself, Cole. Look at what he's done to you, to *us*."

He glances at the ground. "This is mine and mine alone to carry, Charlotte." His eyes carry that familiar guilt, weighed down by the heaviness in his voice.

"What is it, Cole? What's making you this way? Tell me."

Cole doesn't look my way, instead holding his gaze down before eventually looking up to the old oak tree across the lawn.

"Do you remember when you were little and you collected different bugs from the garden to create an insect family in a shoebox?" he eventually asks with a wistful smile. "And how you cried when a bird came and ate them all?"

"I remember. You tried to tell me the caterpillar ran off with the grasshopper and the worm moved out due to renovations."

Cole chuckles. "I scouted the lawn all afternoon for new bugs as a replacement. But you were more interested in why they had to die. You researched what birds ate and decided it would be better to build a bird feeder instead. Then you got your father to install a birdbath, and then you made that bird house together. And now that tree has been home to the same family of finches for generations. You were always determined, trying to find the answers to everything."

This time he doesn't try to hide it. It's almost painful, feeling his energy changing from such a fun moment to such a serious one so quickly. "You deserve those answers."

He turns to look me in the eyes. He opens his mouth hesitantly, the words struggling to form. And just as I think he's about to get it out, the back door opens and Pippi runs up to Dad.

"Charlotte," Dad calls before squinting. "What are you doing?"

I turn back to Cole except there's nothing to see.

"Nothing. Just took Pippi outside."

"Trish and I are about to head off," Dad says as I head inside.

I can't help but smile a little as his face lights up when he mentions this. It's nice to see Dad care about someone else aside from me and the dog for a change.

"Are you sure you're not going to the school prom? You still have time to get ready."

"Nope," I reply.

I had never otherwise considered going to prom. I don't dance, and if Cole can't take me then I don't see the point in going. Even Ryan never asked me to prom, which makes me wonder just how prepared he was to sleep with me then ditch me, yet it also makes me relieved that things don't have to be any more awkward than they already are at school.

Patricia overhears Dad. "Oh? It's the big night. You only get prom once in your life, dear."

"Oh, it's a big night alright. A big night of movies with peanut butter-coated popcorn and Pippi for company. Isn't that right, Pippi?"

Pippi wags her tail, probably at the tub of peanut butter she sees me taking out of the cupboard.

"We don't have to go," Dad starts.

"No, no," I interject with my hand up. "Just because I'm going to spend my evening on the couch doesn't mean you should as well. Enjoy the sushi."

He hesitates, before pointing a finger at me and saying, "No beer. I know how many bottles there are. Just in case you do decide to go, after all."

"Yes, sir."

With a nod of satisfaction they leave. It's just as the car turns onto the road and drives out of sight when Vanessa suddenly appears across the living room. Pippi barks once, but it's followed by a growl, and I don't blame her, because Vanessa's energy is gray, her gaze low, and if she wasn't already dead I would think she is about to be.

I say her name but she doesn't even look my way.

Her voice, for the rarity that it is, is soft and broken when she says, "He was there."

"Who was where, Vanessa?"

"Jordan. When I died. Jordan was there." She looks up at me, her eyes dark and foreboding. "Jordan watched me die."

Fourteen

The twilight sky is clear and the stars can already be seen as the last hues of indigo-blue fade to black. Dylan flicks his car keys and I see the quick flash of the headlights locking behind us as we make our way across the school parking lot to the entrance doors. Under ordinary circumstances I would have taken the time to put my hair in an updo, stop for a photo, or maybe even have a few canapés to start the night. But I need to accept that circumstances in my life aren't ordinary.

"At least act like you don't want to cause trouble." Dylan has to keep pace with my raging stride. "They won't let you in like that. Here."

He pulls my hand back to his and clamps it in place with his fingers interlocked in mine before flashing a smile and pulling out the two prom tickets from the pocket of his tux. I have to hand it to him, he did a very fine job of getting ready on such short notice. Maybe being a guy and naturally good-looking in the way his genetics designed him to be makes such a task easy.

Still, I follow his lead because he has a point. Given how I rushed to look administrable, I need Dylan for his lavish looks and charm as much as his prom tickets. So, tilting my side bangs aside I subtly reposition my dress with my free hand and force a smile.

Even though I am far from the mood of smiling.

The parent on bouncer duty must have heard of Dylan's untimely sexual orientation closet reveal because he raises his eyebrows and pouts slightly at us. I wonder if Dylan also feels the desire to punch the guy in the face. Judging by the way his grip tightens I'd say he does.

Whoever this parent thinks he is, he is not here to preach, however, and he lets us through the doors.

"We're in," Dylan mutters as we walk down the hallway to the school auditorium. "Now what?"

Dylan doesn't know why we're here, only that it's important and to do with Vanessa. That was enough for him to throw on a tux, get in his car, and pick me up. He even handed me a corsage, which I thought was nice of him. It's a dark blue rose, probably to match his tie and whatever dress Vanessa had planned to wear, but since I'm wearing black it does well. I had to make do with the only item of clothing I have that complies with the dress code, which is why I'm wearing my knee-length crinkled halter dress. It's usually something I reserve for serious occasions like funerals, but it's aesthetic enough to cover formal dinners or events too, which now includes gatecrashing prom.

I look at Dylan, but I'm not quite sure what to say. This is the part where I'd rely on Cole to analyze the situation at hand and decide on a plan of action, but he's not here. I gave up on waiting for Cole; I guess he has his own emergency to deal with. So now the plan rests on me. Not that I have a plan, because I don't. But I know Cole, in all his vigilance, would say first and foremost to cover all corners and be sure of the facts before acting upon them.

"You go wait in the hall and I'll meet you there," I say. "I just need to confirm something first."

I don't want to burden Dylan with unnecessary hurt, not to mention lies. Because as much as Vanessa insisted that she remembers what happened, she could still be wrong, the fragmented memories of her death being mixed up with other memories or dreams.

At least I hope so.

Vanessa said that Jordan watched her die. Not just watched her die, but stood over her and did nothing. Blamed her, even.

But why? It just doesn't make sense. That is what I need to find the answer to, and why I'm going up to the one guy I really don't want to see right now.

Ryan is laughing with a group of girls by the photo stage. When he sees me approaching his expression turns to that of bewilderment, then dread. He not-so-subtly removes his arm from the girl next to him.

"Charlotte?"

"Ryan." I force a quick smile as I approach him. "Can we talk?"

He glances at the girl standing cozily next to him who has now also stopped laughing, before asking, "Now?"

"Yes, now."

I notice the girl next to him ever so lightly clasp her hand on his shoulder over his shirt, one finger at a time, in some silly attempt to mark her territory. Little does she know I have no interest in fighting her claim.

Ryan looks at her apologetically and says quietly, "I'll be right back, Anna."

The girl—apparently called Anna—smiles sweetly at Ryan and nods, her stare back at me like daggers as he stands.

But I don't have time for bitch play. Yanking his arm, I guide him into the next classroom and close the door behind us, the music now just a dull bass hum.

He speaks first, "Is this because of Anna? Because really, she's just—"

"It's not about that," I retort. "I just need to know. Why was there a bet about me?"

"Oh, look, Lottie, I already went over this—"

I whip my hand out in front of him. "No, Ryan. Why? Whose idea was it?"

"Jordan's," he simply replies. "As I said before, we all kinda knew you were only half present all the time. Rumors were that you were either talking to imaginary people or dead people. Jordan kept mentioning you, and when I mentioned walking in on you talking to Vanessa it got him interested, and so he came up with the party idea, to, you know . . ."

He doesn't finish, but I get it.

It was Jordan all along.

"But why? Why did Jordan seem so determined to find out about me?"

"I don't know," Ryan replies as he shrugs. "Maybe he wanted to pass on a message to Vanessa?"

Or prevent a message from Vanessa.

"What message, Ryan?"

"I dunno, ask him."

"Drugs."

I look at Vanessa. I didn't notice her appear; usually she enunciates her entrance well enough on her own. I wonder how long she was standing there for. Long enough to hear what she needed to, it seems.

"Drugs?" I ask, my voice strong and aghast.

"What?" Ryan asks.

"Drugs," she says again. "Steroids. Illegal ones. With some others. While we were celebrating I dropped off the flag blood in his locker so I wouldn't have to deal with it later and found them in his bag."

I frown at the thought. Jordan takes illegal steroids? I try to shake my head at this, but I can't. Because as ridiculous as it seems, it makes sense. He wasn't always that muscular, but I guess everyone was putting it down to a growth spurt and working out. And then there's his football performance. He's the star player, after all. Three scouts came out to see it for themselves.

I don't know much about drugs and sports rules, but if what Vanessa is saying is true, the lengths Jordan is willing to go through for his future, to avoid consequences for his decisions and actions . . . I shiver.

I look firmly at Ryan in the eyes. "Does Jordan take steroids?"

"What? No."

"Ryan!"

"He wouldn't . . . no, he wouldn't," Ryan shakes his head. "He'd be off the team, we'd have to forfeit the game win. He wouldn't risk that."

The uncertainty in his eyes shows he's reassuring himself more than me. And that's what it all comes down to: people can believe anything they want to when they're desperate enough. I've experienced plenty of it with grief-stricken relatives and lovers mourning. Heck, I've gone through the same with my own mother. I also saw it with Ryan, believing his grandfather was still around in some form. And he's doing it now too, denying the betrayal, because the truth is so much worse.

I force another quick smile. "Well, that's all I wanted to know. Thanks, Ryan."

"No hard feelings though, right?" he asks.

"Sure, Ryan. Whatever." I'm already out the door before he can say anything else, yet not caring if he even does have anything else to say.

Because my mind is spinning with the truth now set free: it was Jordan all along.

It's not the entrance I planned on making. I think someone says hello to me, and someone else mutters something less pleasant as I brush past. But I don't care. Not even Leslie's corset and lace mesh dress, fishnet stockings, and platform heels take my attention. For me, everyone fades out into a monochrome blur, and like a tunnel, my sight is only set on Jordan across the dance floor.

He looks past me, a background movement in the crowd. But then he double-takes and stares at me pushing past the swaying couples to the slow music, his eyebrows rising as I pass the table of possibly-alcoholic fruit punch and cakes and storm right up to him.

"You saw her," I start, my head pounding with rage. "You went to her, on the bleachers. You saw her passed out drunk, choking to death."

He backs up into Liam, but I step closer, my body directing itself.

"You saw her, didn't you? You could have saved her. But you didn't."

"Charlotte?" Mandy utters something but stops as the lights around us flicker.

"She found the drugs while placing the flag blood in your bag," I continue. "She should have dobbed you in there and then, but instead she took your bag and messaged you that she knew about the drugs and then waited on the bleachers to confront you, hoping for some rational explanation, knowing that otherwise she'd have to let the whole school down, the whole town down, and turn you in."

Jordan's mouth drops at this. Sven asks if what I'm saying is true. Jordan shakes his head angrily, but I'm not done yet.

"She waited in the rain for over an hour. She drank a lot, yes, but she was stressed. So when you saw her, unconscious and choking to death, you knew your little secret would be safe with her gone. So you did nothing. You stood there and watched her die."

I'm pulsing with fury inside myself, unable to grasp how someone could be so selfish as to watch an innocent person—someone he had feelings for, even—die, and for what? A few awards? A bit of fame and fortune? The cheapness of ego surpasses disbelief.

Jordan scowls at me before saying, "You're crazy."

"Why didn't you help me, Jor?" Jor? I say the words like Vanessa's mind is playing in my own, and I then feel an uncontrollable pent-up emotion of anger and sorrow surge within me.

Jordan's jaw drops. His lip quivers. "V-Vanessa?"

"Why?!" I screech the words and the glasses lined with possibly-alcoholic fruit punch simultaneously break and spill over the table and onto the floor.

People quickly step back from the glass and mess, including the glass that was in Jordan's hand.

"I . . ." he stammers, but says nothing more.

Suddenly I feel myself again, only the band has now stopped playing and the prom attendees have stopped dancing to look at me and the mess around me. And once again, I find all eyes are on me with unwanted attention and I'm without an excuse to rely on.

Except Dylan, whose eyes are deep in understanding. He turns to Jordan and hits him hard. And I mean *really* hard, one punch after another, no mercy, until they're rolling on the floor in possibly-alcoholic fruit punch and glass and blood. Stephanie and Mandy scream. Gwen looks on in shock. Liam bobs around them wondering what to do as Sven stands there shaking his head trying to makes sense of what he just heard. Ryan walks up with Anna to see the commotion and seems bemused by the whole spectacle. Two chaperones then come rushing over to haul Dylan off of Jordan, although they appear flabbergasted about what to do.

"You used her phone to delete her previous messages to you and then to message yourself saying she was going to see Dylan to get you off the hook. Then you threw her phone into a puddle to break it. And you actually got away with it. But the suspicion and stress was getting to you. What if you left some evidence? What if someone saw you? That's why you planted the flag blood in Dylan's locker, to try to take any attention away from you. Except you didn't know of his ulterior lifestyle weekend plans. And then there were the rumors of the freak who talks to dead people. You probably don't believe in that stuff, right? You wanted to assume I was a nutcase and shrug it off. Only you couldn't. You watched me closely, and the more you did the more that fear grew within you. So you made the bet with Ryan and got the party planned. Even though the others felt like it was too much too soon after Vanessa died, you wanted my guard down, didn't you? Because you just had to know for sure."

Jordan hisses at my face, "You can't prove anything."

"I can't," I admit before leaning forward, and with a well justified smirk, I add, "But I can communicate with those who can." I whisper the words, "She's here, Jordan. And she's *very* angry."

I swear the blood drains from his face at this. It's certainly draining from his nose; I'm pretty sure Dylan broke it. I stand up straight and pour myself a possibly-alcoholic fruit punch with one of the plastic reserve cups.

"Which is why about five minutes ago the police received an anonymous tip-off about drugs at your address. They won't find the class-A drugs they were informed about when they swarm in, but I'm sure they'll find enough illegal steroids—and who knows what else—with your fingerprints on them to take you in for questioning. Maybe they'll confiscate your phone, too, and trace where you've been. Maybe they'll connect the dots. Either way, you're in for a criminal record, not to mention you'll be out of a future in football and that sweet Ivy League scholarship you've always wanted." I raise my cup. "You better hope you can get a good lawyer; being eighteen you're going to need it."

In one swig I drink the fruit punch in my cup (which surprisingly does not taste of alcohol). I turn to leave but stop and turn back, one final thing I want to let out.

"'It's *your* fault', you said, as you looked down at her taking her last breath." I step closer, seeing the sweat form on his forehead. "But it's not her fault, Jordan. It's *yours*."

By now the room has gone uncomfortably silent, fixated on us. So, one glass-cracking step at a time, I do the only thing I can think of: I walk away.

Letting the door slam behind me, I see Vanessa at the end of the hallway. I stomp up to her, my heels sounding warning of my temper.

"I don't know how you did what you just did, but—"

"I didn't do anything," she replies, totally uninterested in what I have to say. "Or, at least I don't think I did. You did it all for me."

"I did?"

"Yeah, it was briefly like you were saying exactly what I was saying and thinking. Like I *was* you."

I shudder, my own unawareness of myself unnerving me.

I observe Vanessa as she looks at the many messages of love and photos of happier times pasted on her locker. "I wonder if they really cared," she mutters quietly as she traces her finger along the paper hearts. I begin to feel sorry for her, until she shrugs and says, "I wouldn't care about them."

"A bit heartless, don't you think?"

She shrugs again. "Just saying it as it is. School will finish soon, and once the last student walks out of the doors to enjoy summer, I'll be just some little memory left in the past. This will be taken down, and the school cycle will resume all over again in the fall."

I glance around. I don't know if she is trying to be sentimental, but it isn't working. I for one can't wait to be free of the place and would happily be some forgotten memory of everyone here.

"That was a cool thing you did back there, by the way."

I blink at her words. It's the nicest thing she's ever said to me, and effective enough to extinguish most of my frustration over what just happened.

"Yeah, well, don't expect anything else," I reply. "I want to get through the last weeks of school intact, thank you very much. If it's not too late already."

The doors down the hallway open as Gwen storms out of the hall towards the bathrooms in tears, her entourage of cheerleader pals following close behind. It seems like I may not be the biggest drama at school, after all.

Vanessa cringes. "Don't worry, I'm so over this place and everyone in it." She starts to leave but then turns around. "Oh, and by the way, don't be so hard-hearted on Cole. He's a good guy and never meant any harm. Sometimes life just sucks, ya' know?"

What does she mean by that? What has Cole been telling her that I have not been privy to hear? I suddenly feel peeved all over again.

"Bye, Charlotte. And thanks. For everything." She sighs before disappearing, her aura leaving a bright glow in her wake, and it dawns on me that it's the last time I will ever see her.

I stand there, suddenly alone, not quite knowing what to think. I soon hear the door to the school auditorium open and close again, the music still halted, the party over. I guess Vanessa got to be the center of attention at prom, after all. I can't help but snicker at this. Vanessa was such a problem it feels weird she's finally gone. Not that I'll miss her. Because I won't. Definitely not. At all.

I think.

"That son of a bitch is peeing his pants like a sissy, backtracking his own words, admitting this and denying that." Dylan approaches me. "Are you alright?"

"I think so. How's your hand?"

"Painful. But good pain." He looks at his bloodied knuckles with a smirk. "I don't know how you did it, but he's ruined. I'll make sure of it."

"It was a team effort, I guess."

I look back at Vanessa's locker. She certainly made an impact on others, and I guess from that alone she'll live on in some way. Even within me.

I take off the corsage, the one that was meant to be hers, and place it on her locker handle.

Dylan looks at me commiseratingly. "Everyone was so quick to disregard what happened to her. You didn't, though. Thank you, Charlotte."

I manage a resigned smile. "It's what I do."

"Let me drive you home," he offers.

"I think I'll walk; I could do with the fresh air."

"It's dark out; it's not safe." He pats his pants and then scowls in the direction of the hall. "I just need to find my car keys. I'll be right back."

"It's okay," I try saying as he heads back into the auditorium. "I have my own security."

Only I don't, because Cole is still AWOL, but Dylan doesn't know that. I'm well trained in the art of avoiding others and loitering in the dark, at least.

I exit the school, the night air calming and refreshing after the hectic past couple of hours. Then, as if on cue, Cole appears by my side.

"Boo!" he says childishly. "Hello, Earth to Charlotte?"

He waves his hand in front of me and I snap out of my thoughts.

"Cole," I say solemnly, feeling guilty I'm about to darken his energy which is actually normal for a change. "I'm sorry. I think Vanessa's just—"

"I know," he interjects. "She told me everything. We said our goodbyes."

"Oh. Well in that case, where have you been?" I ask furiously before shaking my head. "Never mind. Are you okay?"

"I was going to ask you the same thing." He studies me, although I'm not quite sure what to say. A lot just happened, including things I'm not even sure about.

"I'm fine," I say. "Over being here, though."

"Good. There's something waiting for you at home."

I am about to ask what it is when he chimes in, "Race you there!" before vanishing.

∞∞∞∞∞

Dylan did end up dropping me off home. I refused at first, but quickly realized that the gesture was for him more than me, so I let him make sure that at least I got home safe and sound. I think it helped him, at least a little. I don't know if he'll ever fully get over what happened to Vanessa, but little by little he'll get used to it, the emptiness in his heart he has to live with slowly yet eventually becoming less and less noticeable.

I am also thankful he dropped me off at home because I had forgotten how painful it is walking in heels. As soon as I enter the front door I fling them off with a sigh of relief. I wince as I look at my red feet with the marks of forming blisters. They will need some TLC come morning.

"Cole?" I look around the empty house. Dad's truck isn't here so I don't have to whisper. I call his name again, almost giving in to the conclusion he's doing his brooding disappearing act again when a speckle from outside catches my eye. It starts as one, then another, and as I walk closer I see the entire back patio is lit with fairy lights. And leaning casually against the old oak tree, arms folded across his chest, is Cole. Except instead of his usual white shirt and jeans, he is wearing a white buttoned blazer shirt with black pants and shoes.

Sweet mercy of the dead! And only I am lucky enough to get to see him.

I open the back door. Pippi greets me quickly before settling down. Cole stands up straight as I walk over, and with a small bow he outstretches his arm.

"Ma'am. May I accompany you for this dance?"

"Cole," I breathe, placing my hand on his. "You look . . ."

"Smart, right?" He pulls a smug face in amusement as he tugs on the lapel of his shirt.

I was thinking gorgeous, sexy, handsome, or even god of teen girl fantasies, but I nod. "How—"

"It's imprinted with me through memories. Took a bit of effort, but I got there. I had a good sense of style, you know. Something archeologists will note if they ever dig me up."

I don't know whether to laugh or cry at his comment, imagining his smugness as archeologists conclude he is indeed the handsomest skeleton in the cemetery, yet realizing he's just that . . . a skeleton in a cemetery.

If Cole reads my expression he doesn't let it carry. "I'm quite the decorator, aren't I?"

As much as I want to stare at him all night long I can't help but glance around. "Again, how—"

"Beasey agreed to do it, actually," he replies before muttering, "I made my own bargain with him."

I look at him reservedly, but let it pass, instead feeling my fingers encased around the light feel of his touch.

He leads me from the back porch, past the trampoline to the outdoor patio where the lights are strewn across the wall forming a beautiful little dance floor of our own.

"Every American girl deserves to have a proper prom experience," Cole says, turning to face me before adding softly, "I know you want ordinary. I can't give you that. But I hope this is enough."

"No," I reply. "It's more than enough. It's perfect."

He smiles, those cute dimples of his forming on his cheeks. "Oh, yes. Almost forgot."

He reaches over to the enclosing brick wall. There's a corsage made up of a thin band decorated with little white flowers. He holds his hand out to stop my own hand from picking it up. He frowns, staring hard as he channels his energy to lift it with his own.

And he does so well. It slides half an inch to the left, then bumps to the right a little before it slowly rises on Cole's hands.

I can see the strain on his face, his concentration on the corsage as he carries it the inch-long distance to my hand. And in breathless anticipation he almost does it. Then with one falter it falls to the ground.

"Sorry," he mutters as he slumps to his knees, drained of energy. "I practiced enough times. Maybe a little too much."

"Don't be sorry," I say as I kneel down to quickly pick it up and place it over my wrist. "It's so pretty. Thank you."

For a moment he looks sad, and I wonder if I should have let him try again or at least let him put it in place. But he clears his throat, back to his normal self. He takes my hands as he stands, the gentle feel of him pulling me up with him. "Shall we?"

I nod. He gently pulls me in to him and steps in close. I wonder if he can feel my heartbeat because it's thumping pretty loudly.

"On a positive note, it doesn't matter if you step on my feet."

I giggle as my hands find their way to his shoulders, his own reciprocating to my waist.

We sway slowly, side to side, in sync as one to the sounds of the night, and I conclude that this is the best moment of my life so far.

"You look beautiful, by the way."

Beautiful? Did he just say I look *beautiful*?

Okay, *this* is the best moment of my life so far.

Everything is so wonderful, all traces of the evening and everything before dissipates out of my mind. In fact, I could happily stay like this all night long, wishing this moment will never end.

"Charlotte, whatever happens hereafter I want you to know that you deserve all the love and happiness in the world."

My heart flutters. I smile bashfully. "Thanks, Cole."

"I mean it. I shouldn't dare ask from you, but promise me you'll live to be happy."

"Uh-huh."

I'm so happy I don't even notice the fairy lights go out at first. Not that I care when they do, because I'm too comfortable in the arms of Cole, my suppressed feelings for him setting off within me like joyous fireworks.

Pippi starts barking, probably at a raccoon. It's only when Cole stops that I lift my head up to him then follow his gaze to see Beasey standing across the patio, holding the power extension cord in his hands.

"Beasey?" I frown. Way to go Beasey, gatecrashing what is clearly a magical teenage girl moment.

"Not now, Beasey." Cole shakes his head. "Please, not now."

"This is for her own good," Beasey says, keeping his gaze straight on Cole.

"What is?" I look at Cole and see his jaw is clenched, his energy tense and darkening.

He drops my arms, stepping towards Beasey. "You agreed! Let her have this!"

There's pleading in his voice, not a sound I usually hear from him.

"I agreed I would do what's best for her. She can't fall for you anymore than she already has," Beasey says before turning to me. "You can't."

Okay, now I'm getting concerned. But mostly angry. "Beasey, you're starting to really ruin my evening, and for reference it's been a pretty crazy few hours."

"Why Cole?" Beasey asks, ignoring what I have to say. "Of all the ghosts, why him?"

"Don't!" Cole suddenly implores.

"Why did Cole come to you ten years ago?"

"I . . ." I pause, not knowing what to say. He was a bored spirit who happened upon me at a bad time. I thought he just felt sorry for me, being the helpless little girl scared of the ghosts she could see. Why does that matter, though? Especially right now.

"Charlotte, leave. Now." Cole shakes his head in distress, his muscles tensing as he hunches over.

I notice Beasey chanting and realization hits me.

It's a trap.

Beasey set up a trap.

"Beasey, what are you doing?" I seethe.

"It's just a little chant to keep the spirit in place."

"That *spirit* has a name, it's Cole. And he's off limits, remember? And what do you mean? He's not going anywhere."

Is he? I look at Cole, crouching to the ground, his struggles now just helpless twitches in an aura of darkening gray.

"Cole is his nickname, Charlotte," Beasey says between his chanting.

Cole struggles to speak from his invisible bind. "Charlotte, please!"

"Beasey if you so much as try to exorcise him—"

"Remember," Beasey demands.

"No." Cole looks up at me with begging eyes.

"Don't hurt him!" I yell.

"Remember who you are, Malcolm."

Malcolm?

"Who's Malcolm?"

"No!" Cole shouts in distress.

"Malcom McCroy."

"Malcom McCroy?" I utter. Where did I hear that name before? I don't have time to think as Cole groans sharply.

"Stop!" he pleads as darkness covers him.

"I punched you once before, Beasey, I can do it again!" I warn, my eyes darting between them.

"Tell her or I will."

"Tell me what?"

"Please, God," a whimpering plea from Cole as the dark envelopes over him.

"Tell her how you died, Malcolm. Last chance."

"You're hurting him!" I clench my fist as Cole growls in pain.

"How did you die, Malcolm? Speak!"

"Because!" Cole's voice is loud and strained. He's almost unrecognizable, a ghoulish form, weathered and broken. He slumps forward, limp, and I shudder as I watch the perfectly happy Cole only minutes ago become something so foreign.

For a terrifying moment I wonder if Beasey has killed him to something more than he already was, but then he speaks again.

"Because," his voice falls flat. He looks at me with the eyes of an animal that has given up the fight to survive. "I was the one driving the car that killed your mother."

Fifteen

The world caves in. I feel it fall on me with such force I don't feel the ground I collapse on. It is oddly quiet except for the slight ringing in my ear and there is a pain in my chest. That means I'm not dead, right? It hurts—a lot—but it's reassurance I am still here, one heartbeat at a time.

I feel a grip on my side lifting me up but my limbs don't comply. My line of sight, however, hasn't changed. His eyes, dark and empty, watch me. He hasn't moved—a result of Beasey?—a darkened spirit, exposed to what he was hiding.

He is Cole. My best friend. My only friend, really. The one I could rely on. The one I could be myself with. Heck, the one I love.

I want to deny it, to refuse it, but the fragments come together in my mind. His age. His secrecy. It was there all along. And I was too stupid to see it, too infatuated to believe it.

"Why?" It doesn't come out as a word, so I try again. "Why?" I tremble with each breath I try to take. "Why, Cole? What was so important that you would drive recklessly? Why didn't you stop at the stop sign? Tell me why."

His voice is low, hoarse, but I hear it. "The answer to that question won't bring you any closure, Charlotte."

"Tell me!" I yell manically. "Tell me!"

He hesitates. "Danielle. Remember I told you about her? I was on my way to pick her up. We—"

"No. Stop." I hold up my hand, unable to take anymore, the

feel of vomit building up in my throat. My mother, my baby brother, died because Cole wanted to *get laid*?

"I'm sorry, Charlotte. This spirit lied to you all these years—"

"No!" The sound from my mouth is barely audible. "Don't!"

I can't hear it. Hearing it makes it more real. I want none of this to be real. "I—" I try to speak but my body starts convulsing in short, rapid, uncontrolled breaths. My eyes sting and I realize I'm crying. I try to stand but I can't.

Beasey catches my fall but I yank my arm away from him.

"Breathe, Charlotte. Just breathe," he says.

Breathe? Really? What if I don't want to breathe? What if I just want to just curl up on the grass and go to sleep forever?

I force myself to stand, the need to leave availing as I stumble one foot in front of the other, and it seems to be the only thing I can do to keep from curling up and going numb.

"I. Need. To. Be. Alone." I mutter each word between rhythmic gasps, one at a time. I stagger slowly up the steps to the house and slam the door behind me, and once inside I am greeted, as always, by the photo of my mother smiling at me.

I stumble over to her and light the two candles before collapsing on the couch, looking up at them for judgement under the cross hanging above.

Three people died that night ten years ago. Dad never mentioned the other driver's name, and I never asked. Why did it matter? Some teenager drove recklessly and died for it. He wasn't our problem. Picking up the broken pieces of our own family was. The newspapers never mentioned his name either, or even my mother's name. Such articles are tucked somewhere in the middle pages, the bulletins in small print, not sensationalized like the trigger pieces spewed on the front pages of media nowadays. Because nobody really cares about car crashes anymore; they happen all the time. They were just more statistics for the annual road death toll, numbers among other numbers, a continuing tally.

But I now remember the name, muttered by adults during the darkest days of my life. I remember a police officer saying that name ten years ago to Dad, who was slumped frozen in grief on this very spot on the couch, as I listened on from the staircase banister above. I even remember I was wearing my yellow pajamas, the ones with the poppies on, clutching my teddy bear. He was simply called Bear. Mom allocated him to protect me from the ghosts when she wasn't around.

Before *he* came. Before he *replaced* her.

I lose what breath I have in my lungs. Is that why Cole kept it all a secret? Because I was some sort of redemption for him? Someone to help out a bit until he feels good enough to go on through the pearly gates and level up? Was he ever going to tell me? Or was he going to keep lying, like he always has?

Everything was a lie.

Everything about him is a lie.

And I fell for it all.

I don't hear Dad or Pippi come in, although I do feel the warmth of Pippi's tongue licking my cold hand, and when Dad turns on the lights it makes me squint. Dad mutters something but stops. He is then right next to me, his hands on my shoulders.

I turn to face him. He seems concerned to see me still awake and wearing a dress. Or maybe it's how I'm an incomprehensible blubbering mess that makes him concerned. Probably that.

"I'm sorry," I manage to say.

Tears cloud my vision, but I can't look him in the eyes right now. How can I, when I've been harboring and loving the spirit of the person who ruined everything for us?

Dad pulls me in a close embrace and rocks me back and forth gently. He's not usually one for such closeness, but when the situation calls for it his affection shows through with the reassurance I desperately need.

Like now.

"It will be okay."

"It hurts so much," I sob.

Then the anger grows, and those sobs become uncontrollable wails of protest muffled into his shirt as he holds me tight until I have no energy left, letting the numbing slumber consume me.

I don't go to school the following week. Dad doesn't even bring it up. I sleep a lot. Dad goes out for work, but he comes home when he can and Patricia also pops by frequently, no doubt to keep an eye on me since I'm such an unstable mess. But we do our usual family routines: we take Pippi for walks, we bake a pie, and then we eat the pie while watching sports on television together. I even have a beer. Again, he doesn't bring it up. Things feel as normal as they could be.

There also hasn't been a single ghost come by, including Cole—or *Malcolm*, since that's his actual name. But that doesn't mean he isn't present in my mind, because he is. As soon as I think he isn't, my mind throws it all up again, each reminder as emotionally draining as the one before.

I walk Pippi to the patio one evening, thinking he might be there. Not that I would know what to say or do if he was there because I don't. The humid summer air from the Gulf has arrived and mosquitos are spawning, making me hide my hands into the sleeves of my cardigan and fold my arms. The remnants from the other night are folded away neatly and stored by the pizza oven. Beasey must have tidied up after the night's dramatic end. I don't know why I was expecting Cole to show up. I just thought he'd be on the water tank or lying on the trampoline. I take that place instead and watch the night sky. It's a clear night tonight, the Milky Way stretching out from the hillside.

"Will you ever stop going on that thing?" Dad asks as he walks over.

"Maybe I will, Dad. I don't know anymore."

"Penny for your thoughts, bub."

"Do you think they're up there?" I ask, turning back to the stars. "Why do we always look up when people talk of Heaven? They're not aliens. Heaven isn't on Mars or Sirius or on Titan. Maybe Muslims have it right in that we're meant to pray facing east. Or why not west? We're a ball floating in space; does it even really matter?"

"It's not about direction, Charlotte. It's about feeling. Carrying that love for them in your heart. That's how we live on for them, and how they live on for us."

"Doesn't it annoy you, though? Why them, why then?"

"Oh, Charlotte. I want to be angry that they're gone, to blame God, ask why they had to go so soon. But I can't, because he blessed me to have them in my life, and it's my honor to cherish them in my heart every day."

I look at Dad who holds a soft smile and sparkle in his eyes that matches the stars above. Sometimes I envy my dad with his simple beliefs. Combined with his simple job managing the diner, his simple pastimes of beekeeping and fishing and admiring motorcycles, even his simple relationship with Patricia. It would be hard to think he's ever had hardship. I guess it makes up for having me.

"What about," I swallow, "the guy that did it?"

I feel Dad stiffen. "Oh, bub," he says as calmly as possible. "It's not our place to judge such things. You can hate the who and the what as much as you like, but carrying all that resentment will eventually destroy you. We can only surrender to what is, and trust that in God's judgement there is a deeper purpose to everything."

I huff at the last part, but I guess Dad has a point. Nothing will change what happened. No matter how many birthday wishes Cole makes.

∞∞∞∞∞∞

I wake up early the next morning and pass as functional enough to Dad's relief. He lets me borrow the truck for some errands I say I need to do with the promise I'll study up on missed classes and return to school after the weekend. I fill up the tank and head straight for the highway out of town.

It's amazing what you can find on Google with the right

keywords. Malcolm McCroy is still a mystery except for a small obituary listed in records from a cemetery near Richmond and an old Richmond High School newspaper article about track competition finals dated just over ten years ago. It's the name on the high school newspaper article that captivates my attention however, underneath the picture of relay runners striking the finish line: *Photo credit by Danielle Howell.*

One simple sentence. So many questions.

After a long drive past the state line into Florida, I pull over in front of the house number I am looking for. It's an aged house, not in years but in the way it has had many family memories inside its walls, the way a home should be, unlike those manicured box set houses a few blocks down that look empty and stale.

I walk down the small yard to the door, past the toy trucks strewn on the ground. I hesitate, but knock anyway.

The door quickly swings open. "Yes?"

I note her long, thick brown hair first as it swings around and lands on the side of her chest, her dark brown eyes to match. Her face is slender and diamond-shaped, with full lips sporting a rich red tone. Tan-lines are visible on her shoulders around the thin singlet she is wearing; a tan in the way a true girl from the South has. A bird tattoo, probably a dove, shows through a collection of string bracelets on her wrist, and three distinctive stars are inked on the left side of her waist, just visible above her shorts. She has clearly kept a figure that surely once made her popular with guys.

Guys including Cole.

I know it's her. I don't know how I know as it could have been any Danielle who took that photo, but I feel it. Still, before second thoughts kick in, I ask, "Are you Danielle Howell?"

Even though I found out her married name, I say her maiden name, which makes her blink.

"Yes," she cautiously replies. "Can I help you?"

"I was just wondering if you, uh, if you knew Malcolm McCroy?"

As soon as I mention the name, her outward confidence dwindles to something more sobering. A tiny gasp escapes her that her hand fails to cover up, a reaction that makes it clear she is someone who knew Cole.

And someone who was obviously very close to him.

"Cole," she whispers.

"Sorry," I panic. "I didn't mean to—"

"No," she dithers as she opens the door wider. "Come in."

∞∞∞∞∞

I know I shouldn't be here. Who Danielle is and who Cole was is none of my business. But still, I find myself sitting here, in Danielle's kitchen, twiddling my fingers while waiting for her to finish pouring herself a cup of something before sitting down opposite me.

She moves a toy next to me off the table. "Sorry, I wasn't expecting visitors."

"Don't be," I reply, feeling just as awkward as her. Even so, she was quick to let me inside, eager to talk.

"I haven't heard anyone mention Cole in years, not since I left that bloody town." She seethes at the word "bloody", but based on what Cole mentioned about her ex I don't blame her. I can understand why she would be so nervous speaking to someone enquiring about her past. Heck, I would be, too. Nonetheless, she places her drink on the table and sits down with a sigh.

"Cole." The name is only one syllable but it carries on in her mind, her eyes briefly distant, recounting memories of a person I never got the chance to know.

I guess that's why I'm here.

"How did you say you knew him?" she looks at me and asks.

"Family friend," I lie.

She raises her eyebrow at this, subtle yet clear she's not buying it.

"He used to hang out with my older brother Darren—you remember him, right?—and he played with me sometimes."

She clearly doesn't remember Darren because he never

∞ 215 ∞

existed (unless I chose a very common name of young males in Richmond circa the last decade). But her face softens at this, nonetheless.

"You must have been young to remember that."

"I was seven. He was like a big brother to me. Another one, that is." I glance down at my iced tea quickly. "I don't remember too much, and I don't have contact with my brother anymore since he's doing time. But I remember Darren mentioning a couple of people Cole used to hang out with by the old watermill, including you."

Her face lit up at mention of the watermill. I hope she is buying this.

"And as fate would have it, by chance I saw you at the park across the road and thought, 'My, that looks just like Danielle from the photos my brother had!' so I just had to pop by and ask."

Danielle huffs slightly and mutters, "Small Town Syndrome. You can escape, but never leave. Cole and I joked that it was a curse. It turns out we weren't wrong."

I sip my tea, not quite sure how to respond. The tea is far too weak, but I smile reassuringly. "I was just wondering if you could tell me what Cole was really like, fill in the gaps. For closure."

"Well, I don't really know what to say," she starts. "Cole was a good guy. He really was. Considering everything."

"Everything?" I press.

"Well, we didn't exactly grow up in the best neighborhood, as you would know. We didn't exactly come from loving families, either."

"Oh?" I try not to make it sound like a question, but I want to know more. She doesn't seem to take the hint, though. Instead, she looks down at her untouched tea. Unlike the iced tea she gave me she made herself a hot tea, her fingers wrapping around the cup as if seeking warmth, even though the air inside feels at least eighty degrees. From how Cole described her I expected a strong-faced, articulate woman.

I guess people change.

So instead I ask, "You two were close?"

She smiles. "At times."

I know what that smile is inferring.

"To still be a good person, even when surrounded by so little of them, that's what I remember about Cole. He would always go out of his way to help people who needed it."

My stomach tingles in loving emotion. I guess some people don't change, after all.

"People like me," she adds. "I was in a rough relationship, but he could see it. When others preferred not to notice, he did. He told me what I needed to hear when I didn't want to hear it." She takes a sip of her tea, a grin forming on her face. "I still remember when Tristan—that asshole—told me not to wear any skirts anymore because I would only draw unwanted attention to myself. Well, Cole said that if I didn't wear them then he would. And he did. He wore my skirt all around town, heels as well. The looks he got . . . I need to point out that Richmond wasn't the most liberal place back then. But he wasn't fazed. He did it anyway."

Like Danielle, I can't help but smile at Cole doing such a thing. Then I see it, in her eyes, the bold and free-spirited Danielle that Cole described her as. It's brief, but it's there, hidden behind layers of her past she has since buried.

Layers she's now digging through.

She blinks away something in her eyes. "It was so long ago now."

"Sorry."

"No, don't be. It's good to remember." She squints a little, her mind scavenging for memories. "I was eighteen months older than him so I can't say much about his daily school life. But he seemed to fit in with others. Girls liked him, but he either didn't notice or didn't care."

I can imagine.

"He was quite good at track, too. Actually, I think . . . hang on."

Danielle stands, rummaging in the nearby bookshelf, pulling out a folder. A few papers and crafts fall out which she picks up.

"Yes, here. I took some photos for my cousin doing the school newspaper, including this photo of him. He was rather camera-shy, but I got him. It's my favorite picture of him, actually."

Before I can react she places the picture in front of me. I gasp, peering at the four-by-six-inch glossy paper. Cole, his sandy-blonde hair, his amber-brown eyes, his dimples, his jawline, his muscles, his skin, all there. He has a few freckles too, something not visible on him now. His elbow is resting on someone's shoulder at the edge of the photo, probably another runner. He's in sports attire, possibly not long after finishing a run, but he doesn't look flustered. He's smiling into the camera, the endorphins rushing through his body no doubt, rejoicing in the exhilarating feeling of moving and breathing and being alive.

I pick the photograph up, my finger gently touching his face, longing to feel him, to smell him, to be there with him, to hold him tight and stop him from driving. To tell him to stay alive.

"I'm sorry," I say, unable to control the tears leaking from my eyes.

Danielle flicks me a tissue. I can see her studying me curiously until she says, "You can keep it."

"Thank you," I mutter as I pat the tissue over my eyes. "You don't know how much this means to me."

"I only wish I had taken more."

"What exactly happened? The night he . . ." I choke at the words.

"The night he died?" Danielle sits back down again and sighs. "Cole was good at running, but he was also good at running away from situations he didn't like instead of facing them. I guess that's a trait of a typical teenage guy. He had this silly idea for us to escape town and leave everything and everyone behind. Just like that, without a solid plan. He said we could work at diners, carnivals, live on the road, that sort of thing." Danielle smirks. "And eventually I said yes."

She readjusts herself in her chair, staring at her tea again, finding that comfort in the warmth of her cup.

"The night of the accident I waited, my bags packed. We

were going to leave before Tristan got home from work. Except Cole never showed up. And when Tristan got home and saw me packed and ready to leave . . ." she pauses to swallow. "I was so angry. And then when I found out what had happened to Cole . . . I was still angry. At myself."

She looks to the ceiling and tries to eyeroll away her flustered state. I bite down on my lip, feeling ashamed that I assumed Cole was just after a good time.

"So I stayed," Danielle continues. "I was scared, and I was alone. I guess I didn't want to be another victim to what had happened. Like, if I failed, if Tristan found me or ended up killing me, Cole's death would have been pointless. So I stayed."

"What changed?" I ask, even though I already know—from Cole's account, anyway.

"It was weird . . . I eventually realized that if I did stay, what would have been the point?"

"The point?"

"Of anything. Of Cole dying, of me staying. It hit me, like a whisper in the wind: go. It was always there, at the back of my mind. *Go.*" She lets go of her tea and sits up, taking a breath in. "So I did. I got on a bus and just left. I honored Cole by leaving Tristan, by leaving town. I worked at diners, even a carnival for a short while. I followed the road, and eventually I met Harry, my now-husband." She flashes her wedding ring. "Now I'm an assistant service manager at a restaurant in town, and I volunteer helping other domestic violence victims. And, of course, I'm a mother to Harrison."

On cue to his name, her son walks up to her, half perching himself on her lap as he places his toy truck on the table. He looks about seven, maybe eight years old. Just like his mother, he carries a mane of thick brown hair and dark brown eyes. He looks at me from Danielle's lap, wondering who I am, before picking up the attachment trailer for his toy and running off to his room.

"He's named after his father. His middle name, though, is Cole. Harrison Cole. The two men responsible for his existence, and the two men I want him to take after."

I don't know whether I'm smiling or crying, but either way the emotion I feel is overwhelming. "I'm sure Cole would be glad you escaped and got a happy ever after," I manage to say.

Danielle smiles softly. "I carry that, for both of us. Cole wanted to live, too," she simply says, her words relaying in my mind.

I look away, finding myself doing that same type of flustered eyeroll Danielle was doing only a minute ago.

Cole wanted to live, too.

Danielle must have noticed me. "How did you say you knew Cole, exactly?"

"A family friend," I reply quickly before standing. "Well, I must be off. Thank you for your time. And for the photograph."

She walks me to the door where I smile and say thanks once more before leaving, a long drive back alone to weigh up my emotions and the thought that's stuck in my mind: *Cole wanted to live, too.*

I don't know why I'm at church. I just feel confused, and assume I'll get at least some sort of sign given my supposed gift from the legend Himself. So I am here, not listening to whatever is being spoken in the sermon. I glance around in boredom. Dad seems to be taking it all in, bless him. Two kids, a boy and a girl whom I have seen down my street yet whose names I still don't know, sit on the pew adjacent to me, their faces also clearly bored.

Unlike them, I've at least got my own entertainment. While Beasey has exorcised most of them, I do see an elderly couple nagging at one another down the aisle. I only hear the husband's reply reassuring his wife that she looks fine before they pass through the wall in the direction of the maintenance room.

I wait for a pause in the sermon to whisper to Dad that I'm going to the bathroom, but instead make a detour.

I open the door to find Beasey putting away some candles.

"Where'd they go?" I ask, although from the smell of pine I can make an accurate guess that I'm too late.

Beasey turns in surprise, but as soon as he sees me his reaction goes absent.

"Believe it or not Charlotte, most ghosts appreciate my services. Especially in the house of The Lord."

"Quite the sales pitch. If you could charge your clients you'd make a killing, per se."

"Something tells me you're not here as a union representative for the afterworld."

"Where's Cole?"

"I don't know," he replies laconically.

"Did you send him away?"

"No."

I glower at him, my fist clenched.

He repeats sternly, "*No.*"

I relax a little.

He motions for me to move aside with his broom. "So I take it you haven't seen him since the big reveal?"

"I haven't. And I hate you for that, by the way."

"Hate me all you want. My duty to God is to push ghosts into crossing over back into His Kingdom, not to play Dr. Phil." He eyes me judgingly before sighing. "But you still don't want that, do you?"

He's got me there.

"I don't know what to do," I eventually say.

"You have to forgive him."

"It hurts."

Beasey's eyes turn heavy, the closest thing to compassion I've seen from him. "It hurts because you love him."

"Why do I love him?" I tremble at the words.

"Remember what I told you."

"What did you tell me?"

He sighs. "That The Lord works in mysterious ways. He gave you this gift for a reason. *You.* Maybe *he* is why."

I roll my eyes. My horoscope was right; my patience would be tested with certain people.

"So what does *His Holiness* want me to do?" I ask sarcastically.

Beasey reaches for a cloth and wipes his hands. "Forgive him. Not just for him, but for you. So that you too can move on."

"That's the thing, I don't want to move on. I want things to go back to the way they were before."

"That shows you love him more than you hate him."

I shake my head. "That's wrong. He killed my mother and baby brother. He broke my family."

"He didn't kill them. He may have been responsible for their deaths, yes. So was the local government that failed three other families at the same location since your family before putting a better intersection in place. But he didn't *kill* them."

Damn. I usually hate it when Beasey is right, but not this time.

Beasey continues, "Besides, it was one error. A single bad judgement. How many millions of drivers on the road are there right now and every day making bad judgements? Just a few miles over the speed limit, a rolling stop will be fine, only one drink, officer. Throw in some bad weather or a large truck or a kid crossing the road and what do you get? Carnage, that's what. Too many ghosts have come my way trying to figure out how such a small bad judgement caused so much damage, or why they thought their reasons were worth the risk. But it never changes. My point is, you won't find a single driver with a guilt-free conscience. They don't exist."

I glance at the floor. While I know more than anyone the consequences of car crashes, even I am guilty of less than perfect driving on the road.

"Cole's bad judgement was small but had unfortunate consequences. Nonetheless, he's more than paid the price for it. Regardless of how you feel, he deserves forgiveness."

"What if I find him but . . . I can't?"

"Well, you might not get the chance to."

"What do you mean?"

"Do you not remember anything I tell you?"

"You say a lot of things, Beasey, so cut to the chase."

Beasey exasperates. "You were his anchor, his reason to stay behind. If you reject him, if he no longer feels the need to stay here, he'll cross over."

"Congratulations, you get what you want," I sneer.

Beasey shakes his head. "But he didn't release his pain. He's holding onto all that guilt and sorrow, and if he enters the afterlife in that dark energy . . ." Beasey sighs, looking at me with eyes of concern. "Don't you get it, Charlotte? That *is* Hell."

The hairs on the back of my neck stick up, my head starts spinning.

"No."

"It might already be too late. He might have already gone."

I shake my head in refusal. "He wouldn't do that. No. No, not without saying something first."

"You saw how he was, how he felt."

"Cole?" I call upon him. "Cole!"

"He won't be here."

"Where is he, then? If he's not yet . . ." I can't finish that sentence. The one thing I fear most may just be true: Cole, gone. *Forever*.

Even though he said, even though he *promised* he would be here.

I need to forgive him. Except now there may never be that chance.

"Well, that's up to him." Beasey picks up a mop. "Ghosts have anchors, Charlotte. Not just people, but places. Think. Where does he go?"

I'm already rushing out when he calls out, "Nothing can change the past, Charlotte. The future, though? That choice is yours."

∞∞∞∞∞

The old chapel of the fittingly named Old Chapel Cemetery never had a good life. Built in the 1860s, it succumbed to two fires, a lightning strike, vandalism, and numerous renovations due to low-grade work by laborers who were unamused with the measly pay the Church offered for their services.

I wonder if it was God's doing or just down to misfortune, but with the expansion of the township of Richmond only a few miles away, a newer and more modern church was erected there almost one hundred years later. This resulted in eventually demolishing what was left of the old chapel to make space for a larger cemetery. It turns out its history, combined with low maintenance costs, make it one of the cheapest places around to be buried.

It's unfortunate it has such a bad reputation though, because while I certainly don't care much for the place, it's a quiet, secluded spot bordering the countryside, and if you want to finally rest in peace I can see the appeal.

There are only a few cars in the allocated parking area. Good. Fewer visiting people means fewer visiting ghosts, and there's only one ghost I want to see right now.

I pull in with Dad's truck (he'll have to get a ride from Patricia) and grab the bottle of water, soap, and scrubbing brush on the passenger seat. I enter through the wooden archway, not knowing where to begin. Grave markers and headstones dot the ground with small American flags and flowers of bright colors teeming with life of their own. I begin to wander, little by little, my pace increasing with the anxiety of what I both want and don't want to—yet know I will—find. I scan the names of each marked grave I pass by, each name different to the name I now know so well.

I wasn't expecting it to be *that* one, though.

I halt and do a double take, looking back behind my shoulder.

Shaded by the fence line, an accumulation spot for leaves from the winds, is a plain headstone, half succumbed to moss and with a chip on the right side. Just his name, date of birth, and date of death. I delicately place my fingers over his name, as if it is some long-lost artifact, fragile to the touch, a trick of the light.

"Cole," I whimper. I place my hand on the ground, yearning for the closeness of him. "This is you?"

I brush the grass aside but it's so overgrown I can barely see the markings outlining his grave. The reality then sets in that this is where he is. The real, physical Cole. Or what's left of him. The remnants of a life once living, breathing. I bite down on my hand in emotion and shake the tears from my eyes. I start pulling the scrubby weeds out in tufts until I see the raw soil underneath. My nails quickly fill with dark-brown earth, my hands lightly streaked with grass stains, and I have to fight the urge to not dig more.

Cole's dead, I remind myself. *It's not him. Not anymore.*

"Charlotte?"

I turn and gasp, realizing I'm not alone.

Cole stands across from me, solemn and dark. I must look more of a state however, because Cole's eyes bulge at me. He turns, his jaw drops, and then his lips quiver.

"What are you doing here? How did you find . . ." his voice is cracked and fragmented. His eyes dart between me and the ground beside me before he shakes his head. "What are you doing here?" he asks again in shock. "You shouldn't . . . you shouldn't be here. You should leave." He rakes his fingers through his hair, pacing back and forth around me as I pull out another weed. "Stop that." He pulls at his hair. "Stop it!"

"Cole," I say, pausing only to wipe away a tear. "This is you."

"That's . . . that's not me, Charlotte," he says, pointing at the headstone. "Not anymore. Look at me, Charlotte. I'm right here. You can see me. Just stop what you're doing. Charlotte I said stop it. Please. Stop!" he bellows, before he hollers, "Charlotte!"

"Why are you like this?" I bawl, for once not caring that anyone may see me since kneeling over a grave getting emotional would be fitting right into the surroundings.

"Because I deserve it!" he argues back to me before taking a step back. "This," he says quieter, "is what I deserve. It is my reminder. Of what I carry."

I slowly pull out another tuft of grass and say the only thing that comes to mind. "You wanted to live, too."

I pick up the scrubbing brush and pour water on it.

"You didn't get that, but I am going to make your grave look good at least." I start scrubbing the moss off his headstone and wipe the tears from my face on my sleeve. "Now if you don't mind I'm busy. So either allow yourself the love and respect you deserve or leave me to it."

This seems to do it. Cole looks at me, his face conveying so much emotion yet remaining speechless. He eventually collapses, his side leaning against his headstone. He goes still, his head looking up to the blue sky, his mind retreating elsewhere.

Then he does something that surprises me: he starts talking. About his life. Random, pointless little snippets he remembers, like the time he found fifty dollars on the ground, finished first in track, and snuck into someone's backyard for a swim in their pool one hot summer's night. There is no correlation; just the assurance that he once lived, once loved.

Cole eventually comes back to the present and looks over his headstone. "It hasn't looked like that in a long time."

I don't know if I should ask, but since everything's up in the air I do anyway. "Does your family come here a lot?"

"What family?"

I try not to raise my eyebrows. "Your parents? Or any brothers or sisters?"

"I'm an only child. And no." Cole glances my way when I don't say anything. "There's no mystery, Charlotte. They're alive; they just don't care. Never really did."

Poor Cole. I now know he didn't come from the most stable household, but they must be real scumbags to not even cater to the grave of their only child.

"Why did you come here?" Cole wonders.

"You weren't on the trampoline or the porch. It was the only place I could think of where you may hang around. If you were still here, that is. I thought you had gone. Forever." Tears dwell up in my furrowed eyes. "Don't scare me like that ever again."

"I was going to cross over," he admits. "When Beasey figured it out I begged him not to say anything, to let you be happy. But he said your happiness shouldn't be dependent on me and that I'm holding us both back."

That asshole.

"But he's right. As much as I want you to be happy, it was wrong. And that's unfair for you. So I negotiated with him to keep quiet for a little longer, just until school finishes, for the sake of your studies. Then I would tell you myself. I even said he could exorcise me afterwards. He agreed."

Seriously, that asshole.

"So that night? The backyard?"

"I wanted you to have one last perfect memory of us." He clenches his jaw. "He decided otherwise."

"And everything you said?"

Cole looks at me. "I don't lie, Charlotte. I hid the truth from you, yes. But I never said anything I didn't mean."

So he really did think I looked beautiful, after all.

I swallow, glancing away. Cole is right; his grave certainly hasn't looked like this in a while considering the amount of weeding I just did. I wish I brought some flowers or something to at least make it look a bit more decorative, but it will have to do for now.

I slump down against his headstone, the small amount of shade providing sweet relief from the early afternoon sun. Whether it's the heat or the emotional atmosphere, I feel too frazzled to do much else.

"So now you know." He turns to face me as I wipe my damp bangs off my face, leaving my skin sticky and wet. "I'm no longer your knight in shining armor, your funny big brother to make everything better."

I want to say something reassuring, I really do. But nothing that isn't a blatant lie can restore things back to the way we were. Because those times are over; there is no backwards button.

"Tell me what happened," I say instead. "When you died. Tell me everything."

Cole looks anxious, scared even, but soon nods. He turns away from me, his fingers crumpling in the grass as he leans his head slightly back and focuses his gaze on the sky. It takes him a few long moments, but he gets there, into the darkness I see him entering within himself.

"It was dark and raining. I was running late because of work. I picked up my car from the car yard even though it wasn't ready, but I had to reach Danielle. We were going to leave town that evening before her boyfriend arrived and beat the shit out of her for trying to leave. There was no plan, just to keep her safe." He swallows. "That was the last thought I remember having before seeing the headlights."

I shiver at the thought, the sweat on my neck now feeling cold.

Cole takes another long moment before continuing, "It was quick for your mom. I saw her before I realized what had happened to me. And would you believe it, she actually cared about me. She told me to fight, to hold on. I tried. But I couldn't in the end." He shakes his head at the memory, his face tense and eyes holding back tears. "Your brother, his soul was pure, unborn, so he went straight back to wherever it is we go. He was attached to your mother, though. She couldn't bear to leave him so followed him into the afterlife."

I blink once, twice, remembering to breathe. I don't react though because I need to hear more and Cole's not yet finished.

"But not before going to you and your father." He turns to me at this, his gaze still locked in his memories. "She didn't leave you, Charlotte. She went straight to you, to your bedroom where you were sleeping totally unaware of what had just happened, and said goodbye. She knew you would be scared. She didn't want to scare you with what she had become. She didn't want your last impression of her to be one of fear and distress."

I cover my mouth with my hand to hold the air I feel escape me, but my lips curl anyway. Mom didn't leave without saying goodbye first. Of course she didn't. How could I think so lowly as to assume otherwise all this time?

I only need to look at Cole for the answer to that. As a species we tend to assume the worst in others and ourselves, and experiences so often unfortunately make this rightly so. Throw some raw grief into the emotional mix and it's a recipe for mental trauma.

"She was at peace, Charlotte. I hope it's enough justification to say that. She told me to safeguard you, though. Keep the ghosts away from you. I promised her I would." Cole takes another long moment before adding, "I had no idea you would be able to see me, though. I was only going to hang around until you stopped crying, but you just seemed so lonely and sad, I couldn't leave you. Making you smile, and helping other broken souls by helping you, I felt useful. Like maybe this is where I'm supposed to be. That maybe I am better off dead. Because with you I have a purpose. With you I feel loved, which is more than what I had when I was alive. Is that weird, feeling more alive being dead? That I died to live?"

I don't know how to reply to that. I don't think I can, because I'm on the brink of succumbing to the emotions that are brimming over me.

Thankfully he takes it as a rhetorical question because he continues, "To fulfill the promise I made to your mother, I decided I would look after you and do what I could to make your life better. And that meant suppressing who I was and what happened. And as for Danielle, I could do nothing but look on helplessly as her ride never came, and as Tristan . . . as he . . . I failed both of you." He starts sobbing uncontrollably. "I'm so sorry, Charlotte. Not a dawn or dusk passes where I don't think about what happened, the pain I caused."

Okay, *now* I break down and cry. I'm not quite sure what else to do. I want to be angry, to shout and punch something, but that something isn't Cole. Because regardless of what he did or what happened, he held back and kept his trauma for all these years, not *because* of me, but *for* me.

"As much as I wish to go back and change things, I can't. But I'll do everything I can to make up for it."

I wipe my eyes with my sleeve. "A bad mistake doesn't make you a bad person, Cole. You're a good person. You've always been a good person. Which is why I forgive you."

"I don't want forgiveness, Charlotte."

"You need it though. You need to accept what happened so that you can cross over. So that you can finally be at peace."

Cole looks at me, his eyebrows slanted. "Is that what you want? For me to cross over?"

No.

"Yes."

No!

"No!" I shake my head. "I mean, if that's what you want then I'll support you."

"What makes you think I want that?"

"Well, now that your karma is cleared 'n all, Beasey said—"

"Forget what Beasey said," Cole growls.

I don't argue with him there. I'm just about to offer my agreement when he leans in close, his fingers trailing over my muddy hand with his feather-touch.

"Charlotte, if you tell me to then I will leave right now—into Hell even—if that's what you want. But know that you weren't just my redemption. In fact, I thought you were the one who needed me, yet the only place I want to be, in this world or the next, is with you."

I'm dying. Am I dying? No, I'm living. Because my heart is pounding in my chest, pumping blood and chemicals and emotions all at once, making me feel both giddy and flushed.

Which is why, in the heat of the moment, as birds sing and fly around the nearby trees and the faint fragrance of butterfly weed lingers in the air, ignoring my hesitation, I place my hands on his neck and in one swift motion I close my eyes and kiss him.

I don't know what I was expecting. I guess I wasn't really expecting anything because I hadn't thought this far ahead. The only kissing experience I've had was with Ryan Hill, so I assumed it would be like that.

Only this is nothing like kissing Ryan Hill. This is so much *more*.

I feel the gentle touch of his lips on mine which is met with a surge of energy through me that makes me feel both lightweight and joyous. It only lasts a moment, but it's there—a connection that feels whole and true and complete as if I was only ever something less before.

Cole flinches back and looks at me, eyes wide and confused. Yet his presence lingers on my lips, tingly and light, the remnants of that moment still alive.

I wonder what he's thinking, but I know he feels it, too.

Because his aura is now glowing bright.

And he kisses me back.

I finished the school year without incident. It was close; with what happened at prom, alongside my tardiness and absences, I have gotten quite the collection of misdemeanor reports. I wasn't expelled, however; probably because it was so close to the end of the school year that they couldn't be bothered, not to mention they couldn't really pin me for anything that had happened that night.

So I went to school, and with no more unwanted visitors I managed to attend classes on time and pass everything I needed to. I seemed to have a new streak to my name, one which was feared, because after the prom confrontation people dared not hassle me, which also meant I didn't need to provide any explanation as to what exactly happened. Because, like the teachers trying to pin me for it, I too had no rational explanation to give. The rumors of what happened differ from person to person. Leslie said it was "the coolest thing ever" and asked how I did it. The teachers put it down to poor-quality glassware.

Psychic mediums were suddenly rife at Foxton High School. Many of the more open-minded students said it was Vanessa, except those same people used various movies and television shows based on ghosts as their justification. Jordan, however, was adamant it was all my doing and that I was a possessed demon. Not that anyone believed him. He has since been ostracized and is under investigation from the police following the discovery of his illegal drug stash. Needless to say he was kicked off the football team just before Ivy League scholarship applications went through. His lawyer has told him to prepare court appeal applications and plea deals instead.

Regardless, the general agreed consensus is that what happened at prom night was "freaky" and will no doubt go down in school history, passed on as whispers through future school years. Maybe they'll make a tradition of it like the flag blood, or come up with Halloween stories about the slain cheerleader haunting the school on prom night. Maybe my name will always be attached to what happened too, as part of some school legend.

Oh well. I just have that impact, I guess.

With everything finishing off for the better, I managed to smile brightly as I shook hands with Principal Headley to receive my high school diploma. Dad and Cole watched on proudly in the audience, of course. When it was all over, Leslie and I hugged; a gesture of congratulations and parting since our social contract had come to an end. We talked about college and promised to stay in touch, but we both knew that promise would be empty. I then cleared out my locker, and subtly slithered through the crowds of selfies and yearbook signings, walking away with no intention of ever looking back.

∞∞∞∞∞

I'm sitting on the front porch, finishing a cold glass of lemonade when Cole appears next to me. It's raining, a light passing shower with sunlight fighting to break through. There's probably a rainbow somewhere over Foxton, but I don't care to look. My attention instead is on Cole as he casually leans on the railing in front of me. His mouth twitches into a smile, both his hands resting in the pockets of his jeans with his legs crossed.

"I didn't mean to interrupt your thoughts."

I wave my hand dismissively. I don't let him know my thoughts were of him—or, more specifically, *us*—but my unwavering smile probably shows it enough.

∞ 233 ∞

"Your hair looks nice."

I feel my hair, styled loosely into a French braid, the wavy ends flowing out freely behind me. I'm glad he's noticed; I seem to put more effort into my morning routine lately.

"I think my hair and I have found a compromise for now. I only wish it'll stay this way," I reply, knowing the humidity will set it off soon enough. "Speaking of wishes, what was your birthday wish, by the way?"

"Charlotte, I can't tell you my wish, that'll jinx it."

I raise an eyebrow. "I thought you didn't believe in that stuff?"

Cole comes up to me without a word and focuses intently on trying to move the lock of loose hair hanging on my face. I give him patience to try, just as intrigued as he is to see if he can. He gives up, but does so with an unyielding smile.

"This wish *will* come true. One day." He winks, leaning back to the railing where he was just before. "What are your plans now?" he asks, changing topics.

I ponder this. High school is over and I feel like anything is possible. But summer doesn't mean beach trips and barbecues every day. It means college applications and apartment hunting. It also means helping Dad at the diner to start saving for the costly expense of adulthood.

But then again, the world can wait.

"I'm thinking I'll finish this lemonade, then take Pippi for a walk, and then lay down and watch passing clouds while holding your hand."

Cole's smile grows. We haven't spoken of that particular moment we shared by his grave, but it's there, the connection between us still alive. And it's evident it's put a positive spin on things, because Cole's aura has been bright and clear since. He'll open up about it when he's ready. Maybe about other things, too. And I'll be here, ready to listen and support him the way he has for me.

Cole opens his mouth to reply with something but suddenly clenches his teeth and turns to his side, rage and fear flaring up inside him.

"It's *him*."

I don't need to ask who because I now see Beasey standing by the mailbox, seemingly oblivious to the rain.

"Stay here," I order as I reach for my umbrella and then make my way down the driveway.

Cole instinctively hesitates but then nods. He's accepting that I'm not as helpless as I used to be, but he still has that protective instinct about him, something I'm certainly not complaining about.

"This inn is full," I say through the receding rainfall. "Try the stables down the road."

"Don't worry, I'm just stopping by to congratulate you on your graduation."

"So kind of you." I glance at his motorhome parked on the roadside. "You're leaving?"

"Lord's bidding, Charlotte. Foxton isn't the only place with ghosts, although it'll remain one of the most memorable."

I shake my head. Why do I even care? If I never see Beasey again then that's fine by me.

"Cool," I simply say.

"I can't say I'm a fan of this humidity."

"Welcome to the South. Or should I say farewell on behalf of the South?"

"That would be the one," he replies.

"So . . . northbound?"

"Nowhere in particular. Just following the breadcrumbs."

"I hear Alaska has a lot going for it this time of year."

Beasey gives me a look, one that is shown through his eyes because his face remains as blank and untelling as it usually does. "Don't worry, I won't be pestering you back here anytime soon. I am curious, though, as to how things went." He glances at Cole standing so, well, *ghostly*. "All is well, I assume?"

"Stronger than before."

"You are a different one, Charlotte. Are you sure there's nothing I can do to persuade you to join us in Italy? Flights, finances, accommodations are all taken care of. And they really do have the best food in the world."

"You're right, Beasey. I am different. And a European getaway with a lifetime supply of lasagna sounds great. But I'm not going to join some cult to feel like I belong, especially one with principles I don't morally align to."

"Don't you? Don't you want the chance to find out for sure? The chance to reach your full potential? Regrets are those not taken, after all."

"Regretting would be not doing what I want to do and giving in to you."

"It can be a very lonely life being a Communicator," he persists.

"Yeah, it can be lonely," I agree. "But I'm not alone."

"Ah." Beasey sighs, glancing back at Cole. But it's the disappointed type of sigh that lingers from his mouth. "So young, so naïve."

"Maybe so. But I make my own choices, and I will accept what happens from them. As you said yourself, the future is mine."

Beasey flashes that judgmental half-smile of his. "Charlotte, you actually remembered something I said. And on that note I bid you goodbye."

He heads to his motorhome, but stops to take out his wallet and hands me a business card. It's plain white, with the name 'BEASEY' in small type on one side and a telephone number on the back. Basic, but the *Communicator Club* probably doesn't have a graphic designer in the mix.

"When you need me," he says. "And remember, I don't charge for the Lord's work."

I stand here as he drives off, spinning the card between my fingers with my thumb. I have every intention to rip it up and throw it to the breeze, but Beasey's words stop me.

When you need me, he said. Not *if* you need me.

I eventually slide it into my phone case, somewhere always on hand *if* I need it, yet with no intention of ever having to use it.

The rain has now died off to a mildly refreshing drizzle, the type that feels good on the skin on a warm day like today. Like the weather, change is in the air and it feels refreshing.

Cole appears by my side as I walk back to the house. "You seem content."

I guess content is a good word to describe how I feel.

"I am." I smile. But as I look up at him my heart drops. Beasey's words come to mind, about how I should help him cross over and let him go if I truly love him. Because although I fight the idea with the pull of my heart, Beasey is—as much as I despise it—right, and I wonder how long things can be between us as the way we are.

"Hey, Cole," I stop walking and turn to him. The sun is now shining down on us and he has a slight silvery reflection, one I could happily stare at all afternoon. "I just need you to know for sure, whatever you promised my mom, you've fulfilled it." I swallow. "I don't want you to linger behind for me. You can move on now if you want to. It's okay."

Cole's forehead creases slightly as his eyes narrow. But then his face brightens up, the dimples showing on his cheeks as he gently strokes my chin with his thumb.

"Move on? Why would I want to do that when things are just getting good here?"

I didn't think I could experience my heart swooning any more than it already has before, but I've just been proven otherwise.

"Yeah, one day it will be time for me to leave," Cole admits before smiling as he moves in close to me. "But not today."

I smile back. Not today.

From The Author

It is no easy task putting a novel together, but it has certainly been one I have enjoyed. I would like to acknowledge those who helped support me, especially you Nicola who encouraged me through the rough patches.

I hope you, the reader, enjoyed reading this as much as I enjoyed writing it. Please feel free to leave a review if you did! If you are on this page wondering if it is really the end then I have some good news for you: Charlotte's story continues!

The Way We Go

Charlotte is off to college, excited for a new start. With Cole by her side and newfound friends, she's optimistic for what awaits her. Except it's never that simple when the dead get involved, and Charlotte must soon decide the fate of not only her but those she cares about . . .

Coming Summer 2024

About The Author

A perpetual global nomad, Olivia Norton has so far lived in five different countries over three continents. With a background in English teaching and outdoors instructing, you'll either find her exploring the great outdoors or curled up reading a book with a cup of tea (no milk!)
She currently resides in New Zealand with her foster cat named Blanket.

Stay tuned for updates and upcoming releases on
www.instagram.com/olivianorton_author
www.goodreads.com/author/show/42842710.Olivia_Norton